Quail Crossings

Jennifer McMurrain

Quail Crossings
By Jennifer McMurrain

©2012 by Jennifer McMurrain

All rights reserved.

This book or parts thereof may not be reproduced in any form, stored in or introduced into a retrieval system, or transmitted, in any form, or by any means (electronic, mechanical, photocopying, recording, or otherwise) without prior written permission of the copyright owner and/or publisher of this book, except as provided by United States of America copyright law.

This book is a work of fiction. Names, characters, places, and incidents are a product of the author's imagination or are used fictitiously. Any resemblance to actual events, locales, or persons, living or dead, is coincidental.

Cover Design/Interior Design: Linda Boulanger
www.TreasureLinePublishing.com

Published by TreasureLine Publishing
www.TreasureLinePublishing.com

ISBN: 978-1-61752-136-2

Also available in eBook publication

Dedication

To my Grandparents, Elmer and Tiny Collar and Bill and Lou Anne Johnson. Thanks for sharing your stories with me and being my loving muses.

Chapter One

August 1934

"Norman, I'm in no mood for your nonsense. I need to milk the cows." Dovie Grant stared at the large grey goose guarding the old barn.

Norman raised his wings and released a loud hiss. Dovie knew that if she took another step the goose would start biting, and having left her broom by the house, she had no way to defend herself. She sighed and stretched her back, feeling every one of her thirty-two years.

"You're a plum evil goose. Little Charles Garber needs that milk, and just like in the Bible, good will prevail." She shook her finger at the bird. "You better watch out, or you'll be Thanksgivin' dinner!"

Distracting the animal was the only way to get her chores done. Knowing Norman was notorious for biting people on their backsides, she turned her fanny to the beast and shook her slender hips a little. She prayed she was quick enough to spin around and catch the animal by the neck before he could give her a good nip.

Dovie peeked under her right arm to stare at the goose. Norman gazed at the tempting treat.

"Hurry up, you big oaf. I'm startin' to get a cramp."

Dovie swayed back and forth, trying to make her backend look more appealing.

Norman tucked in his wings and stretched his neck to the right, watching to see if she was bluffing. When Dovie didn't move, he took his opportunity and tottered toward his target. Just as he went in for the strike, Dovie grabbed him by his neck with one arm, tucked his feet up with the other, and tossed him in the direction of the pond.

"My word, Norman, you're heavier than a pig after slop." Dovie wiped her hands on the blue apron that covered her tan dress.

Norman, lowering his head in defeat, waddled back toward the pond.

Finishing her milking, Dovie pulled a couple of hay bales down off the stack to feed Poppy, the milk cow. A flash of red caught her eye. Bending to retrieve the mysterious item, Dovie choked back a cry. Hidden beneath the stack of hay, she uncovered a dingy black-haired doll wearing a red polka-dot dress -- Helen's doll. How long had it been there? she thought. Why haven't I noticed it before?

Dovie threw the doll to the side. There was far too much work to be done to dwell on the past. She continued forking hay to Poppy, trying hard to ignore the doll's beady eyes bearing into her back. It was no use. Setting the pitch-fork in the corner, she once again bent to retrieve the forgotten toy. Even though Helen didn't have any siblings, she was notorious for hiding her most prized possessions in the barn, certain no bandits would be able to find her treasures.

A sharp sting in her heart sent Dovie sinking to the ground. She held the doll tight to her chest and wept.

Dovie's father stirred his coffee in the Knollwood Cafe. Taking a sip of the steaming beverage, he grimaced and added more sugar. He watched as a plump woman wiped down the wood tables. With each wiping, the towel turned a darker shade of brown. James could feel a fine layer of grit burrowing into his forearms as he leaned on the table. Just another day on the plains, he thought. It's all getting a bit too normal. He glanced out the window and searched for at least one dark rain cloud.

All he found was the constant haze that stained the Texas sky during these endless dry times. Dust storms came regularly nowadays and varied in strength. Some sent Dovie scurrying to clean the thin coating of dust that slipped into their house while others left James digging out his truck and tractor. Any crops he managed to nurse through the winds and dirt, shriveled up due to the drought. James glanced down at his calloused hands and then rubbed them together in a silent prayer for rain.

The jingle of the front door caused James to look up and nod at the new customer.

"Well, I'll be. It's James Murphy," said the man taking a seat across from James. "Didn't expect to see you in Knollwood today."

"Mornin', George." James shook the man's hand. "Had to bring the Ford in for some repairs. Can't seem to get myself under the truck anymore."

"You should've brought it by," said George. "Ben could've fixed it in no time for you."

"That's mighty nice of you to offer. Since Simon died, I need help with the everyday stuff. I'm no spring chicken, and Dovie's got her hands full with her own chores. But I'm sure Ben has his own duties keepin' him busy. Thanks all the same."

"Hey, Annette, can I get a cup of coffee?" George said, smiling at the lady cleaning tables. "Thanks."

George scratched his head. "How's Dovie doin'?"

James felt his eyes sink as he thought of his daughter. "Better than expected, bein' it's only been a few months. She stays busy helpin' the Garbers and the Clarks. We've got more than we need, so she takes 'em milk, cream, and such. It's good for her to get out, takes her mind off things."

"I heard the Garber farm's goin' under -- too much debt after the war. Bein' north of the crick don't help. He's got no trees to shelter his wheat. Seems what the winds don't take, the dusters bury." George shook his head.

James sniffled as the dust tickled his nose. "Feels like the whole town's goin' under. Gonna have to go to Wilson just to get parts for the tractor since the Bailey place closed. That's one of the reasons I brought the Ford to Sonny. Hate to see him go under too."

The door jingled as three skinny kids entered the cafe and settled at the table behind the men. James's heart lurched at the sight of a young blonde girl holding the hand of an older girl. He wanted her to turn around. He needed to see her face. He needed to see his granddaughter, Helen. James shook away the thought. There was no way that was his Helen.

"We're doin' better than Willow Creek. Hear 'bout their banker?" George asked, gaining James's attention.

He shook his head as he watched the young teenaged girl fuss over a scrawny red-headed boy. The little blonde girl turned and gave James a little finger wave, reminding him of his granddaughter. His heart ached as he remembered he'd never see her again.

"He flew the coop!" George banged his hand on the table, making James jump. "The people went to do their banking, and there was a sign on the door sayin' there ain't no money. Can you believe it? All those poor people trusted the bank, and now it's gone. Their entire savings just wiped out."

James shook his head. "Seems like yesterday we couldn't grow enough wheat to sell." He took a sip of his coffee and tried to steady his nerves. "Now we can't give it away, and good hard working folks, just like us, are losing everything. I'm just growin' a feed crop this year. Can't afford to lose what little stock I have left."

James's eyes shifted back to the table of kids, hoping the young girl was still facing them. She wasn't, but the young boy trying to roll up the arm of his shirt caught his attention. James wondered if the shirt was a size too big or if the boy was just too skinny. The boy's emaciated arm answered the question.

"Can I get you somethin'?" Annette asked the trio of kids as she pulled a pencil from behind her ear.

"I'll have fried eggs, bacon, taters, and hot cakes," said the young girl licking her lips. "And make them eggs runny so I can mix 'em with my taters."

"Alice, you know better," scolded the older girl before looking at Annette. "We'll just have a glass of milk."

"Well, you're in luck today." Annette winked, placing the pencil back behind her ear. "We have a three-for-one special on the milk."

"Ohhh, ma'am, do you have any of them drinkin' straws?" asked Alice, sitting up on her knees.

Annette shook her head. "No, honey, sorry."

"That's too bad." Alice slid back down in the old wooden chair and picked at the wood table. "I got to use one in Armadilla. It was so much fun."

"It's Amarillo, Alice," chided the older girl. "Don't

bother the lady with your nonsense."

As Annette stopped to refill the men's coffee cups, James grabbed her hand. "Get them kids a decent breakfast and add it to my coffee, please."

"Sure thing, James. The little one sure looks like Helen." Annette placed her hand on her heart.

"Yes." He patted Annette's arm. "She sure does."

Annette rushed to prepare the breakfast surprise, barely missing a skinny young man standing in the doorway.

The young man looked at James and took off his hat, exposing a full head of red hair, matching that of the skinny boy's. "Excuse me, sir?"

"Yes." James looked up at the young man.

"Couldn't help but hear your conversation with the waitress. I appreciate your kindness. Can't remember the last time I was able to feed 'em a decent meal."

James raised an eyebrow. "Them your kids?"

"They're my brother and sisters." The young man extended his hand. "The name's Bill Brewer."

James stood and shook it. "Good to meet ya. I'm James Murphy, and this here's George Wheaton. Please have a seat, Mr. Brewer."

"Call me Bill," the young man insisted as he sat.

"Ok, Bill." James looked to the table behind him. "Do y'all have names?"

"I'm Evalyn." The older girl pointed to the young boy. "This is Elmer."

Elmer did a quick nod at James before returning his stare to the table.

"And I'm Alice," said the youngest.

Annette came from the kitchen carrying a tray of toast, oatmeal, and milk.

"Hope y'all like oatmeal." Annette sat the plates in

front of the children. "It'll sure stick to your bones."

"We didn't order this." Evalyn shook a confused face at Bill.

"It's ok, hon, Mr. Murphy's takin' care of it." Annette smiled.

With a nod from Bill, the kids started to inhale their breakfast gift.

"Slow down," Bill said softly. "You don't want to make yourselves sick. Remember small bites until your stomach gets used to it."

The kids nodded at their brother and slowed down.

"Bill, would you like some breakfast?" asked James. It hadn't escaped his notice that Bill was just as skinny as his siblings.

"If it ain't too much trouble," Bill answered. Annette hurried back to the kitchen.

"'Bout breakfast," Bill continued. "As much as we appreciate it, we ain't accustomed to handouts. I don't have much, but I'd like to repay you. If you have some work that needs to be done, we'd be more than happy to see to it."

"Bill, how old are y'all?" George asked, sipping his coffee.

"I'm eighteen, sir. Evalyn's fourteen, Elmer's ten."

"And I'm six," stated Alice with a mouth full of oatmeal.

James turned his attention to Bill. He knew it was only a matter of time before one of the kids got sick from starvation. Just the thought made him shudder.

"I hate to pry," said James, twisting his coffee cup, "but what brings you to Knollwood?"

Annette slid a bowl of oatmeal in front of Bill.

"Well," said Bill, "I was workin' for the railroad over in Bryerville helpin' to lay tracks. They was headed north, and

I didn't want to take the kids that direction with only a truck to sleep in." He took a big bite of his oatmeal before continuing. "We grew up a few towns over, in Tuckett. We came back to see if our old home was still vacant, but it wasn't. So now we're just lookin' for some farm work with possible room and board. If you know of anyone lookin' for help, I'd appreciate the opportunity."

James gave a knowing look towards George. He knew it would be impossible for George to take on these four kids as well as his own brood. There was only one thing left to do, but he knew Dovie wouldn't like it. Taking another look at the three children eating oatmeal like it was steak and eggs, he made up his mind. His daughter would just have to make do with his decision.

James looked at Bill. "I just happen to know someone who needs a whole mess of help."

Chapter Two

James inched his battered truck down the road leading to Quail Crossings. He wasn't concerned about losing control on the loose dirt. He was dreading the upcoming conversation with his daughter.

How could he tell her that he had just hired Bill and agreed to take in his three siblings? She wasn't going to appreciate his generosity no matter how bad off these kids looked. He'd told Bill to give him half an hour before coming out to the farm. James hoped that would give him enough time.

Pulling into the driveway, he saw Dovie fishing in the pond east of the two-story white house. Her curly brown hair escaped from the floppy straw hat that shaded her face from the blazing summer sun. Getting out of the truck, he leaned on the hood and searched for the right words. Taking out his handkerchief, he wiped his brow. Glancing up at the sun he knew it was going to be a hot one in more ways than one.

Dovie looked up from the pond and waved at her father. He ran his hand through his salt-and-pepper hair. By the way she tilted her head, he knew she could tell something was wrong. She gathered up her fishing pole and tackle and bit her lip. Dovie had lived with her father all of her thirty-two years on God's green earth, and the simple gesture of biting her lip told him she dreaded what he had to say.

As he watched her walk toward him, his heart grew heavy. She had endured so much tragedy lately. Would she be able to bear the burden he was about to place on her? James shook his head. She would have to; he'd already set the wheels in motion, and his conscience wouldn't let him go back on his promise to Bill now.

"No fish today, Dad." She gave him a peck on the check. "I'll put some beans on."

She turned towards the house. He knew she was trying to avoid his stare.

"You better make a big pot," James called after her. "We're having company."

Dovie stopped. "Dad, we haven't had company in a long time. Since…"

She lowered her head and continued to chew on her lip. The last time they'd had company was six months ago, after the funerals of Dovie's husband and only child. James walked to his daughter and hugged her tight.

"I know, but I think it's time," he said, rubbing her back.

"Yeah, I guess you're right." She wiped the tears with the back of her hand and forced a smile. "I'll fry a chicken instead. Who's comin'? The Clarks? The Spauldings? Oh, I hope it's the Clarks. I haven't seen Sara in a coon's age."

"The Brewers." James wiped his forehead again.

"The Brewers?" Dovie raised an eyebrow. "Guess they're new in town?"

James nodded. "You could say that."

"Where do they live?" Dovie asked, leaning her pole against the old truck and wiping her hands on her apron.

"The old Patton place?"

"No." James shook his head. "They live at Quail Crossings."

"Dad, you didn't!" Fresh tears flowed from Dovie's eyes. "You sold our home? I knew money was tight. Why didn't you tell me? I could've sold some more eggs and cream." Dovie twisted her apron into knots.

"Calm down. You know I'd never sell this place," James reassured.

Dovie shook her head. "I don't understand, Dad."

"I hired a man to help me today. His name is Bill Brewer." James placed his handkerchief in his back pocket.

"Ya could've just told me that." She slapped him on the arm. "You scared the livin' daylights out of me."

"There's more. Let's go inside." He ran his fingers through his hair causing Dovie to frown.

"He's not some criminal?" Dovie placed her hands squarely on her hips. "I know you've got a generous soul, Dad. But we have to be careful who we invite in here. You know there are scoundrels all over these parts just looking for the next sucker fish."

"He's no criminal," said James. "Let's talk inside."

Dovie turned slowly and walked toward the house.

James pulled his silver pocket watch from his overalls. He didn't have much time. Running his finger over the inscription, *I'll love you forever*, he wished his wife, Sylvia, were here to help. Saying a quick prayer for strength, he closed the watch and went to face his daughter.

The smell of lavender filled the kitchen, causing James to once again think of Sylvia. Dovie's bath soap was her one vice. Her mother had bought her a bar every year for her birthday, and Dovie saved a little of her egg money to continue to buy the flowery scented soap.

Dovie sat at the table, twisting a dish towel.

James sat beside her. "Bill has three younger siblings, and I told him they can all live here with us."

"You did what?" She bolted up, knocking her chair over.

As James leaned down to turn the chair upright, he heard Bill's truck drive up. He prayed they'd stay outside for a little while.

"Their ma and pa left for California two years ago, and Bill's been tryin' to take care of them ever since. One look at these kids will tell you they need our help, and we need theirs. They're all willin' to help around here to earn their keep. We've got two empty rooms upstairs and more food than we can eat." He motioned out the back door as he stood. "It's our duty as God's people to take care of these children."

"Don't tell me about my duty to God. God took my child away, remember, Dad? And now you're telling me it's my duty to care for these orphans. What about God's duty to me?" Dovie braced herself on the back of the chair and took a deep breath. "Dad, I can't handle this. How could you bring children into this house and expect me to take care of 'em? I'm not ready." Dovie began to cry again. "Dad, I think of Helen every day. I wake up and wait to hear her laugh, but I don't. There's nothing but silence. I'm used to the silence. I've accepted it. Now you want me to hear kids running through the house again, to get my hopes up that it might be Helen."

James rubbed his daughter's arms and choked down his own set of tears. "Dovie, I know what I'm asking ain't easy. Truth is Quail Crossings will go under if I don't get some help with the crops and livestock. We can't afford to take the truck and tractor into town every time something breaks, and I can't fix it myself any more. Bill's offering to help in exchange for room and board plus a small wage so he can build some savings. I can't turn that offer down, not and make ends meet."

Dovie shook her head. "I can hardly take care of the two of us. The last thing I need is a bunch of young'uns gettin' in my way."

"I assure you ma'am we will *not* be in your way." Evalyn stood in the doorway, her green eyes narrowed. "And you will not have to take care of *my* family."

"Oh great, Dad," Dovie gestured toward Evalyn. "This one's all sass. How old are you, girl? Not old enough to know how to respect your elders apparently."

"The name's Evalyn, not girl, and I'm old enough to know when we're not wanted. I'm gonna talk to Bill. I'd rather go hungry than be in *your* way." Evalyn slammed the door.

"Good riddance," Dovie called after her.

"Now, Dovie, that wasn't very Christian of you. These kids have been through a lot," scolded James.

"So have I!" She threw her hands in the air. "Do you think this is easy? How is this going to help? Like I don't have enough reminders? I'll go into town and get a job. We'll make ends meet some other way."

"There's no work in town, you know that, Dovie." James put his hand on his daughter's shoulder. "I can tell these are good kids that have been dealt a bad hand. I need help 'round here, and Bill's got a truck which will help come harvest. I know you're hurtin', but in times like these, Dovie, how can we turn our backs on these children? Would you want someone to turn their back on Helen if the roles were reversed?"

The minute he said it, he wished he could take it back,

but it was the only way to get Dovie to see what needed to be done.

Her blue eyes stared through him. "Dad, I can't--"

A soft knock interrupted Dovie. They turned to see a young girl with braided blonde hair standing in the doorway. Her little blue dress hung around her fragile body.

"Hello, ma'am, I'm Alice," she beamed handing Dovie a small bouquet of yellow weeds. "Thanks for givin' us a home. We'll work real hard for you, I promise. I can't wait to sleep in a real bed again. That ol' truck has the lumpiest seats. Plus have you ever tried sharing a bench seat with your sister? Half the time her feet are right in my face."

She wrinkled her nose before wiping it on her sleeve.

Dovie grabbed her chest as she stared into Alice's big emerald eyes. Spinning around she looked at her father and blinked back tears. "Dad, I can't. She looks like…"

James furrowed his brow. "They're staying, Dovie, and that's the end of it." He turned towards Alice. "Go get your family. Dove will show y'all where you'll be sleepin'. You'll still have to share a bed with your sister, but I think you'll wake up a lot happier without feet in your face." He tweaked her nose, causing her to giggle.

Alice ran down the steps. "Come on, guys. She's going to show us our rooms!"

"I know you can make this work." James walked out the door. "I'm gonna show Bill 'round."

With Button, their brown and white cow dog, on his heels, James left the kitchen to find Bill. He knew he had to explain Dovie's reaction. He just hoped Bill hadn't already decided to leave. James turned the corner of the barn to find Elmer slumped down, drawing in the dirt.

"Where's your brother, son?" James asked.

"By the chicken coop, sir." Elmer concentrated on the

ground. Bags shaded Elmer's eyes. It looked like the kid hadn't slept in weeks.

James wiped his brow. "You alright?"

Elmer nodded, still staring at his dirt art work. Button sniffed the boy's shirt and then flopped down in front of him belly up. Dropping his stick, Elmer gently rubbed the dog's belly. James shook his head. Lord knows what these children have been through, he thought.

As he approached the chickens, James could see Evalyn pointing her finger at Bill's nose.

"We can't stay here," Evalyn yelled. "That lady don't want us here. Said I was full of sass and we're gonna to get in her way. She's no right to talk to me like that! I'm 14, not some baby. I've been takin' care of Elm and Alice for a long time. What does she know about raisin' kids? She ain't got none!"

"Young lady," James stepped forward, "you might want to get the facts before tellin' tales to your brother. Dovie has her reasons and as confusing as they might be now, they are valid. That's why I'm here to talk to your brother."

"Why? Cause she's an old maid? That ain't our fault." Evalyn crossed her arms.

"Evie, hush up and go help with Alice," Bill ordered.

"But Bill," she stomped her foot, "we don't need these people."

"I do believe you enjoyed a hearty breakfast this mornin' thanks to Mr. Murphy. Now stop bein' ugly and go help."

Color flushed Evalyn's cheeks as she swallowed hard. Lifting her head high, she turned and stormed off.

"Sorry 'bout that, Mr. Murphy. If Miss Murphy..."

"It's Mrs. Grant." James ran his hand through his hair.

"Let me explain. 'Bout six months ago, Dovie lost her husband and daughter, and she's still grievin'."

"The last thing we want to do is cause her trouble." Bill checked a wire on the chicken coop. "Please forgive Evie, sir. She gets out of line sometimes. A lot of responsibility has fallen on her shoulders since our parents left."

"It's not my place to ask, Bill, but do you really think they're comin' back?"

"It's hard to say, but I reckon not." Bill tightened the wire on the coop gate. "I'd be obliged if you didn't repeat that to the kids. It just seems like some hope is better than none. If Mrs. Grant's unhappy about the arrangement, I won't hold you to it. We'll just stick around long enough to pay for breakfast and then be on our way."

"You'll do no such thing. Dovie's got some healin' to do that's all. With a little prayin' we'll work it all out." James put his arm around Bill's shoulder. "Let's get you and the kids settled."

Evalyn saw the curl of Bill's mouth and knew they were going stay. She stomped her foot and leaned against a tall cottonwood. That nasty ol' woman had talked to her like she was a child. Now Bill expected her to smile and be thankful for a bowl of stupid oatmeal when they should be on their way to California. Bill had some nerve, yelling at her like she was a child. She'd show him. She smirked. She'd show all of them.

Chapter Three

September 1934

"Bill! Bill!" Alice jumped on the bed, waking Bill from a dead sleep. "Get up! I don't want to be late for school!"

"The sun ain't even up yet." Bill wiped the sleep out of his eyes. "Go gather the eggs and feed the fowl. Tell your sister to go help with breakfast."

"I ain't tellin' her." Alice ran to the door. "She's crankier than a treed opossum."

Bill sat up and took a deep breath. He had a feeling he'd have trouble getting Evalyn to school.

"Elm." Bill nudged his brother. "Get up and start the milkin'. I'll be there as soon as I can."

Elmer nodded as he stretched, and Bill left to get his sister out of bed.

"Evie, get up!" he hollered leaning on the door jamb.

"I'm not goin'," said Evalyn, throwing her pillow over her head.

"One of the conditions of stayin' here," Bill tried to steady his breath, "is that y'all go to school. We've been here a couple of weeks, and you've been pouting like a mule pulling the cotton wagon. The least you can do is help with breakfast and go to school."

"Well, I don't want to stay here, and I don't want no more schoolin'," Evalyn grumbled. "I've learned everything I need since Ma and Pa left."

"Evie, don't be a brat. I need this job. Get your behind out of bed and go help with breakfast. You keep sayin' you're not a child, so quit actin' like one."

"You're the one acting like a child, Bill." Evalyn faced her brother. "All we have to do is go to California. There are plenty of jobs, and we might be able to find Ma and Pa. I don't think you want to find them because then you're not the boss anymore."

Bill sighed. "Evie, we've been over this a dozen times. There are more people headed to California than there are jobs. Half the country's been swindled to believe there's jobs there. It doesn't make sense that the whole country's struggling, but California has enough jobs for everyone."

"You think you know everything," Evalyn scoffed. "There are more fields in California than anywhere in the country. The crops are full, and they can't get enough people in there to pick the harvest before it rots."

Bill laughed. "This is why you need to go to school, so you can get your facts straight. Bottom line, I'm not giving up a job that puts a roof over our head and food in our mouths for what might be in California."

"What about Ma and Pa?" asked Evalyn.

"There's a reason they left while we were all at school. Evie, it's time you realized they're…"

"They're what, Bill?" Evalyn lifted up on one elbow and raised an eyebrow.

Bill shook his head. "I'm done with this conversation; you're going to school. End of story."

Bill ran down the stairs before Evalyn could continue the argument. Sitting up, she crossed her arms. How was she going to get out of this God forsaken place? Throwing off the covers, she started pacing as she brushed her long, strawberry blonde hair. Bill was right. The kids did need breakfast, and it was her job to make sure they had a good one. She changed and tied her hair in a quick ponytail.

As she walked down the stairs, the smell of biscuits made her stomach growl.

"'Bout time you got out of bed." Dovie grabbed another pan of biscuits from the oven. "No wonder your sister's so skinny."

"There's nothing wrong with Alice," Evalyn snapped back, silently forbidding herself a biscuit.

"I'm sure you see it that way, being you're skinnier than a fence post yourself." Dovie wiped the flour off her hands. "There's leftover beans and cornbread for your lunches. Do you think you could manage, or is that too much work for your delicate constitution?"

Evalyn rolled her eyes. "Better than nothin', I suppose."

"There's a small basket in the pantry we use for picnics and such," said Dovie. "Y'all will have to eat together come lunch time."

"You want me to eat with the children on my first day of school?" Evalyn gasped.

"That or go hungry." Dovie placed the biscuits on the table. "Makes no difference to me."

Evalyn turned to retort but stopped as Bill and James entered the back door, followed by Elmer and Alice.

"Bill, when you get back from takin' the young'uns to school, meet me over at Bud Clark's. He lives just south of here at the end of the road." James hung his hat on a peg.

"We're gonna help him get his winter wheat started while Dovie and Sara do some cannin'."

Evalyn ran up to tell Bill how unfairly she was being treated, but he shook her off with a quick shake of his head. She stomped her foot, knowing she wasn't going to get her way this morning.

"Yes, sir," said Bill turning his attention back to James. "The kids haven't been in school for a year or more, so it'll be a bit while I get 'em settled."

Bill sat at the table and glared at Evalyn to do the same. Alice plopped down by his side and started playing with her fork. Across the table Elmer sat tracing the rim of the small tin plate. Evalyn slid next to Elmer and sighed dramatically. Bill ignored her, as Dovie and James took their places at the ends of the table.

"That's fine." James said to Bill and then folded his hands. "Bow your heads, everyone. Let us pray."

Dovie gasped as she and her father pulled into the Clark farm. The barn door hung on broken hinges and beat the side of the warped barn with each gust of wind. The chicken coop sat empty, filled with sand dunes from the last duster. It was clear it hadn't housed chickens in a long time. Sara's little garden sat to the south of the barn, her vegetables shriveled in the dry heat of the September sun.

Dovie looked at Bud Clark standing in the driveway waving to them. He had a look on his face that Dovie couldn't quite place. Scanning the homestead that had once flourished, she looked back at Bud. It was hope. Bud looked hopeful. It was a look she hadn't seen on many faces in a long time.

"So glad y'all could make it this mornin'." Bud shook James's hand as he got out of the truck. "Have you had breakfast? I'm sure Sara has some grits left."

"Thanks, Bud, but we ate at home," said James. "My new man, Bill Brewer, should be out here shortly to help out."

"I'm afraid I'm a bit of a mess," confessed Bud, rubbing his hands on a red handkerchief. "Sure I grew up here, but I'm an accountant at heart, not a farmer. Daddy tried to teach me a few things, but between his bouts of forgetfulness and the stroke, it wasn't much. I confess since Daddy died, I'm pretty lost."

"I'm sure you're doin' fine, Bud," James reassured. "It's a hard time for all of us. Why don't you show me your seed?"

"Guess I just spent too much time in the city," said Bud, his nervous laughter filling the air.

Bud turned to Dovie. "Sara's inside with Ruth. She's expecting you."

"Thanks, Bud," said Dovie. "You boys have fun playin' in the dirt."

Dovie turned and walked towards the house. Knocking gently, she stuck her head in the door. "Sara?"

"In here," called an airy voice from the kitchen.

Dovie walked through the house and started fanning herself. "Goodness, Sara, it's hotter than a grassfire in August in here."

"I know." Sara wiped her forehead. "Tiny got carried away this morning when she started the oven. I told her we were canning, so she made sure we had a hot fire."

"I wish I had your daughter's energy." Dovie tied her apron. "Well we've got the heat, so let's get started, shall we?"

"There really isn't much." Sara looked sadly at her two baskets of vegetables. "I'm afraid my garden isn't doin' too well. What I did get started was either eaten by rabbits and grasshoppers or died 'cause it's too dry. Even with all Tiny's energy, we can't keep up the waterin'. The water well's almost a half a mile from here. But we sure are thankful for it since the one up here by the house went dry." She turned and looked at little Ruth playing on the floor. "I don't know how we're gonna make it through the winter."

Sara turned, and Dovie could see her shoulders shaking.

"Please don't cry." She rubbed her friend's back. "We'll make it through this pickle. I brought green beans and some apples from our orchard. You know it's right by the crick, so it does pretty good. We have more than enough. We'll make some applesauce for Ruth and some jelly for Tiny and Junior's biscuits. I'll talk to Dad about gettin' y'all some chickens. I'm sure our new farmhand, Bill, will help mend that ol' coop out there. Plus we got an extra sack of potatoes and onions in the cellar. I'll bring them by in a couple of days. Maybe we can even get that ol' windmill by the barn to workin' again so you don't have to go so far for water. I bet Bill knows a thing or two about windmills."

"Dovie, I heard about all them kids you've got to feed now. You can't be givin' us all that stuff. Besides Bud will never take charity." Sara wiped her eyes. "You know how hard it was for him to ask for your dad's help."

"Forget that charity nonsense. Do I look like FDR to you? This is neighbors helpin' neighbors. It's what we do. If we can't lean on each other, then who can we lean on? Tell Bud the birds are a loan. When you get a good flock goin', give us some back. Same with the taters and onions." Dovie twisted her apron. "Besides, the apples will just rot, so you're doin' me a favor. And don't be afraid to shoot them rabbits, they cook up pretty good. You can also can their meat for the winter."

"I'm sorry I'm makin' such a fuss. I get so scared sometimes. Guess I've been in the city too long. Aren't you scared, takin' on all them kids?" Sarah asked.

"More annoyed than scared." Dovie snapped some green beans. "That oldest girl's a thistle. Thought she was too good to eat out of a picnic basket today with her younger siblings. Barely made it down to breakfast to help. Dad swore these kids would be helpful, but she's been nothing but a lazy goat. Just keeps bleating all day long without actually doing anything." Dovie threw the green beans in a deep pan.

"Don't you think it'll heal your heart a little, Dovie?" Sara asked, her voice cautious. "I mean, nobody will ever replace Simon and Helen, but won't it be good to have children's laughter in the house again?"

"No!" Dovie snapped. Sara took a quick step back.

Dovie flattened her apron. "I'm sorry. Now who's sounding like a goat?" She looked at Sara and smiled. "It's just that I don't want a bunch a kids 'round who could leave on a breath of wind and upset Dad." She turned toward the window and took a deep breath before silently adding, "and me."

Dovie returned to snapping green beans. "Oh, look at us cacklin' like a bunch of hens when there's work to be done."

James popped his head in the back door. "You ladies seen Bill?" he asked.

"No, Dad," answered Dovie, "haven't even heard a truck on the road."

James shook his head. "Probably still up at the school getting the kids settled."

Dovie gave a worried glance to Sara before answering her Dad. "I'm sure that's it. I bet he'll be here any moment."

Chapter Four

"Alice, school may be a little scary at first," Bill said as he sped down the dirt road towards town. "But Elm and Evie will be there to help you out. When they're not around, remember your teacher's there to help you. I expect you to treat her with the same respect as you do with Mrs. Grant and Mr. Murphy."

Evalyn grunted.

"I do hope she's nice. Besides I'm not scared, I'm excited," Alice said, smiling. "Do you think there'll be any girls in my class?"

"Of course there'll be girls in your class. Don't be stupid," Evalyn said, frowning at the vast dusty farmland that surrounded the truck. Alice stuck her tongue out at her older sister and crossed her arms.

"Alice, you're not bein' stupid. I'm sure there'll be some girls in your class." Bill gave Alice a little pat on her leg. "As for you Evie, I don't want no trouble from you today. You respect your teacher too, you hear?"

"What kind of trouble do you think I'm gonna get into out here?" Evalyn gestured towards the empty horizon. "Chase some chickens, let the cows out? Really, Bill." She rolled her eyes. "Besides I wouldn't put it past this backwards little excuse for a town to still have a one-room schoolhouse. They'll probably seat me right next to the first years and expect me to babysit."

"Well, I don't think you have to worry 'bout that. We're here," Bill said pulling in front of the two-story brick building.

Alice's mouth dropped open. "That sure is a lot of kids. I hope they like me."

"Who wouldn't like you?" Bill reassured as he parked the truck. "I'll make sure you're settled before I leave."

Two girls approached as the family piled out of the vehicle.

"Hi, I'm Charlotte Wheaten," said a blonde girl as she brushed her long ponytail off her shoulder. She was just a tad shorter than Bill, with a long face and petite nose. Every time she moved, Bill caught a whiff of strawberries. "I believe you met my father at the coffee shop with Mr. Murphy a few weeks ago."

"Ah, yes, good to meet you." Bill tipped his hat. "I'm Bill. This here's Alice, Elmer, and that's Evalyn." He tilted his head towards the hood of the truck where Evalyn lingered.

"This is my friend, Lou Anne Garber," said Charlotte as a striking girl with raven hair stepped forward.

"Nice to meet you, Miss Garber," said Bill as he studied the way her dark hair flowed over her shoulders in soft waves. Her eyes were as gold as ripe wheat, causing Bill to stare. He'd never seen such a lovely creature. She met his eyes, and an unnatural shade of pink flushed her cheeks as she quickly looked away.

"You can just call us Charlotte and Lou Anne," said Charlotte, breaking Bill's trance. "There's no need to be formal here. We're all bound to be fast friends. In a town this small, everyone knows everyone. We all get very close." She grabbed Bill's arm.

"Come on, Bill." Evalyn pulled Bill away from Charlotte. "We wouldn't want Alice to be late on her first day."

"So, it's your first day?" Lou Anne bent to meet Alice's gaze.

"My first day ever," said Alice, her voice serious.

"Well, I would love to show you to your classroom if it's ok with your brother." Lou Anne glanced up at Bill, a fresh round of color flushing her cheeks. "My sister, Joan, is in your class. I'll introduce you. Would you like that?"

Alice nodded as her smile returned.

"And I'll introduce you to her teacher, Mrs. Spaulding." Charlotte grabbed Bill's arm again. "She and I go way back."

"Thank you both very much." Bill looked at Lou Anne. "That'd be great."

Evalyn watched her brothers and sister walk into the school. The nerve of them girls, she thought, just throwin' themselves at Bill. Are there no boys in this school? Looking around the schoolyard, all she saw were boys Elmer's age tumbling in the dirt. No wonder Bill was pounced on the minute he got here.

"I just hate it when she does that." Evalyn turned to see a skinny blonde standing behind her, the spitting image of Charlotte Wheaten, only shorter. "She thinks she's God's gift to everyone. I should know; I have to share a room with her." She extended her hand. "Hi, I'm Harriet Wheaten."

"Evalyn Brewer." Evalyn shook Harriet's hand. "So, are there no older boys here?"

"Most of the boys 'round here quit school after the eight grade. They go to Amarillo in search of jobs or are working their daddy's farms. When you grow up in a town as small as Knollwood, they're all kind of like your brothers anyway. So when a new guy comes around, all the girls start acting crazy. My sister's a prime example. She's dated all the boys in the county, but there's something intriguing about an out-of-towner like your brother."

"Trust me there's nothing intriguing about my brother." Evalyn strummed the hood of the truck, and then laid her cheek on her fist. "So if there ain't any boys, what do y'all do for fun 'round here?"

Harriet's eyes twinkled as she looped Evalyn's arm with her own. "I'm sure we can think of somethin'."

Elmer entered his classroom, glancing up only long enough to spot an empty seat. The two-story schoolhouse boasted four classrooms and a gym that doubled as an auditorium and dining hall during bad weather. Kindergarten through third grade and fourth grade through sixth grade were in the bottom two classrooms; seventh grade through seniors were in the top two classrooms. It was easy enough to find his room after the two girls had shown Bill where Alice would be. Elmer just silently walked across the hall. He didn't want anyone to make a fuss. I'd rather be on the farm, he thought as he maneuvered through the desks. Suddenly, he was blocked by two worn brown lace ups.

"Jeepers, I thought I was the only redhead on the entire planet. Though Molly claims to have red hair, hers is more blonde than red, and Peter's doesn't count 'cause he got red paint in his hair and when his ma tried to wash it out, it turned all pink. Can you imagine walkin' around with pink hair? It ain't always been pink. It used to be white like snow, not the dusty snow but real snow, the kind you can eat without getting' your mouth gritty."

Elmer followed the shoes up to see a short freckle-faced girl, in a patched flour sack dress, missing a front tooth. Being short a front tooth didn't stop the girl from grinning from ear to ear.

"Oh, my goodness, you've got freckles too! We're gonna be best friends, I can tell. Are you at the Murphy place? You have to be. There ain't no other new kids in town. It's just a hop, skip, and a jump from my house. I can ride my Dad's horse, Biscuit -- he calls him that 'cause he loves biscuits -- my dad, not the horse. Can you imagine a horse eatin' biscuits? Anyway, we're just at the end of the road, and I ride Biscuit to get milk from Mrs. Grant all the time for my little sister, Ruthie. It's real nice of Mrs. Grant to give us milk. We have a milk cow, but her milk tastes like it's been sitting in sagebrush."

Elmer sidestepped around the babbling girl and took a seat at the vacant desk. He concentrated on the contents of the desk, hoping the chatty girl would find someone else to tell her life story to.

"Oh jeepers, how silly of me, here I am honkin' like a lost goose, and I didn't even tell you my name!" She sat on his desk. "It's Mary Sara Florence Lillian Clark. My parents couldn't decide which of their mamas to name me after, so they named me after both grandmas and my ma. You should see my name in the family Bible, takes up the whole page. But you can just call me Tiny; everyone else does on account of me being so short. I don't think I'm all that short. I can just about reach anything I put my mind to. I just have to be clever about it. Rose Calliway used to be my height, but this summer she grew like a corn stalk. I thought we should call her Tiny Two, but it never stuck. You got a nickname?"

Elmer nodded slightly at the girl and whispered, "Elmer Brewer."

"Well, that's a silly nickname." Tiny slapped her thigh. "We're gonna have to come up with something better than that -- maybe E.B. or Red. How 'bout Freckles?"

Elmer cringed and then let out a deep breath of relief as the teacher entered the room and clapped her hands, sending everyone scurrying to a seat. Tiny grabbed his hand and pulled him out of his chair before he had time to protest. "I like to sit on the front row. Come on, you can sit with me."

Alice tightened her grip on Bill's hand as they entered her classroom. He watched as she took in the kids huddled in groups around the large two-person desks. She tugged on Bill's sleeve. He looked down and gave her his best big brother smile.

Her lips started to quiver. "Bill, I don't know no one."

Bill glanced at Lou Anne.

Lou Anne motioned to a little dark-haired girl sitting in the middle of a giggling crowd playing jacks on the wood floor. The girl skipped over and hugged Lou Anne. Bending down between the two young girls, Lou Anne smiled at Alice.

"Alice, this is my sister, Joan." Lou Anne looked at Joan. "Joan, this is Alice. Will you help her out today? This is her first day, and she really needs a friend, and you're one of the best friends I know."

"It's my first day too," Joan said. "But I know most of these kids from Sunday school." She grabbed Alice's hand.

"Do you play jacks?"

"I don't know how," confessed Alice.

"I'll show you," said Joan, patting one of Alice's dog-eared braids. "I love your braids. Mine never come out smooth, so my Ma just puts my hair in a ponytail."

"My sister, Evie, does mine. She pulls my hair so tight, sometimes I think my eyeballs are gonna pop out of my head." Alice tried to bulge her eyes.

Soon both girls were laughing and skipping back to the group on the floor. Alice turned to Bill and gave him a short little wave, signaling that it was time for him to leave.

Bill looked at Lou Anne. "Well, I guess she's settled. Thanks for all your help. Can I walk you to your class?"

Before Lou Anne could answer, Bill was whirled around by Charlotte who was standing next to a young woman that Bill recognized as the preacher's wife. "Bill, this is Mrs. Spaulding," said Charlotte. "She teaches Alice's class."

"We've met at church," said Bill, extending his hand to Alice's teacher. "Nice to see you again, Mrs. Spaulding. We've tried to keep Alice up with her studies, but we've moved around a lot in the last two years. So I'm afraid she's a little bit behind."

"I'm sure she'll do just fine," said Mrs. Spaulding, giving Bill a reassuring smile. "Having a smaller class is a benefit. We'll have her caught up in no time."

"Thanks," said Bill, "I'll be picking her up today, so if you have any issues or concerns please let me know."

Mrs. Spaulding nodded, turned to the class, and clapped her hands three times. "Take your seats, children. We're ready to begin." The kids scuttled to their seats, Joan saving Alice a spot beside her.

Bill exited Alice's classroom and turned towards Lou

Anne and Charlotte. "I really appreciate your help today. It made things go a lot easier."

"It was really no problem, Bill," said Charlotte, leaning on his shoulder. "You know, as one of the oldest girls in this school, I take it upon myself to make sure everyone's taken care of." She leaned in closely. "You know, I'm 17 and very mature."

Bill dropped his hat, and Charlotte bent to retrieve it, running her hand down his chest. Lou Anne rolled her eyes and started upstairs toward her class. Charlotte handed Bill his hat, winked, and whispered, "Very mature," before following Lou Anne.

Chapter Five

"I'm sick of all this dust. It's driving me crazier than a bee tied to a string." Dovie watched the thick cloud of dirt chase the truck in the side mirror as she tried to swallow the grit. "The good Lord has to let it rain sometime. What was it Grandpa Oce used to say?"

James stared ahead. Dovie nudged her father. "Dad, I asked you a question."

"Sorry, honey, I'm just wonderin' what kept Bill." James downshifted the truck. "He doesn't seem like one that would go back on his word. I just hope he didn't run into trouble in town. Surely the school took those kids right in."

"You have a good heart, Dad, but we don't know these folks from Adam. They could be long gone, lookin' for greener pastures." She looked at the dry, cracked fields. "Though I'm sure the whole world is brown."

James shook his head. "I just don't believe that, Dovie. Bill doesn't seem like the type. You can tell he wants to do right by those kids. It's one of the reasons I hired him."

Pulling into the driveway, they spotted Bill sitting in the back of his truck, his red hair plastered to his even redder face. He had a blue bandana tried around his left forearm. Sitting just under the tailgate in the shade, was their goose Norman, head high in a triumphant pose.

Dovie and James glanced at each other and smiled.

"I guess you're right, Dad. He does have a good reason for not showing this afternoon. You still got that stick in the back?" Dovie asked.

"I don't go anywhere without it. I should've known it was ol' Norman." James parked the truck. "I'll take care of Norman. You see to Bill."

James eased out of the truck and reached into the bed of the truck to grab a large tree branch.

"Get!" He growled as he waved the branch at the large bird. Norman hissed at James. "You better get to the barn, you ornery ol' bird, or I'll sic Button on you. She'd love to ring your mean ol' neck." James let out a loud whistle.

Norman let out a series of laughing honks as Button rounded the corner. Norman retreated toward the barn. Button sat by James's side, eyeballing the offending goose.

Dovie got out of the truck and walked to Bill as James leaned on the side of the bed. "So, Norman wouldn't let you out of the truck, huh?"

"That bird is the devil," Bill said, hopping down. "Why haven't you cooked it yet?"

"Norman is better than any guard dog when it comes to keepin' the chickens safe," said Dovie. "We've seen him fight off foxes, badgers, and even a coyote. That bird's so mean, not even a bear could get to them birds. The only thing he's actually scared of is Button. I think he knows that dog would lie in the middle of the road if Dad asked him to." Dovie reached for Bill's arm. "How bad did he get you?"

"Not bad. Broke the skin a little. Hurt like a bugger." Bill took off the bandana and showed Dovie the small gash. "I just pulled in for a minute to grab my canteen. Next thing I know, I'm diving head first into the truck bed. Every time

I tried to move, that bird started throwing a fit and bitin'. I feel like a fool letting that mangy bird trap me, but he's evil." Bill rubbed his nose. "Do I have a sunburn?"

"Norman has trapped all of us at one time or another. It's a rite of passage here at Quail Crossings. Why do you think Dad keeps that branch in the back of his truck?" Dovie said. "Come on. Let's get you cleaned up. I bet you could use some water before you get the kids, and we'll break you off an aloe leaf for your nose and the bite."

"Why don't you rest up a bit? I'll see to the kids," offered James.

"I couldn't let you do that, Mr. Murphy. I told Mrs. Spaulding I'd be there in case Alice had any problems." Bill glanced at his arm. "I'm fine, really. Nothin' a little water and some humble pie won't fix."

"I insist." James held up both hands. "You've been in the back of the truck for most of the day without water. I've seen the sun do a number on people, and we can't have you blacking out while driving down the road. If Alice had any problems today, I'm sure Mrs. Spaulding and I can work 'em out. Now get inside and rest up a spell."

Bill nodded and turned to walk into the house.

"Dovie," said James, "every time it rained my father would say, 'Oh come down these sweet drops of rest.' Somethin' we could surely use right now." He looked at the cloudless sky before getting into his truck.

Less than an hour later, Alice burst through the door and bounced into her brother's lap. "Oh, Bill, it was so much fun! My teacher, Mrs. Spaulding, you met her, she's so nice. Of course, I knew she would be 'cause she's the pastor's wife and all. She said I was smart 'cause I already know my numbers and ABC's. In fact, she invited me to her Bible School class. I hope I can go. I really like her, but Sally put a tack in her chair, and when she sat down, she let out a little squeak. The whole class laughed, and Mrs. Spaulding's face turned redder than Evie's does when I use her hair ribbons. I tried not to laugh, really I did, but I laughed anyway. Then Mrs. Spaulding started laughin'. She said she sounded like a cricket, and she really did. Then she got real serious, and this boy, Ralph, told on Sally, and she had to sit in the corner during recess. I would never do somethin' like that to my teacher. She's too nice, and I'd hate to miss recess. So can I go to Bible School on Sunday?"

Bill swallowed a laugh and smiled at his sister. "Of course you can go to Bible School on Sunday. Sounds like you had a very good day, and you learned a good lesson 'bout not hurtin' people for fun." He turned toward his brother. "How about you, Elm?"

Elmer shrugged and stared at his feet. "I'm gonna go feed the dogs."

He walked toward the door with Alice on his heels. "I wanna help!"

"Change out of your school clothes first," Bill hollered, and the two changed course and ran upstairs.

Bill raised an eyebrow. "How was your day, Evie?"

"Just awful, Bill. I had to listen to Charlotte Wheaten talk about how gorgeous you are all day. She even had the nerve to ask me if you were courtin' anyone. Does anyone even say that anymore? Seriously, Bill, it made me sick to my stomach. I swear she's much too forward if you ask me." She noticed the gash on Bill's arm. "What happened to your arm? Did Mr. Murphy put you in harm's way?" Her face turned red. "I knew Mr. High and Mighty wasn't the saint he claims to be."

Bill lost his smile. "Don't speak about Mr. Murphy that way. He's a good man. Probably one of the best I've ever met." He forced his smile to return. "I just had a run in with that big oaf they call Norman."

"The goose?" Evalyn raised an eyebrow.

Elmer and Alice ran out the back door.

"Slow down!" Evalyn chided.

Bill laughed. "Yep, the goose. Don't underestimate that crazy bird. Get changed and then get the laundry off the line for Mrs. Grant. I want you and Alice to help her with supper tonight. At the very least, I want you to make the biscuits for breakfast so Mrs. Grant doesn't have to do it in the morning."

Evalyn's mouth dropped open. "I've had to put up with girls oglin' you all day, and now you want me to help *her* with laundry and dinner? I won't be…"

Bill held up his hand. "No arguin'. I've had one long day, and I'm not puttin' up with your nonsense."

Evalyn closed her mouth and stomped upstairs to change as Bill left to find Elmer. It didn't take long for him to locate his brother in the barn. What surprised him was seeing James leaning next to Elmer, both concentrating on the contents of the stall.

"Now, son, do you think you can handle trainin' all these pups?" James asked, chewing on a piece of straw. Six small black and white balls of fur lay in the hay, suckling on their mother, Pancake, as Alice gently petted each one. "I want 'em ready by Christmas or at the very latest, ready for the market in March, to sell as huntin' dogs."

"Yes, sir," Elmer said.

"I'll give you ten cents on the dollar for every one we

sell. The rest will go towards food," explained James. "Do you understand what that means?"

Elmer nodded and extended his hand to James. "Thanks, Mr. Murphy."

James shook Elmer's hand. "Better go help your brother with the cattle. He'll wonder where you got off to."

Elmer ran towards the pasture. Bill walked past James and gave him a thankful nod, which James returned.

Alice carefully traced the desert rose embossed on the ivory dinner plate. She loved setting the table with Mrs. Grant's fine china. She couldn't remember a time when her family hadn't eaten off tin plates. Dovie insisted they use the china for Sunday lunch and daily supper. Her grandmother had passed the dishes on to her mother with strict instructions to use them daily. "No use for dishes to sit and collect dust," she'd say.

Of course, these days it didn't matter if you used it or not, everything collected dust. Alice couldn't set the table until all the plates, bowls, forks, and spoons were rinsed and dried. Dovie and Evalyn made bread early in the morning, before the dusters hit. Sometimes the bread was gritty, but it was eaten anyway.

Alice thought about her parents and pictured them sitting in a green valley eating oranges. "I sure do miss Alice," her ma said.

"Yeah," said her pa. "She used to love eating oranges."

Alice remembered how their neighbor, Opal Lutz, always gave them an orange at Christmas. Licking her lips, she could almost taste the sweet, juicy flesh.

"Watcha doin', child?" asked Dovie, placing some

folded towels in a kitchen drawer. "You're gonna catch a fly with your mouth open like that, or worse a stink bug."

"I was just thinkin' 'bout the oranges we used to get from Ms. Lutz. She had a sister who lived in Florida, and when she would visit at Christmas, she'd always bring a bag of oranges. Since Ms. Lutz lived alone, she shared them with us." Opening her eyes she grinned. "Do you think they'll have oranges at the church potluck on Sunday?"

"I don't reckon," said Dovie, placing the laundry basket in the bottom of the pantry closet. "I haven't seen oranges 'round here in a coon's age."

"Oh well, I'm sure there'll be good food there anyway." Alice dried the silverware. "Watcha makin' for it, Mrs. Grant?"

"Just some ol' baked beans."

"She means her famous baked beans," stated James as he hung his hat on the long nail by the door. "She makes the best beans this side of the Mississippi, probably the best beans in the whole country."

"Hush, Dad, there ain't nothin' famous 'bout my beans." She hit him playfully with a dish towel.

"She's bein' modest. Folks line up for her beans. They got to have one of the ladies stand there and spoon 'em out so everyone gets some." James smiled at Alice. "I'm sure they'd line up for seconds, but there ain't never any left."

"Don't know why anyone would get so excited over beans," snorted Evalyn as she placed the meatloaf on the table.

"Just wait till you taste 'em, young lady," said James, winking. "You'll see."

"Well, I never really cared for baked beans. They just turn to mush in your mouth." Evalyn looked at Alice. "Or oranges either, they were too sticky."

"Evie, why do you act like you've always got a splinter in your hiney?" Alice sneered causing James to belt out a laugh. "You know you liked them oranges just as much as I did. Remember that year I ate yours? You were madder than a cat thrown in a stock tank."

"Alice Brewer, do you want your mouth washed out with soap?" said Bill, standing in the doorway.

"No sir." Alice bowed her head. "It's just she's lying, Bill, and she's always so cranky."

"Never you mind," said Bill, washing his hands at the sink. "Sounded to me like Evie was just stating her opinion. You need to respect that and respect your older sister. Now apologize."

Alice swallowed hard. "I'm sorry I said you have a splinter in your hiney, even if you act like you do." James choked back another laugh as Dovie slapped his arm. Alice continued. "I just want you to be happy." Alice looked up at her older sister. "Don't you think you could at least try to be happy here?"

Chapter Six

The day of the potluck started before dawn. Not only did they have to get to church on time, but the beans had to be perfect. Dovie's reputation depended on it. She silently chastised herself for thinking of her reputation and not the needy folks the potluck would feed as she stirred the beans that had been soaking overnight. They were ready for cooking. Dovie cut a sweet red onion and fried the last of the bacon. They'd have to do without until the next slaughter in October, but not having bacon for a few weeks was not the end of the world. After adding the onion and bacon to the beans, she grabbed the brown sugar and molasses. Next came the delicate process of adding half a cup here and there of the two ingredients until the consistency and taste was just right. All it took now was time for all the flavors to blend.

"Evalyn," Dovie said, after a breakfast of grits and sausage, "it's customary for the young girls of the congregation to tend to the table, helping with the dishes and carrying plates for the older patrons. Is that somethin' you think you can handle, or do I need to tell Pastor Spaulding that you're unable to do your part."

"She'll be more than happy to help," answered Bill, winking at his sister.

"Oh, yes." Evalyn plastered on a fake smile and batted her eyelashes. "I can think of nothin' better to do than tend to a bunch of folks eatin' your famous beans. Why it would be the highlight of my year."

Dovie stared at Evalyn, wishing she'd kept her mouth shut and let Evalyn look lazy at the dinner. But she liked having Bill around to help her dad. It was just a shame he came with so much baggage.

"Well, we better get a move on it, or we'll be sitting next to deaf ol' Velma," said James.

"Now, Dad," Dovied chided, "that's not very Christian."

"I know, I know, but that woman sings like a peacock."

Dovie couldn't help but chuckle as she grabbed her beans. "Yeah, and you sound just like a canary."

Her Dad was right. Poor Velma had lost most of her hearing, but that hadn't stopped her from singing the Lord's hymns at the top of her lungs and largely out of tune. Guess God didn't care if you had the voice of an angel or a cat in heat, as long as you were singing his praises, thought Dovie.

When they arrived at the church, Dovie rushed inside to stick her beans behind the old wood-burning kitchen stove so they'd stay warm during the service and not burn, while James secured them a good pew away from Velma's vocals.

Her beans securely in place, Dovie fanned herself at the back door as the Brewers piled out of their truck and were greeted by different folks. Tiny grabbed Elmer's reluctant hand and pulled him toward the playground, followed by a skipping Alice and Joan. Harriet whispered something to Evalyn, making her grin from ear to ear, as they headed to the far side of the little church. Bill's arm was instantly grabbed by Charlotte as she escorted him into the sanctuary, nodding to people as they passed. Dovie chuckled to herself as she watched Bill politely fight the urge to snatch his arm away from Charlotte. He was gonna have his hands full, Dovie thought. It wasn't every day a good-looking bachelor found his way to Knollwood and decided to stay.

As the church bells rang, everyone hurried to find a seat so the service could start. Dovie scanned the pews for the Brewers. Bill sat next to Charlotte and was listening to George Wheaton. From his gestures, Dovie figured George was telling Bill his famous fish story. Elmer sat just behind his brother, next to Tiny who was chattering on about one thing or another. Alice and Joan sat next to James and played Patty Cake while everyone else filed into the small sanctuary. But Evalyn was nowhere to be found. Frowning, Dovie sat next to James and opened her hymnal to the song posted on a wooden plank at the front of the church. She inhaled deeply, taking in the scent of wood polish and the fragrance of the roses that sat in two vases flanking the pastor's podium.

The crowd grew silent as Pastor Spaulding stood in front of the congregation and welcomed everyone to another Sunday of worship. As they were finishing the first hymn, Dovie saw Evalyn and Harriet sneak in and take the empty seats next to Velma. Serves them right for coming in late, Dovie thought. She'd have to speak to Bill about Evalyn later. No one living under her roof would be sneaking into the sanctuary after the service had begun. It wasn't right.

Dovie could tell Pastor Spaulding was keeping the service short, with the knowledge that his congregation was looking forward to the feast ahead. So many families were just scraping by; today's potluck would be a feast for everyone. It was getting hard to ignore the chorus of growling stomachs, and soon Dovie's own stomach began to growl in anticipation of the dinner ahead. Pastor Spaulding said his final prayer of the service and blessed the upcoming meal.

As soon as the "amens" were said, all the ladies rushed out to get their food on the tables that had been set up by the playground before service, while the men moved around a few of picnic tables. Dovie sent the younger ladies to put out the tins, forks and napkins for the patrons to use and sent others to start heating water on the old stove for a washing station.

She brought her beans to the serving table and stirred the thick concoction. The sweet aroma filled the area, and a line started to form. As she stirred, something strange caught her eye. There was a twig in her beans. Using her serving spoon, she carefully fished out the twig, only to find a body attached. It wasn't a twig, but a big brown grasshopper. How in the world did a grasshopper get in her beans? she thought. Flicking it behind her, she stirred again, blinking back tears as she saw grasshopper upon grasshopper. Picking up her pot, she hurried toward the kitchen.

"You better bring those back, Ms. Dovie," a gentleman joked from the line. "I've been waiting all year for those beans."

Evalyn blocked her path.

"Oh, I do hope there's nothin' wrong with your famous beans," Evalyn said dramatically. "I was so looking forward to trying 'em. You know, to see what the fuss was 'bout."

"You did this, didn't you?" accused Dovie. "That's why you were late to service this mornin'."

Evalyn placed her hand innocently on her chest. "Why, Mrs. Grant, I have no idea what you're talkin' about."

"You little devil." Dovie brushed by Evalyn. Once in the kitchen, her tears would no longer stay put and rushed down her cheeks, though she tried diligently to brush them away before Evalyn saw. She didn't want to give that little brat the satisfaction of seeing her upset.

"Dovie, what's wrong?" asked Sara, wiping her wet hands on her apron.

"That little heathen, Evalyn, put grasshoppers in my beans! They're ruined," Dovie bawled, no longer able to maintain her composure. Thankfully Evalyn had ventured back onto the church grounds.

"Well, I never." Sara stirred the beans to see for herself.

"Dovie, we're ready to serve," sang Kathleen Wheaten entering the kitchen. "We just need your beans. There's about to be a riot."

"No beans today, Kathleen," said Sara. "Looks like someone put grasshoppers in the pot. I don't think there's any way we can save 'em."

"Not someone, it was Evalyn," said Dovie, "I ought to tan her hide."

Kathleen raised her delicate hand to her mouth and peered into the pot. "Grasshoppers you say?"

"Yes, the pot is full of 'em," gasped Dovie between sobs.

Kathleen hurried to the door. "Harriet Christine Wheaten, you get in here right now!"

Dovie could tell by Kathleen's tone that she felt Harriet had something to do with the grasshopper beans. "Evalyn all but confessed, Kathleen. That heathen has been mocking my beans for days. Plus she was late to service this morning, givin' her an opportunity to mess with 'em. I'm sure Harriet had nothing to do with it."

Harriet entered the kitchen with Pastor Spaulding on her heels. "Is everything alright, ladies?" the pastor asked.

"Yes, Pastor," said Kathleen. "Y'all go ahead and get started."

"But Mrs. Grant's baked beans aren't on the table yet. Surely, we can't start without them," insisted the pastor.

"I'm sorry, Pastor, but they'll be no beans today," said Sara, rubbing Dovie's back gently.

"But…," said Pastor Spaulding, a pout forming on his lips, "everyone looks forward to Mrs. Grant's beans."

"They'll have to make do," stated Kathleen. "Could you please ask Bill and Evalyn Brewer to join us in here?"

"Sure." Pastor Spaulding hung his head in disappointment and went to find Bill and Evalyn.

Kathleen turned to her daughter. "So you and the girls are goin' fishing after church? That's why you needed all them grasshoppers?"

Dovie gasped.

"Yes, Mother." Harriet locked her hands behind her back, ignoring Dovie's astonished stare.

"Where are the grasshoppers? I want to see 'em." Kathleen folded her arms tight.

"We let 'em go," said Harriet as Bill and Evalyn walked in the door. "We just didn't have the heart to kill 'em."

Kathleen tapped her foot. "How convenient they found their way into Dovie's baked beans."

"Mom," Harriett said dramatically, "I don't know what you're talking about. How do you know they're my grasshoppers? The pests are all over the place."

"Sorry to interrupt, ladies," Bill said, holding up his hand. "The pastor said you wanted to see us?"

Kathleen turned to Evalyn. "Do you know what

happened to Dovie's baked beans?"

"I'm guessin' there's somethin' wrong with 'em." Dovie could tell Evalyn was trying not to smile, but her right dimple was giving her away. "She did run in here bawling like a baby."

"What did you do, Evalyn?" asked Bill, eyes wide.

"Why do you always assume it was me?" snapped Evalyn.

"You know you did it, you monster! I saw you and Harriet come in late to service. I can't believe y'all would do that -- to waste all that food when people are goin' hungry." Dovie glared at Evalyn, fresh tears wet her cheeks. "Do you know there are some folks out there who haven't had a decent meal in weeks? This potluck might be the last full belly they have till spring."

"Well, I'm sure they'll get along just fine without your beans." Evalyn crossed her arms.

"Harriet, you and Evalyn should be ashamed. Now I want y'all to apologize to Mrs. Grant and then to those folks out there," ordered Kathleen.

"I will not." Evalyn stomped her foot. "And you can't make me."

"But I can." Bill crossed his arms. "You'll do as Mrs. Wheaten says. We'll talk 'bout the rest of your punishment at home."

"She's been braggin' about those beans all week. Maybe it was God who knocked her off her high horse."

The ladies gasped at Evalyn's statement.

"You've just earned yourself barn duty," said Bill, face as red as his hair. "Keep it up, and I'll throw you over my knee in front of this entire congregation."

"Bill!" Evalyn protested and then looked at her friend. "Harriet?"

"Ain't no use. They've done made up their minds." Harriet turned to Dovie. "Mrs. Grant, I really enjoy your baked beans, I'm sorry they got ruined. I hope you find the real culprits and that they are severely punished."

Dovie glanced at Kathleen, who rolled her eyes.

"Oh, they will be, sweet daughter, don't you worry about that," said Kathleen, pushing Harriet toward the door.

"Evalyn," warned Bill, "you will apologize to Mrs. Grant and those people out there, or you'll walk home after your whoopin'."

"You wouldn't dare." Evalyn eye's narrowed.

"Don't think for one second I wouldn't leave you here after giving our family a bad name," Bill said.

Evalyn slowly looked towards Dovie. Face as red as Bill's, she spoke in a low controlled voice, "I'm sorry."

"Now, outside." Bill gestured to the door. "When you're done with the apology to those folks out there, you can relieve Lou Anne and Betsy at the washin' station."

Evalyn stomped out the door.

"Mrs. Grant," Bill reached into his pocket, "please allow me to pay for the beans."

Dovie waved her hand at Bill. "You shouldn't have to pay for Evalyn's misdeeds. You didn't know what she was doin'."

"Then she'll need to work it off. She knows better than to waste food."

"Sounds fair." Dovie glanced at the ruined beans. "The dogs will feast like kings tonight. I'm sure the ol' mutts won't mind some bugs in their beans."

Grabbing her bean pot, she walked quietly to the pick-up and waited for her father to take her home.

Chapter Seven

October 1934

Alice stared at the big goose blocking her path to the chicken coop. She fought the urge to run back inside and get Evalyn, who'd been cranky since the potluck. Alice took a hesitant step forward. Norman also took a step forward, staring her down. Alice reluctantly took another step toward the coop. Norman followed her lead and took his own step forward. This continued until the two were a foot apart. Alice squatted on her haunches to be eyelevel with the bird.

"Are you gonna bite me, Norman?" She tilted her head to the right. Norman mirrored her behavior as he tilted his head to the left

"Do you wanna play?" Alice stretched her head to the left and smiled as Norman copied her actions. Raising her left hand, she watched as Norman raised his right wing. She giggled at the bird, and he honked lightly. Alice and Norman continued their game until Alice laughed so hard, she fell on her behind. Sitting with her legs crossed, she patted her thighs, and Norman took a seat in her lap.

"You wanna be my friend?" she asked the bird as Norman lay his head on her shoulder. "K, then it's settled. Let's go gather eggs."

Norman jumped off and waddled towards the coop. He let out a loud honk when they reached the gate, causing the chickens to run from the door and allowing Alice to enter without any trouble. Every time a hen would cluck in disapproval of the egg gathering, Norman would let out a gruff honk that would quiet even the nastiest of hens. Alice exited the coop and grinned down at Norman.

"Didn't get pecked one time." She patted Norman on the head. "Thanks for your help, Mr. Norman. You're quite the gentleman."

Norman followed Alice as she finished her morning chores. As the kids left for school, he chased the truck to the end of the drive and let out a loud pitiful honk good-bye. When Bill returned from dropping off the kids, Norman met him at the door. Bill grabbed his stick and shook it at the bird.

"You're not going to trap me in the truck again, you ugly ol' fowl." Bill glared at Norman.

Norman looked around Bill into the empty truck, bowed his head, and waddled away.

"Norman's actin' weird today," Bill told James as he went inside.

"How so?" James furrowed his brow.

"He chased the truck down the drive when I took the kids to school. Thought he was gonna jump in the bed at one point. When I came back, he was sittin' by the road. I was sure he was going to try and trap me again, but he just looked into the cab and then waddled away. Now he's out by the road again, lookin' like he's waitin' for somethin'."

"I'm sure he's fine," said James as they walked to the barn. "Norman's a bit of a bird brain, you know."

James slapped his knee and laughed as Bill shook his head at the joke.

Bill watched Norman sit by the road all day. He never moved, just concentrated on the dusty highway. Feeling sorry for the fowl, Bill took him a bucket of water. But Norman wouldn't touch it. Bill shook his head and continued his chores. While tending to the horses, Bill watched as Dovie tried to herd Norman back to the pond using a broom. But Norman just sat there as she poked him over and over with the straw end.

"Fine," yelled Dovie after fifteen minutes of poking, "but if you end up road kill, it's your own fault for being more stubborn than an jackass on a July afternoon."

At one point even James tried to coax the bird away from the road. Having no luck, he examined the goose. Coming back to Bill, James shook his head. "I don't get it. He seems to be fine. Most likely he won't make it to the morning, and we'll have no idea why." James ran his hands through his hair. "If he's not better by nightfall, I'll put him down. No need for him to suffer, ornery ol' bird or not. Probably shouldn't eat the meat being we have no idea what ails him."

Norman continued his vigil all day by the road staring in the distance. Bill's heart broke as Norman let out a low honk as Bill left to pick up the kids from school.

Half an hour later, Bill watched as Norman's head perked up at the sight of his truck pulling into the drive. The bird jumped up and waddled toward the truck. Alice jumped off the front seat as Norman approached.

"Watch that bird! He might be sick," warned Bill, pulling on Alice's arm and grabbing his stick.

"Oh, I sure hope not." Alice brushed off Bill's hand and gave Norman a pat on the head. "Mr. Norman and I are friends." Norman flapped his wings in the air and let out a joyous honk. Stunned, Bill watched as the two new friends waddled off towards the pond, Alice telling Norman all about her day at school.

Bill shook his head in disbelief. If he didn't know any better, he'd swear the bird was listening. He had to find James and let him know Norman was only suffering from a case of loneliness, if geese could feel such a thing.

He entered the house and found Dovie giving Evalyn her list of extra chores for the day.

Bill took off his hat and shifted it from side to side. "Mrs. Grant?"

"Yes, Bill," answered Dovie.

"Norman's fine now. Turns out he was waiting for Alice all this time."

Dovie choked back a laugh. "Well, I'll be. Who would've thought?"

"How's Evie doing?" asked Bill.

"She's keepin' her sass to a minimum." Dovie paused for a minute and then added. "She hasn't ruined anyone's beans lately."

Evalyn rolled her eyes at her brother and sighed.

"Good to hear." Bill grinned. "Keep it up, Evie, and you can go to the fair next Saturday."

"Really, Bill?" Evalyn's face lit up. Bill knew she was dying to get out since she hadn't been able to do anything but extra chores for three weeks.

James shot through the back door with Elmer. "Are all the kids inside? There's a duster comin'. Looks like a big one."

"Alice is at the pond with Norman. Elm, go get her. Can we get to the cattle?" asked Bill.

James shook his head. "No time, just help me with the horses. Evalyn, get the chickens locked up and the laundry off the line. Then help Dovie get sheets and towels on the doors and windows."

The four hurried to finish their tasks before the clouds of dust blew in. As Elmer and Alice returned, Alice locked Norman into the barn with the horses and then helped Evalyn with the clothes. Once done, the three ran inside. Elmer and Evalyn nailed wet towels over the windows with Dovie, while Alice covered all the dinnerware with flour sack towels. Bill and James hung wet sheets over the doorways.

"I got all the windows upstairs," said Elmer, panting.

"Everything's done down here," said Dovie, and they all sat down at the table. "Sure goes a lot quicker when you've got six people instead of two. Can't remember the last time Dad and I got all the windows covered before the duster actually hit. Maybe it ain't as big as you thought, Dad?"

A hard gust of wind plowed into the house, causing the boards and windows to creak. The dust followed, blocking out most of the sun. It turned from late afternoon to dusk in an instant. "Guess I'll eat my words," said Dovie, eyeing the roof.

Alice climbed in Bill's lap. "I'm scared."

"It's ok, sweetie. We've been through these before." Bill caressed the child's head. "Remember when we got caught in the truck? We made it through that, didn't we?"

"And that was really scary," said Alice, nodding.

"So, Dad, are you takin' Poppy to the fair for the milkin' contest?" Dovie asked looking at Alice with concern. Bill could see she was trying to get their minds off the storm.

"Of course," answered James, "the lady's got a title to defend. I bet she's still the best milk cow in the county, if not the country. If FDR knew about Poppy, he'd scoop her up and take her to the shantytowns to feed those poor people. I bet they'd even put her on a poster next to ol' Uncle Sam."

"Makes you thankful for what you have." Bill looked at Evalyn, who strummed her fingers on the table.

"What else is at the fair?" asked Alice, climbing out of Bill's lap and into her own chair closer to James.

"Well, it changes a little each year." James scratched his head. "But I hear there'll be some pony rides, games, a livestock show, and, of course, the hayride and hoedown."

"I wanna go to the hoedown!" Alice clapped her hands in delight.

"I suspect we'll all go," said Bill watching Evalyn. Even in the dusty air he could see her eyes light up.

"Oh, what will I wear?" Evalyn placed her hand on her chin and began to daydream.

"Are you gonna enter your apple pie this year?" James asked Dovie.

"I reckon," she answered. "Don't know why I bother. Hannah Garber always wins with her pecan pie."

"Is that Lou Anne's mother?" Bill asked catching another eye roll from Evalyn. She was getting too good at those, thought Bill.

"Yes, she is," said Dovie. "How do you know Lou Anne?"

"She's just one of the girls in this town who insists on throwing themselves at Bill," Evalyn answered. "You'd think he was Clark Gable the way they all fall over themselves at him."

Now it was Bill's turn to roll his eyes. "I met her the first day of school. She helped me get Alice settled. Plus I've seen her at church."

"Mrs. Grant, will you teach me how to make a pie?"

asked Alice. Bill was glad for the change in subject.

"Of course she will," promised James, obviously ignoring the glare from his daughter as he continued to look at Alice.

"Only if you don't mind, Mrs. Grant," said Bill. "But it would be nice for Alice to learn her way around the kitchen, and it would give Alice more of an opportunity to help out around here."

Dovie sighed. "You're right. She does need to learn how to cook. Sure she can help make the pies. But you'll have to help with the dishes too. That goes hand in hand with cooking."

"Yes, ma'am." Alice glowed. "Will we get to go to school tomorrow?"

"Probably not. Everyone will be cleaning up, includin' us," said Bill.

Alice glanced towards the muddy sheet covering the door. "Sure hope Mr. Norman's ok."

"Mr. Norman?" Dovie raised her eyebrows at Bill.

"Yep." Bill shook his head. "I told you, she and the devil bird are now buddies. I thought that bird was going to jump in the truck with us this mornin'."

"Your buddy?" Dovie said raising an eyebrow at Alice.

Alice popped up on her knees. "I was headed to the chicken coop this morning, and he blocked my path. At first I was scared he was gonna bite me, but then he started playing. I asked if he wanted to be my friend, and he said yes."

"He said yes?" It was James's turn to raise an eyebrow.

"It's like this." Alice placed a finger on her chin. "He don't speak English, but he let out this low honk and then sat in my lap. So I took that as a yes."

"Well, I'll be," said Dovie. "I didn't think that bird

liked anything that walked on two legs."

"He likes me. He even held the chickens off, so I could gather the eggs without getting pecked. That nasty ol' rooster didn't even get me." Alice smiled. "Mr. Norman's a good listener too. I told him all about my day at school, and he didn't interrupt once to talk about himself." She glanced at Evalyn, who was still daydreaming.

"So that's why Norman was acting so weird this afternoon," said James. "He missed Alice while she was at school."

"He did!" Alice beamed. "I missed him, too. He was all I could think about. We were adding pictures of apples, but I kept seeing little Normans instead of apples."

"How 'bout we play some rummy till this thing passes?" suggested Dovie.

Everyone nodded, and Dovie went to find cards. They played until supper and then attempted to eat leftover ham and biscuits. No one had much of an appetite since each bite contained a side of grit. After dinner, they played Slap Jack until Alice and Elmer went to bed with the duster still raging outside.

The four adults played bridge for a few hours before calling it a night.

"Gonna be some diggin' tomorrow," said Bill as he headed for bed. Listening to the dust hit the windows, he feared for the cattle, crops, and his family's livelihood at Quail Crossings.

Chapter Eight

Dovie took down the muddy sheet that blocked the back door, wadded it up, and threw it in a corner. She'd be doing laundry most of the day with all the sheets and towels they had used on the entryways and windows. It was nothing out of the ordinary these days; they had gotten into a routine after the first couple of storms. Dovie shook her head at how repetitive it all was and how with every storm came bad news.

Some people lost livestock, cars, even houses, but the saddest stories were of those who had lost their lives in the dusters. Many folks, kids especially, were coming down with the dust pneumonia, and some, especially the babies and the elderly, couldn't fight it off. Dovie wiped away a tear at the thought and headed to the back door.

The storm was over, and the morning sun displayed a sea of tan. Sand was everywhere. Grabbing her big push broom, she forced the back door open and started sweeping the stoop. James and the kids would be in and out all day. It wouldn't do her any good to clean the inside if they kept tracking dirt in from the porch.

As she swept, her mind drifted back to the first dust storm she had ever experienced. It had been two years earlier. She had been hanging laundry out to dry with Helen, who had just turned three at the time, on another dry windy day, in a series of dry windy days.

The wire gave her a nasty shock as she hung Helen's Sunday dress, and she bit back an oath.

"Mommy, are you ok?" Helen asked.

"The laundry line just shocked the tar out of me."

Helen giggled.

"Oh, you think that's funny, huh?" Dovie advanced towards Helen, hands held up in tickle position. "How 'bout I release the tickle monster. Then you'll have somethin' to laugh about."

Helen let out a delightful squeal and rushed behind a fresh sheet hanging to dry. Dovie lifted up the line only to be shocked again.

"Ouch! What in the dickens is going on?" she asked looking around the yard. Scanning the horizon, she spotted some light clouds rolling in.

"Get in the house, Helen. It looks like it might rain. Thank the Lord." Dovie raised her hands to the sky.

"What 'bout the clothes, Mommy?" Helen asked.

"Don't worry 'bout them. I'll get 'em. You just get in the house." Dovie shooed her daughter toward the house.

Helen skipped away as Simon sped into the driveway.

"Get in the house, Dovie," Simon yelled. "There's a storm comin', the likes of which I've never seen before."

"Ok, Simon, don't get your knickers in a bunch." Dovie turned back toward the laundry. "Let me get the clothes off the line."

"There's no time. Where's your dad?" Simon scanned the horizon.

"In the barn." Dovie continued with the clothes. "Simon, it's just a storm. I've got time to get the laundry. A little water is just what we need."

Simon grabbed his wife by the shoulders.

"There ain't no rain in that storm. It's nothin' but dirt. I was at Johnson's when they got a call that a duster was headed our way. Get in the house. Cover all the windows with wet towels."

"'K, just let me get the laundry," Dovie said stubbornly. "Helen's Sunday dress is out here."

"Forget the damn laundry, Dovie!" Simon yelled, giving her a good shake.

Dovie sucked in a deep breath and ran into the house, tears flowing down her cheeks. Simon had never cussed at her before. She grabbed the pile of towels she had just taken off the line and threw them in the sink. As she pumped water over them she mumbled under her breath, "How dare he talk to me that way. Now Helen's good dress is gonna get rained on, and I'm gonna have to do all the washin' again. Just who does he think he is? Well, I'll let him know exactly who he is when he gets back in here. To think I can't stand a little rain. It'd be a blessing to dance in it after the drought we've endured. I'll show him I ain't no prissy pants."

She felt a gust of wind strike the house. Helen began to cry.

"It's ok, honey; it's just the storm. See, come look outside. I know it's been a while since we've had some ra..." She stopped at the door as she saw the figures of Simon and James making their way through, not rain, but dirt. Soon the air in the house was thick with dust. Helen started coughing.

Dovie rushed to the sink. Grabbing a wet flour sack towel she wrapped it around Helen's nose and mouth. "Go sit at the table and keep your eyes shut, baby."

Simon and James rushed in, carrying nails and

hammers. A cloud of dirt followed as they shoved the winter door shut.

"You got them towels, Dovie?" asked Simon.

Dovie grabbed a pile and shoved them in Simon's arms.

"Good. I'll get the den. You start in here. James get some sheets to put over the doors."

The three worked hard covering every window, doorway, and crack. As soon as the last nail was hammered, the wind stopped and the dust settled. Simon, Dovie and James looked at each other and laughed.

Helen cried harder seeing the three adults laughing like loons.

"What's a matter, sunshine?" asked Simon sweeping up his daughter.

"Y'all are laughin', but I don't know what's funny," his daughter cried.

"It's ok, sunshine." He gently removed the makeshift handkerchief. "We're just laughin' cause we're glad the storm's over."

He pulled Dovie close and embraced the two of them in a family hug.

"I'm sorry I yelled at you, honey. I'd do anythin' to keep you safe, even if it means cussin' at you." Dovie nodded and buried her head in Simon's shoulder.

They had lost four chickens, two piglets, and half their garden in that first storm. Dovie had thought it was a fluke of nature, something they would probably never see again in their lifetime. But that duster was soon followed by many others, most much stronger than the first one.

Alice bumped Dovie's foot with the door, breaking her from her trance, as she tried to slide past. "Sorry, Mrs. Grant, but I gotta get to Mr. Norman."

Alice ran down the stairs followed by Bill, Elmer, and James. She ran to the barn door and started digging with her hands. "We're comin', Mr. Norman. Please, please, be ok."

Kicking the dirt away from the shop door, James forced it open and grabbed three shovels, handing one each to Bill and Elmer.

"Bill, help me with the barn. Elmer, start on the chicken coop. Once we get the barn open, we'll check on the cattle and crops and then tend to the trucks and tractor. All the animals are gonna need fresh water. Lots of work to do today. Let's get to it."

He turned to Alice who was still digging with her hands. "Alice, we'll get ol' Norman out. He's a tough one. I'm sure he's fine. Go help Evalyn in the garden. Make sure to sweep off every plant, then water."

Alice hesitated, glancing at the barn door, and then did as she was told. Dovie could hear her squeal with delight as Norman joined her just a few minutes later.

"Oh, Mr. Norman, I was so worried about you." She hugged the bird's long neck as he wiggled the dust from his tail feathers.

The day was a blur of sweeping, dusting, and digging, stopping only for a biscuit or two when hungry. All the bed sheets, towels, and dishes had to be washed. Even with the towels and sheets over the windows and doors, the fine grit had found its way into every nook and cranny.

Dovie was putting on a pot of potatoes when she heard James stomping his boots on the back stoop. He came in, placing his hat on the nail, and sat in the chair with his head low.

"Is it real bad?" asked Dovie, sitting.

"Lost two calves. Too soon to tell on the wheat. What seed didn't blow away is buried so deep." James shook his head and looked at his daughter. His eyes telling of the worry he wouldn't speak.

"Can we get any meat off the calves?" she asked choking back a tear.

James shook his head. "Still too little, such a shame."

"Oh, Dad," Dovie walked behind her father and hugged him, "is there anything I can do?"

"Pray for rain," he said softly. "Pray like you've never prayed before."

Elmer sat in the shady branches of an old cottonwood tree and squinted at the rider coming in the distance. It was a girl alright, but not tall enough to be Evie, and Alice wouldn't be riding alone. His groan was followed by a hard pounding in his chest as he realized it was the one and only Mary "Tiny" Clark riding in his direction.

He swung his legs up onto the branch and prayed she wouldn't see him. What in the world was she doing out here?

Tiny rode right under the cottonwood tree. "Jeepers Elmer, whatcha doin' in the tree? What are you, a chicken hawk?"

"No." Elmer sighed. "Just restin'."

Tiny nodded. "I bet. It's been a busy day at our farm too. We lost a couple of chickens, and I haven't been able to find my dog, Jelly. I named her that on account I love jelly so much, just like my dad loves biscuits." She pointed to the horse. "This is Biscuit. You know I told you about him at school. Anyway, Jelly was off huntin', or whatever dogs do, when the duster hit yesterday, and we haven't been able to find her. I was hopin' she was over here with Pancake and

Button. She's got a red rope tied around her neck for a collar. Would've tied her up in the barn had she been at home. She sure hates dusters."

"Haven't seen her," said Elmer as he hopped down from the tree. "But I'll help you look."

He let out a loud whistle. A few short minutes later, Button came blazing up the trail.

"Jeepers," Tiny said, hopping off Biscuit, "I wish I could whistle like that. Can you teach me? My pa tried to teach me a bunch of times. He tells me to put my lips together and blow out, but I just can't get the hang of it." She tried to whistle, a small whine escaping from her lips. "See, just plain pitiful if you ask me. He can whistle entire hymns. I swear he makes birds jealous. I bet Biscuit, here, could do a better job if he tried."

"Try breathing in when you do it," said Elmer, walking toward the far side of the orchard.

Tiny gave it a try, letting out a low whistle. "Jeepers! It worked. Now I just got to practice." She blew in again, making the whistle a little louder.

"Where does Jelly like to go?" Elmer asked, trying to save his ears from her continuous tries at whistling.

Tiny shook her head. "She never leaves the farm. This is unlike her. I can always count on her to meet me at the road when Pa brings me home. Not yesterday, though. Pa thinks she'll come back on her own, but I'm more worried than a hen collecting her chicks."

"I bet your dad's right," said Elmer. "Dogs are smarter than most people. They used to be wolves you know."

"Jeepers, that sounds like a load of chicken poop to me." Tiny laughed.

Elmer felt his face go red. "It's true. I read a book about it in the Amarillo library. All dogs come from wolves."

Tiny stopped and put her hands on her hips. "Are you tellin' me that Mrs. Fine's little dog she keeps in her purse during church, used to be a wolf?"

"I sure am," said Elmer, planting his feet.

Tiny laughed again. "Oh, Elmer, you're a riot. There's no way that pipsqueak of a pup came from a giant wolf. No way, no how. That's the silliest thing I ever heard."

Elmer turned back toward the house.

"Where ya goin'?" asked Tiny.

"Home," Elmer grunted.

"Jeepers, Elmer, I'm sorry. I didn't mean to make you mad. I just want to find Jelly. Please help me find her," she pleaded. "Come on, Elmer, she's the only dog I've ever had. The only reason we got to keep her is cause Ma convinced Pa she'd eat only scraps and keep the coyotes away. There's no way he'd let me get another one. She's my only friend, other than you."

Elmer shook his head and kept walking, ignoring Tiny's cries as she galloped by.

Chapter Nine

Two days later, the duster was forgotten in the excitement of the County Fair. Dovie collected the ingredients for the pie and called Alice to come help. What was her father thinking? She had been trying to win that blue ribbon for years, tweaking her recipe a little each time. Now she had to teach a six-year-old how to make a pie. Might as well say good-bye to that ribbon right now. Dovie sighed. Making a pie was just one more thing she wasn't going to be able to teach her Helen.

She felt her throat tighten and tears threaten as Alice ran into the kitchen, dragging Evalyn's blue apron on the floor.

"What is this?" Dovie asked, pushing her thoughts of Helen away.

"My ma always wore an apron. Evie always wears an apron. And you always wear an apron, so I thought I needed an apron."

Dovie couldn't help but smile. "I see. Here, let me help."

She tied the top strings around Alice's neck, careful of her fine blonde hair. Then, taking the waist strings, she doubled them around Alice's growing figure. The child had put on at least twenty pounds in the last three months, a good sign. Grabbing a couple of safety pins she kept in her pocket, Dovie temporarily hemmed the apron at Alice's knees.

"Did you wash your hands?" Dovie asked.

"Yes, ma'am. We don't want no dirt in your pie."

"Show me," said Dovie.

Alice held out her hands palm up, then turned them so Dovie could inspect her clean fingernails.

"That'll do. No fidgetin' with your hair. We don't want no hair in our pie, either." Dovie dragged a chair to the counter. "Here, stand on this so you can see. We're gonna do the crust first. Watch me measure the ingredients, and then you can help mix it."

Alice watched Dovie measure the ingredients. Her eyes beamed as Dovie slid the mixture of ingredients in front of her. "Ok, now get your hands in there and mix everythin'. Make sure to get it all."

The little girl squished and mixed with all her might. Soon she paused and let out a loud sigh.

"This sure is hard work, Mrs. Grant." Alice panted. "Whoever said 'easy as pie' didn't know what they was talkin' about."

"How 'bout you take a break and let me mix for a while." Dovie took the bowl as the little girl picked at the dough between her fingers.

"Feel this, Alice?" Dovie handed Alice a piece of dough. "It's too dry, so we need to add a little bit of water."

She added a couple of splashes to the bowl and mixed it some more. "Ok, feel it now."

"It's really soft." Alice said as she rolled the dough between her fingers.

"Yes, but not too soft, or we'd have to add more flour," explained Dovie.

Dovie handed Alice the flour sack. "Now sprinkle the counter with flour, so we can roll the crust out."

Alice grabbed a handful of flour and threw it on the counter, causing a white cloud to puff up in Dovie's face. Alice bit back a smile, waiting for Dovie's reaction.

"We'll have to work on your sprinklin' technique." Dovie waved her hand in front of her face so she wouldn't sneeze. They both giggled.

Placing the dough in the center of the flour lake, Dovie realized the ache of missing her daughter that she had felt less than an hour ago was gone. Not only was it gone, but she was giggling. Something she hadn't done much lately. Maybe it was ok having these kids around. They didn't seem to be going anywhere, and Bill looked to have a good head on his shoulders. She let out a sigh as she thought about the cold day she had buried her family.

"You ok, Mrs. Grant?" asked Alice.

"I'm fine," she said, rolling out the dough. "Just thinkin' 'bout the past."

"'Bout your daughter?" asked Alice.

"Yes."

"What was she like?"

"A lot like you. She asked too many questions." Dovie handed the rolling pin to Alice. "Now you roll for a while. We want nice even strokes. We're trying to make a circle not a rectangle." Standing behind Alice, she showed her how to make nice even runs over the dough.

The couple continued to work through the afternoon as Dovie peeled the apples and then handed them to Alice. With her brow furrowed, she cut them into halves. As Dovie cut the apples into smaller pieces, Alice asked the big question. "How we gonna beat Mrs. Garber?"

"Well, I've been thinkin' about that for a while," said

Dovie. "Why don't you go to the cellar and bring up a jug of apple cider?"

The smile dropped from Alice's face.

"The cellar, Mrs. Grant?" she asked, her voice shaky.

"Yes, you'll find it on the left side - in the corner," Dovie said, not noticing Alice's face. "Dad left the door open this mornin' to let it air a bit."

"Ummm... Mrs. Grant, I can't go down there."

Dovie paused mid-cut and looked at Alice. "Why on earth not?"

"It's scary down there. There might be monsters," explained Alice.

"Nonsense, there's nothin' but food down there. Now go on."

Alice reluctantly headed for the door. As she grabbed the handle she looked at Dovie, hoping that she had changed her mind, but she had gone back to cutting apples.

Taking a deep breath, she walked slowly towards the cellar on the north side of the house. The big wood door that she used as a stage for her and Norman's plays lay open next to the black pit. She walked to the edge and peered down the steep cement stairs leading into the unknown abyss. Looking around the farmyard, she searched for someone to run this errand for her, but saw no one, not even Mr. Norman.

Alice started singing '*Jesus Loves Me*' as she took the first step, placing her right hand on the dirt wall for balance and continued the song as she gingerly walked down the stairs. With every step, her voice grew smaller as her eyes grew larger. She reached the dirt floor and stared into the darkness. She prayed her song would keep the cellar monsters at bay.

Her eyes adjusted to the dark, and she let out a slow

gasp. It was so colorful! On every shelf stood a rainbow of jars. There were potatoes and onions in the right corner and on the left was the cider. As she walked to get the cider, no longer feeling afraid, she scanned each ledge and tried to identify the canned goods.

"Green beans, peas, tomatoes, squash, applesauce." She took a closer look at a jar filled with purple liquid containing odd red squares. "I wonder what this is?"

Finally reaching the cider, she grabbed the heavy jug and waddled to the stairs, wondering if she could get Mr. Norman down here to play house with her.

"Mrs. Grant, I did it!" exclaimed Alice, bouncing through the back door. "At first it was really scary, so I sung *'Jesus Loves Me'*, so the monsters wouldn't get me. It worked! I got down there, and it was wonderful. I've never seen so much food and all them colors. What's the purple stuff?"

Dovie tilted her head. "Purple stuff?"

"Yeah, they was sittin' by the applesauce."

"Oh, the pickled beets."

"The what?" Alice heaved the cider onto the table.

"Beets. Have you never had pickled beets?"

Alice shook her head.

"Well, if you think you can handle another trip to the cellar, we'll have 'em with supper."

Alice ran out the door before Dovie could say another word.

When Alice returned, the duo finished their pies and sat them on the windowsill to cool.

"We're gonna beat Mrs. Garber. I can feel it." Alice gazed at the pie.

After cleaning the pie mess, Dovie started roasting a couple of chickens, one for supper and the other to take to the picnic at the county fair. Alice carefully picked the beets out of the jar with a fork and put them into a bowl. Dovie had warned her not to get the juice on her dress because it could stain, and Alice had heeded the warning.

Before long the family gathered around the table, stomachs growling at the potpourri of apple pie and roasted chicken that filled the air.

"Looks like you've outdone yourself again, Dovie." James grabbed a chicken leg.

"I helped," chimed Alice.

"You did?" James scratched his head. "What did you do?"

"The pie, it's the bestest ever." Alice bounced up on her knees. "We're gonna beat Mrs. Garber for sure. I also put the beets in the bowl."

"Beets can be tricky," said James seriously.

"They sure can. Mrs. Grant said if I got the juice on me, it could stain my pretty dress."

"Well, I don't see any stains, so I guess you did good." James smiled.

Alice beamed from her seat, and with a simple nod from James, everyone bent their heads.

"Dear Heavenly Father, thank you for this food you've blessed us with and for the lovely hands that prepared it. Thank you for bringin' the Brewers into our home and family. Please be with their parents and keep them safe in California. Dear Lord, please bless us with rain and please bring peace to those who are less fortunate. We put our lives in your capable hands. In Jesus's name we pray. Amen."

Alice quickly picked up her fork and stabbed a beet. Taking a huge bite of the purple vegetable, she smiled. "It don't taste like a pickle at all. It's kinda sweet."

Everyone chuckled, except Evalyn, who slid the beets to the side of her plate. Her family was getting just a little too cozy in this one-horse town with these back country folks. She was going to have to step up her plan if she wanted to get them on their way to California. A smile twitched at the corners of her mouth while she formed her plan. If this didn't get them kicked out of this Godforsaken place, then nothing would.

Chapter Ten

Dovie watched Bill wipe the sweat off his forehead with his blue bandana. Getting Poppy, the milk cow, into the truck had been a huge task. Building the ramp from the ground to the bed of the truck had been the easy part. Poppy didn't want to take one step onto that wobbly plank. James pulled as Bill and Elmer pushed while Dovie watched, barely breathing. She could just see one of those boys getting kicked in the head. Poppy was a well mannered cow, but even she had her limits. Inch by inch the boys finally got her tied to the back of the cab as the ladies loaded the last of the picnic goodies.

Today was the opening picnic at the fair, and everyone would get their livestock settled. Tonight would be the hayride and hoedown before tomorrow's contests.

They pulled into the fairgrounds, and Poppy gladly backed out of the truck, happy to be on solid ground. Elmer brushed her while Bill piled some hay into her trough. As the boys got the cow settled, the ladies went to the picnic area where Alice helped Dovie spread out a huge blue and white quilt.

"My mother made this quilt while she was pregnant with me," said Dovie as she smoothed out the wrinkles.

"Sure is pretty." Alice traced the stitching. "Wish my

ma would've made a quilt for me when I was a baby."

"There's nothing stopping you from making one yourself," said Dovie.

Alice's face lit up. "So you'll teach me how? Just like the pie?"

Dovie silently groaned. Why had she said that? She looked at Alice's excited face and shrugged. "I don't see why not. Every girl should know how to make a quilt."

Alice jumped up and hugged Dovie. "Oh, goody, I sure am glad Bill got a job with Mr. Murphy."

Dovie gave Alice two quick pats on the back and grabbed for the basket of food. "We better get a move on or the boys will be belly achin'."

The meal of cold chicken and potato salad satisfied the hungry group, and after clean up, they all headed in different directions. Dovie and Alice took their pie to the contest booth. Bill and Elmer went to check out the midway games while James and George Wheaten looked at tractors. Evalyn had one goal: find Harriet and fill her in on the plan.

Harriet had confided in Evalyn that she would one day be in the movies. After watching "Grand Hotel" with Greta Garbo and John Barrymore, Harriet couldn't get enough of Hollywood. Evalyn had promised her a ride to California if she helped get Bill fired. Walking the midway, Evalyn daydreamed about her and Harriet living in Hollywood, rubbing elbows with Cary Grant and Bette Davis.

The first step was to get Bill on board with going to California to search for their parents. Even if they didn't find them, he could still get a job. Maybe he could get work building the movie sets she and Harriet would act on. There was wealth and fame to be found in California and only dust and skinny cows here.

Finally, Evalyn found Harriet standing by a shed of chickens with her mother. She ran to her friend's side.

"Well, I didn't think they'd spring you in time for the fair." Harriet grabbed Evalyn's hands and giggled.

"I'm out on good behavior and slave labor." Evalyn rolled her eyes and turned to Kathleen Wheaten. "Can Harriet come with me to the crafts building?"

Kathleen stared at the two girls suspiciously. "Well, if Dovie feels you've earned your way then who am I to disagree?" She looked directly into Harriet's eyes. "But I'm warnin' you, Harriet, if you even think of doin' somethin' disgraceful, you will be cleanin' out every stall in the barn, you hear?"

"Yes, mother," said Harriet, innocently looking at the ground.

"So are you thinkin' of doin' something disgraceful?" Harriet asked as soon as they were out of earshot.

"I have a great plan," Evalyn squealed. "If this don't get Bill fired, then nothin' will."

"Oh, I knew it." Harriet clasped her hands together, and the two walked the midway in whispers.

The rest of the day flew as people hurried to prepare for the hayride and hoedown. Bob Johnson had brought in his green wagon, top-heavy with hay, and attached his two black geldings to the front. Mounds of woolen blankets lined the bed of the wagon. The ride included a mile trek to Old Tree Park, around the big cottonwood tree, and then back to the fairgrounds.

The younger kids lined up first, most with their parents, while the teenagers lagged behind waiting for the rides at dusk when young Ben Wheaton would take the helm.

Bill was helping Alice off the wagon when Charlotte popped up behind him.

"How was the hayride, Bill?" She batted her eyelashes.

"It was good. We had a great time. Didn't we Alice?" He yanked on Alice's braid.

"Sure did, Bill. Thanks for takin' me." Alice rocked on her heels and glanced at the playground.

"Bill, do you mind if I go play?" She pointed to a group of kids who were swinging.

Bill reluctantly nodded his head. He didn't like being alone with Charlotte, but that was no reason for Alice to stay. He let out a breath of relief when he saw James and Elmer.

"Y'all goin' for a ride?" he asked, hoping Charlotte would get bored.

"Told Bob I would make sure Ben was doin' okay. Elmer's my excuse," said James.

"I was hopin' to go on the hayride, but I don't have anyone to ride with." Charlotte pouted her lips and looked at Bill.

"You could ride with us if you want," said James, noting that Bill was looking at someone else.

Bill nodded as he watched Alice being pushed on the swing by Lou Anne Garber. "Would y'all excuse me?"

Not waiting for an answer, he walked away. Charlotte watched as he approached Lou Anne and removed his hat. Stomping her foot on the ground, she glared at the two exchanging words and at how Lou Anne blushed as she nodded yes to something he had just asked. It didn't take her long to realize that Bill had asked Lou Anne to ride the hayride with him as he took her hand and guided her toward the horses.

Charlotte's eyes narrowed as she watched Bill, her

Bill, help Lou Anne into the wagon. She was not going to let Lou Anne Garber get away with stealing the only good-looking man in Knollwood. She stormed off down a trail parallel to the road.

Bill playfully touched a curl framing Lou Anne's face. "You've done somethin' different with your hair."

Lou Anne fluffed the bottom of her locks. "Do you like it? Clare put it in pin curlers for me last night."

"It looks nice." Bill brushed a curl off her forehead. "It shows off your eyes. I hope you don't find me too forward, but will you let me take you to dinner sometime?"

"Why, Mr. Brewer, are you askin' me out on a date?" Lou Anne playfully covered her mouth with her hand and batted her eyelashes dramatically.

"I do believe I am, Miss Garber." Bill took her hand.

The two looked at each other, and Lou Anne leaned forward. Bill followed her lead and bent to kiss her soft plum colored lips.

Closing his eyes, Bill anticipated the taste of Lou Anne's lips when the horse on the left let out a loud cry and reared, causing the horse on the right to do the same. Lou Anne screamed as the wagon tipped on its side, sending the passengers crashing to the ground.

Bill opened his eyes. His head was cloudy. People groaned all around him.

"The horses reared," he thought as he jumped to his feet.

"Elmer!" he yelled, "Lou Anne! James!"

Elmer was the first to sit up as he rubbed his knee. "Over here. I'm ok."

He heard a soft cough on his right. Quickly lifting a hay bale, he found Lou Anne fighting her way through a heavy blanket.

"Lou Anne, you okay?" he asked lifting the blanket.

She brushed the dirt off her face and nodded.

"I think so," she said grabbing his hands to stand.

As she stood, she felt a bolt of pain shoot through her ankle, causing her to sink in Bill's steady arms.

"My ankle," she said, choking back a cry.

Without another word, Bill swooped her up and carried her to an uprighted bale. "I'll be right back. I'm gonna see if anyone else needs help. Just stay put till everyone's accounted for, and then I'll get you back to town."

Bill turned and could see most of the riders were standing, brushing the dry grass and hay off their clothes. Ben talked softly to the horses while a few of the men, including James, tried to raise the wagon to its correct state. Bill rushed over and grabbed a corner of the wagon in time to see James wince as he helped lift the back end.

The wagon upright again, Bill approached James.

"You all right?" he asked, nodding towards James's wrist.

"Just twisted it wrong." James examined the wagon wheel.

"It's busted," he said looking at Ben. "Better unhitch 'em. Looks like we're walkin'."

Most of the passengers had already headed back to the fairgrounds to spread the tale of their frightening ride. Bill walked over to Lou Anne.

"The wheel's broken. The way I see it, we have two choices. We can wait for someone to come with a truck, or I can carry you back."

Lou Anne looked around. "It's gettin' pretty dark. I'd hate for you to trip while carryin' me. Will you wait with me?"

"Of course," said Bill. "Let me catch up with Mr. Murphy to let him know we'll be needin' a truck. I'll be right back."

Lou Anne watched Bill jog awkwardly to catch up with James and Elmer, who were just over a small hill. Her attention turned to the sound of a breaking branch just beyond the road.

"Who's there?" she called out.

"It's just me, you big scaredy cat," said Charlotte, coming out of the bushes. "I heard about the accident and wanted to make sure everyone was okay."

She looked over at Ben who was still talking softly to the spooked horses as he unhitched them.

"Why didn't you walk on the road?" Lou Anne crossed her arms. "Shouldn't you be checkin' on your brother? He fell too."

Charlotte flipped her wrist in her brother's direction. "Oh, Ben's fine."

She sat next to Lou Anne.

"So did you and Bill get cozy? Have you no shame? Lettin' a man kiss you in public. Good thing it didn't happen, or your reputation would be ruined. I'd say I did you a favor."

Lou Anne blushed, and then her eyes widened. "What did you do?"

"I didn't mean to hit the horse with the rock; I was aiming for you. But it's nothing I wouldn't do again, even with the same outcome. Bill is the man I'm gonna marry, and I won't let anyone get in my way." She leaned in close to Lou Anne's face. "Keep that in mind my pa and James Murphy are good friends. I'd hate to see anything happen to Bill's job. You know with all those siblings to take care of. It would be such a shame to see little Alice go hungry again."

"Charlotte?" Bill stood at the crest of the hill, looking puzzled. "What are you doin' out here?"

"Oh, Bill." She ran to him and flung her arms over his shoulders. "Was it just awful? Are you hurt?"

Bill gently unwrapped her arms, keeping a hold on her wrists. "I'll ask again. What are you doin' here? I know you didn't come up the road 'cause I was just there talkin' to Mr. Murphy."

"Well, Bill," she jerked her hands away, "I decided to go for a walk since you wouldn't take me on the hayride. I didn't walk on the road 'cause I wanted to be alone. I heard all the commotion and came running."

"I'm sorry, Charlotte, I didn't mean to accuse." Bill scratched his head. "I just can't figure out what spooked them horses."

He walked towards Lou Anne who quickly wiped the tears off her cheeks. Bill knelt and looked at her ankle. "I know it hurts." He winked at her. "Won't we have somethin' interesting to talk about on our date."

"Bill, I have somethin' to tell you," Lou Anne said.

Lou Anne looked at Charlotte who stood behind Bill with her hands on her hips. The scowl on Charlotte's face confirmed what Lou Anne already knew. Charlotte wasn't exaggerating when she said she would stop at nothing, even if it meant hurting innocent people. Her actions that evening were proof enough.

"I'm seein' someone else, John Gates from Wilson. I should've told you before the hayride. I just got caught up in all the excitement. So I can't go to dinner with you. It wouldn't be right."

Bill looked at Lou Anne and nodded slowly. "I think Ben needs some help with the horses. The truck'll be here soon."

Lou Anne watched as Bill took the reins from Ben. "You better treat him right, Charlotte."

"Oh, silly Lou Anne," Charlotte said as she wrapped her arm around Lou Anne, "if there's one thing I know, it's how to treat a man."

Chapter Eleven

George Wheaten hurried toward James and Elmer. "Glad you're okay. Sorry to add to your troubles, but your milk cow's gone missin'. We've looked all over the fairgrounds and can't find her. Some folks are searching in town now. We've never had anything like this happen at the fair before."

James scratched his head. "It's all right, George. We'll find her. Could you take a truck up the road and get Lou Anne Garber? She's got a busted ankle from the accident." He placed his hand on George's shoulder. "You got a good boy in Ben. His cool head kept the horses from boltin'. If it weren't for him, there'd be a lot more injuries."

"I'm just glad everyone's all right." George ran to get his truck.

"Mr. Murphy, where do you think Poppy is?" asked Elmer.

"Not sure. She probably got spooked with all the noise and ran off."

Elmer shook his head. "Doesn't seem like Poppy. You don't think someone stole her, do you?"

"Let's hope not." James checked the latch on the stable gate. "It's in good shape. I must've not gotten it shut when I left for the hayride."

"No, sir." Elmer lowered his head and kicked dirt. "I was the last one out. It had to be me. I'm the reason Poppy's missing."

"Don't worry." James patted the boy on the shoulder. "She can't be far."

"Mr. Murphy!"

James looked up to see Junior Clark running toward them. "We found your cow. She's in the schoolhouse."

"How in tarnation?" James closed the stable gate.

"One more thing, Mr. Murphy," said Junior, wheezing. "She's on the second floor."

"Someone had to put her there." James grabbed a lead rope and muttered under his breath. "Poppy wouldn't have climbed them stairs on her own."

As they arrived at the school, Junior led them to an upstairs classroom. When James opened the door, his nose wrinkled as the stench of manure assaulted him. It would take most of the night to clean the room and probably more than a week to get rid of the smell.

"Good, you're here," said Bud. "We waited. Didn't want to spook her anymore than she already is." Bud looked at his son. "Junior, go find Mr. Wheaton and let him know we found Poppy and Mr. Murphy, so he can call off the search."

Junior nodded and ran back down the stairs.

"Any idea how she got up here?" asked James, running his hands through his hair.

"Tiny saw two girls runnin' out the back door about an hour ago. Came in to check it out and found Poppy. She then came and got me," Bud explained.

"Two girls, huh?" said James, looking at Elmer. "Let's get her out of here before she can add to the smell, what do you say?"

James whispered to Poppy as he walked toward her and attached the rope to her harness. She let out a low moo in appreciation as he led her out of the room and into the hallway. As they approached the stairs, Poppy planted her feet and grunted in disproval.

"Come on, Poppy. It's okay," cooed James, rubbing her nose.

The cow didn't move, and, with each tug of the rope, her eyes got wider.

"Elmer and I could push her, while you pull," suggested Bud.

James shook his head. "Afraid one of y'all would get kicked."

"What if we lead her down backwards?" asked Elmer. "Like when we got her out of the truck."

James and Bud looked at Elmer with raised eyebrows.

"If she can't see where she's goin', maybe she won't be scared," Elmer explained.

James shrugged at Bud. "Worth a try, I guess."

Walking Poppy back down the hall, James turned her rear toward the stairs. With the careful movement of each leg, Poppy gingerly backed down.

"Good work, son," said James, patting Elmer on the back when they reached the safety of the first floor.

"Who would have thunk to back the cow down?" said Bud, scratching his head. "Genius."

Bill met them as they reached the back door of the school.

"I heard." Bill patted Poppy on her head. "I didn't believe it when Tiny said Poppy was in the school, but here she is."

James handed the lead rope to Elmer. "Why don't you take her back to the stables and get her some water and give her a good brushing."

Elmer nodded and glanced at his brother. Bill let out a sigh. "It was Evalyn, wasn't it?"

"We don't know for sure," said James. "But Tiny saw two girls running from the school and then came in to find Poppy on the second floor. I hate to speculate, but after what she did with Dovie's beans, I'm not sure who else would've done something like this."

"For the love of Pete!" Bill punched the air and then sat on the shallow step leading out of the school. "If you need to take Poppy to the vet, I'll cover the bill and for any damages she may have done to the schoolhouse." Bill shook his head. "If there's any way you could help me cover the cost for now, I'll pay you back. I don't think we've got enough saved to cover it up front, but you can have what we got. I would appreciate it greatly if we could settle this between us and the principal; hopefully we can leave the sheriff out of it."

"I've got no reason to go to the sheriff. Poppy's fine." James sat beside Bill. "And the school doesn't need anything but a good scrubbing. As far as I could tell nothing had been damaged. I'll talk to the principal and work something out. Just let me know how you want to handle Evalyn."

"I'm not sure if I know how to handle her, sir." Bill rested his head in his hands. "She wants to go to California to find our parents. She's been harpin' on me to go there for months. Now it seems she's resorted to tryin' to get me fired, as if that'll convince me to go to California."

"Well, I hope that's not gonna happen," reassured James. "Your job is safe as long as you're here."

"Thanks, you and Mrs. Grant have been too kind. Most people wouldn't put up with Evalyn's antics." Bill looked up. "I guess I need to go find her and see if she has an explanation."

"No need," said Bud, "she and Harriet are walkin' this way."

The men watched as the girls strutted toward the school.

"We just heard there was a cow in the school and wanted to come see for ourselves," said Evalyn, rocking on her heels.

Bill stood. "Any idea how she got there?"

"I put her there." Evalyn smiled down at James. "I was sure that Clark girl would've told you by now. We made sure she saw us."

James stood and patted Bill on the shoulder. "You should find everythin' you need in that storage shed over yonder. I'll let the principal know you're taking care of it. See you in the mornin'."

"You mean he's not fired?" Evalyn stomped her foot.

"Now why on God's green earth would I fire your brother?" James asked. "As far as I can tell he's just tryin' to take care of his family, though you seem to makin' that job harder than it has to be. Poppy's fine by the way." James narrowed his eyes at Evalyn. "In case you were wonderin'."

He turned his attention back to Bill. "We'll take Alice and Elmer home after the hoedown, so you can stay here till the mess is cleaned. I'll send over George and Kathleen."

"Y'all heard Mr. Murphy," said Bill. "Go get some shovels and a wheelbarrow. The longer you dilly-dally, the longer we'll be here."

"Sorry, Evalyn, but I gotta skedaddle before my mother hears 'bout this," said Harriet, walking towards the parking lot. "You know how she gets."

"You're not gonna help?" whined Evalyn.

"This isn't my fault." Harriet planted her hands on her hips. "You said your brother would get fired, and we'd be on our way to California. I can't take the blame for this and live with them. I'll be mucking out stalls for months. You know no director is going to put me in the movies if my shoes smell like manure."

"Harriet Christine!"

Harriet cringed.

"Where in the world do you think you're goin'? Did you think I wasn't serious when I warned you earlier?" Kathleen grabbed her daughter by the arm. "What if that cow had been hurt? Mr. Murphy has been a good friend to your pa for ages, and here you are embarrassin' us with your foolishness."

"It was all Evalyn. I thought she was just playin' around. When I saw she was serious, I tried to stop her."

Evalyn rolled her eyes. "Thanks a lot, Harriet. Some friend you are."

"Harriet, if you think for one second that I believe you didn't have a part in this, you're seriously daft. Go get a shovel," ordered Kathleen. "You girls are lucky Principal Miller isn't getting the sheriff involved. I've never been so embarrassed in my entire life."

Harriet looked at her father.

"Do as your mother said, Harriet." George looked away from his daughter.

Harriet turned and huffed to the shed, followed slowly by Evalyn.

"I'm sorry Evalyn has gotten your daughter mixed up in her nonsense." Bill traced the rim of his hat.

"I know you do your best, Bill," George said to Bill. "I don't blame you for the trouble Harriet's in, and you shouldn't have to be here pickin' up after your sister. You're just a kid yourself. Why don't you go on to the hoedown? We'll make sure the girls get things cleaned up."

Bill shook his head. "I couldn't leave you to watch over Evalyn. That ain't right."

"Nonsense," said Kathleen. "George's right. You go and have fun. I won't take no for an answer."

Bill watched Kathleen and George walk into the school before turning and heading towards the dance. He could hear the band playing a rowdy two-step number. People laughed and shouted "yee-haaa" as he approached the huge slab of cement. Strings of lights came from every corner and met at the huge pole in the middle of the dance floor.

Standing back, Bill scanned the crowd. He saw Alice standing on James's toes as he swung her around the floor. Her cheeks glowed from giggling. Elmer was trying desperately to remain seated as Tiny pulled him towards the dance floor. Dovie sat nearby and clapped her hands with the music. It was the first time he had seen a smile reach her eyes since moving to Quail Crossings.

Next, he found Lou Anne sitting by the stage with her foot resting on a box. Bill watched as Jon Gates babbled in Lou Anne's ear, paused, and then kissed her on the cheek. She flinched in surprise.

Bill's gut burned with jealousy. He started across the dance floor, his face red with frustration. Approaching the middle pole, he came face to face with Dovie.

"Dance with me, Bill," she said, and he could tell she wasn't asking.

The music slowed, and he took a deep breath. Relaxing his shoulders, he let the music take over as he led Dovie in a slow two-step.

"Give her time," Dovie said softly. Bill looked at her in

confusion.

"Dad told me you two were getting' pretty cozy on the hayride, and now she's here with Jon. That can't be easy to watch but goin' over there won't help. She's young, and she'll come around. Trust me."

The music ended and the crowd clapped.

"Thanks," said Bill.

Dovie waved her hand. "Don't think nothin' of it."

Bill took another glance at Lou Anne. She met his gaze; a small embarrassed smile appeared but soon dissolved as Jon patted her on the shoulder to get her attention. Bill turned and walked toward the darkness.

Chapter Twelve

James woke up the next morning and moved his wrist in a slow circle. Grimacing, he rubbed his aching joints. Turning the wagon upright had been a little much for his arthritis. He got up and put on his overalls, careful of his tender wrist. He could hear Dovie in the kitchen preparing breakfast, whistling a tune from the hoedown.

He was surprised she was whistling after the argument they had had the night before about Evalyn putting Poppy in the schoolhouse.

"How much of this nonsense are you going to put up with?" she asked once they'd returned home from the dance.

"What do you suggest I do?" James ran his fingers through his hair. "It ain't right to fire Bill because of Evalyn's attitude."

"And if Poppy would've been harmed or one of you guys gotten hurt, then what? We'd be in a real pickle, and the Clarks would be finished if Bud couldn't work."

"I know," said James, "but Bill is trying to do right by his brother and sisters. This is the first real job he's had since his parents left. I promised I wouldn't fire him, and I won't. Firing him means Alice and Elmer go without, and I won't do that. God put them in our lives for a reason."

"Then put that girl on a train to California before she brings the whole family down. That's where she wants to go."

"I'm not putting a fourteen-year-old girl on a train to California alone when we have no idea where her parents are. Besides, Bill would never allow his family to be broken up. He'd quit before sending her off alone. They're staying, all of them, and that's the end of it." He turned toward his bedroom. "You better get your head on straight, Dovie. The path you're on is a slick one with the devil right on your heels. We have always lived by the golden rule in this house, and we always will. Doesn't matter what Evalyn does. We will rise above it with compassion and understanding because she is a young girl going through a confusing time."

His mouth watered at the smell of bacon filling the morning air, snapping his mind back to the chores of the morning. Entering the kitchen, he gave Dovie a knowing smile. "We okay?"

She returned his smile with a hug. "Of course we are. You're right, Dad. I will do my best to turn the other cheek."

Reaching into the cabinet over the sink, James grabbed a can of ointment and began rubbing it on his wrist.

"You all right, Dad?" Dovie eyed the wrist.

"Yeah, liftin' the wagon was a bit much." He put the ointment away. "Doesn't look like I'll be milkin' Poppy for the contest."

"I can do it," came a voice from the corner.

James turned to see Elmer standing by the stairs.

"I won't be as fast as you, but I'd like to try. If you don't mind takin' me to the fair today. Bill says he has to stay here with Evalyn."

Elmer glanced up the stairs as Bill slammed the door leading out of the girl's bedroom. Bill took the stairs by twos, stopping briefly to acknowledge Dovie and James, and then flew out the door. Two minutes later he returned carrying a bucket full of water.

"Y'all might want to plug your ears. I have a feeling this is gonna get loud," Bill said, advancing up the stairs.

Dovie raised an eyebrow at James as a bloodcurdling scream echoed through the house, followed by a large thud and muffled arguing.

"I told you to get up," came Bill's angry voice as Alice skipped down the steps.

"Bill just threw a whole bucket of water from the stock tank on Evalyn," said Alice, giggling. "She's madder than a wet cat; looks like one too." She looked at James and stopped laughing. "Serves her right for puttin' poor Poppy in the schoolhouse. Poppy never did nothin' to her. Mr. Murphy, can Mr. Norman and I go to the fair with y'all?" Alice pouted her lips. "Bill said he ain't goin', and I didn't sleep at all last night, wonderin' if our pie got the blue ribbon. I just can't wait till this evenin' when y'all get back to find out. I just can't!"

"If it's okay with your brother, then you can come with us. Same with you, Elmer," said James. "But Norman has to stay here and keep the chickens in line. You know how those hens can get." He tweaked Alice's nose causing another giggle before Alice and her brother sprinted upstairs.

"Don't forget to ask if you can enter the milkin' contest," Dovie hollered up the stairs and walked back to her frying bacon.

Evalyn lumbered down the stairs, biting her bottom lip. Her wet hair was pulled into a tight ponytail.

She turned to James and inhaled deeply. "Sorry I put your cow in the school. It was a wrong and childish thing to do, and I'm glad no one, especially the cow, got hurt."

She then turned and stared at Dovie. "I've been told to inform you not to worry about supper tonight. I'll be cookin'."

"And," Bill said from the stairs. Elmer and Alice crowded behind him.

"And," Evalyn growled, "for the next month I will do the dish and clothes washin' and anything else you and Mr. Murphy ask me to do until further notice."

"You'd' think that apology tasted like sour milk the way her lip was curled," Dovie mumbled to her father.

Evalyn faced Bill.

"Now, may I go, oh, Master Brother?" she asked with pursed lips.

"Better grab some breakfast first." Bill gestured to the table. "It's gonna be a long day."

Evalyn reluctantly sat at the table and grabbed a couple of pancakes.

"I've told Alice and Elm it's okay for them to go back to the fair. No reason they should miss out 'cause of Evalyn." He turned to his two younger siblings. "Do as Mr. Murphy and Mrs. Grant say or join your sister."

They both nodded their heads eagerly.

"Okay, kids," said James, "we leave in half an hour."

Evalyn started cleaning as soon as breakfast was finished, while Bill walked out with the others. She grabbed the tub of dishwater off the stove and stared at her family gathered around Mr. Murphy's truck.

"Have fun at the fair," she mocked. "Make sure to milk that cow real fast and bring home the biggest, bluest ribbon ever for your crackerjack apple pie. And make sure to do everything perfect Mr. Murphy and miss priss Mrs. Grant ask of you or become a slave. Don't you dare talk back or think for yourself. No, that kind of thinkin' won't be tolerated. Go ahead, act like a bunch of stupid sheep."

Her eyes narrowed as Bill approached the house. She was sure he'd go do his own chores while she cleaned the kitchen.

"We need to talk," he said walking in the door. "No scratch that. I need to talk, and you need to listen."

He pulled out a chair and pointed. "Sit."

Evalyn sighed and plopped herself down. It had been one lecture after another since the Poppy incident. Even Harriet's parents had laid into her, as if they had any right to act like her parents. That's the problem with a small town. Everyone's in everyone else's business.

"I understand you miss Ma and Pa. So do I." Evalyn opened her mouth to speak, but Bill shook his finger at her. She snapped her mouth shut. "You can speak when you're not in trouble. Until then, I want you to listen and then to think." She sighed again and crossed her arms.

Bill rubbed his hands together and took a deep breath. "I don't know no other way to say this, so I'm just gonna say it straight. They ain't comin' back, Evie. And goin' to look for them would be like findin' a needle in a haystack. It ain't gonna happen. I ain't takin' Alice and Elm to California, and gettin' their hopes all up that we're gonna find Ma and Pa. I won't do that to them. I won't do that to you. Mr. Murphy has made it clear he's not goin' to fire me because of your antics, so it's time to stop playin' these games. Don't you understand? For the past two years, we've been doin' what Ma and Pa should've been doin'. We both had to grow up so fast, especially you, Evie."

Bill rose and started to pace. "I want this job. Not just

for me or Alice and Elm, but for you too. So you don't have to work so hard. So you can go out and be with your friends and not have to worry about where the next meal is coming from or having to do our laundry in the cold crick. We've got a good thing here. This is our opportunity for Alice to never feel hunger, for Elmer to have friends, for you to be yourself, and for me to feel like I'm doin' right by y'all for the first time since Ma and Pa left."

He walked to the door. "Don't say nothin'. Just think about it. Think about how it was before, sleepin' in the truck and not eatin' for two or three days at a time. When you get done in here, come help me in the barn. We need to clean out the stables."

Evalyn watched him walk out the door before she blinked, knowing tears would follow. She never noticed how stressed he was about their situation. He always appeared to be so optimistic, always saying there would be work in the next town, a good meal, and a warm place to sleep. She went back to the dishes and began to weigh her options.

Bill kicked the stack of hay. The last thing he wanted to do today was clean out the stables and babysit Evalyn. He wanted to watch Elmer in the milking contest and see if Alice won a ribbon for her pie. He was glad Mr. Murphy and Mrs. Grant took the kids to the fair. He didn't know if he would've had the strength to stay home had they refused.

Grabbing the pitchfork, he began to muck out Poppy's stall. It was probably best he wasn't at the fair. He was sure he'd run into Lou Anne. He pictured Jon giving Lou Anne a kiss on the cheek and felt his heart drop. He had been sure Lou Anne was making up her relationship with Jon for some reason, until he saw the kiss. Lou Anne wasn't the kind of girl that would just let anyone kiss her.

But then how would he know? Just a few hours earlier, she had been ready to kiss him on the hayride before the horses spooked. She didn't know him from a jelly jar. Maybe she was that kind of girl. On the other hand, she had looked surprised when Jon kissed her.

Bill shook his head as he scooped up another batch of dirty hay. It just didn't set right. Lou Anne couldn't be like that. The way he felt for her deep down in his belly was different. There was no way he was getting that feeling wrong. He had known girls in high school before he dropped out. But none of them made him feel like Lou Anne did, which was silly because he had just met the girl. He was never one to be romantic, but Lou Anne felt right, as if he had been waiting his whole life for her.

Maybe he should go to the fair. He could drag Evalyn along and make her stick to him like molasses. He shuddered when he thought of having to talk to Lou Anne with Evalyn glaring over his shoulder. Talk about uncomfortable.

Evalyn grabbed the push broom as she entered the barn. She paused briefly to tie a blue scarf over her hair and then started sweeping the leftover hay out of Poppy's stall.

"I've been thinkin' about what you said," Evalyn said, breaking the silence.

Bill leaned on the pitchfork. "Well?"

"I'll try," she whispered.

"What?" Bill grinned. "I couldn't quite hear you."

She glared at her brother. "Don't push your luck, brother dear. I said I'll try."

"That's all I ask," Bill said returning to his farm work.

Chapter Thirteen

Alice bounced on the front seat of James's pickup and rubbed her hands together. "Oh, I can't wait to see if we've won! I'm so excited I could just burst."

"You know, Alice," said Dovie, "there are a lot of mighty fine cooks in Knollwood. We might not win." Dovie glanced back to check on Elmer sitting in the bed of the truck.

"I just can't stand it," Alice squealed. "I've never been in a contest before."

"Well, you don't have to wait any longer," said James. "We're here."

Alice crawled over Dovie and jumped out of the pick-up.

"Come on, Mrs. Grant." She held out her little hand. Dovie stared at it.

"Dovie, it ain't gonna hurt to hold that little girl's hand." James patted his daughter's shoulder.

Dovie shook her head, took a deep breath, and grabbed Alice's tiny hand. She felt a tickle in her heart from having the soft, warm fingers in her palm. Dovie tried not to giggle as Alice pulled her through the midway making their way to the pie booth. A small crowd had gathered around the shelves of pastry. As they reached the back of the crowd, they met Hannah Garber.

"Good mornin', Dovie," Hannah said, her voice dripping with sweet sarcasm.

"Mornin', Hannah." Dovie plastered on a smile.

"Just gettin' here I see."

"Yes, took our time this mornin'," answered Dovie. "Didn't see any need to rush."

Hannah looked down. "And you must be Alice. Joan talks about you all the time." Looking back at Dovie, she gestured towards the booth. "Shall we take a look?"

"After you," said Dovie.

The two ladies walked shoulder to shoulder as the crowd parted to let them through. Alice jumped up and down tugging on Dovie's arm. "There's ours! We got second!"

Hannah's smile grew large. Dovie looked at the shelves behind the counter, searching for the blue ribbon.

"Why, Hannah, it looks like Cathy Johnson has taken first this year with her cherry pie." Dovie smiled.

Hannah's face turned an unnatural shade of pink as she swallowed her disappointment. "Well, good for her," she choked out.

"Oh, look, there's yours." Dovie pointed to the bottom shelf. "You got third. Congratulations."

"Guess the judges went for tart over sweet this year." Hannah turned and hurried away.

"Mrs. Garber doesn't like to lose," Dovie whispered to Alice. "But at least she's tryin' to be a good sport about it." Alice covered her mouth and giggled.

"The milkin' contest's going to start soon," said Dovie. "We better get a scoot on, so we can get a good seat to watch your brother."

Elmer sat on the milking stool with James leaning over his shoulder pointing at the udders. He couldn't help but notice his sister perched on the gate, both she and Dovie watching his every move.

Dovie rubbed Poppy's nose and whispered into her ear. "I know you had a rough night, but help him out a little ok?"

"She must think I'm gonna get stomped, asking the cow for help. Maybe I shouldn't do this," Elmer thought.

"Now don't let ol' Ted Newberry scare you," said James, bringing Elmer's attention back to the cow. "The man milks like a machine, but he ain't gentle, so his cow will stop workin' with him. Carl Weinder's cow looks a little skinny this year. I don't think you'll have to worry about it filling the bucket, much less beating Poppy. Bud, Jr.'s slow, but steady. Don't underestimate his milkin' skills. Then there's Randy Koller, good guy and fast. Comes in second most years. Try not to pay attention to anyone else, just concentrate on you and Poppy. Be gentle, steady, and go as quick as you can without hurtin' her." James patted Elmer on the back. "You'll do great."

"Good luck, Elm," said Alice as they left to go find seats.

"It's time," said Bud, holding his clipboard. "James, you ready?"

"Elmer's sittin' in for me. I'll be holder. He'll be the milker."

"Those are some big shoes to fill, Elmer," Bud smiled. "You up for it?"

Elmer nodded slightly.

Bud acknowledged the nod, grabbed the pencil he had

stashed behind his ear, and made the changes on his clipboard.

"Take her to the arena. You'll be right in the middle between Ted Newberry and Randy Koller."

James attached the lead rope to Poppy's harness and led her out of the stable while Elmer held the gate. Grabbing the milking stool, Elmer looked at his feet trying not to notice the massive crowd that had gathered. His belly did somersaults as they entered the large corral that doubled as the livestock arena. Taking his place between the older men, Elmer let out a deep breath and stared at Poppy's udders.

"Please don't let me mess up," Elmer muttered.

The crowd fell silent as Pastor Spaulding bowed his head. "Thank you, dear Lord, for bringin' us together in a day of fun and competition. We are truly blessed to have these animals in our lives to fill our bellies and the bellies of our children. Please, dear Lord, keep these animals and their handlers safe. And a special thank you, Lord, for protectin' those on the hayride last night. We are very thankful no one was badly hurt. In your name we pray. Amen."

A hum of amens followed as Pastor Spaulding lifted his megaphone and changed from pastor to sports announcer.

"Ladies and Gentleman... Welcome, welcome, welcome to the greatest milkin' competition in the world!"

The crowd cheered as Elmer shook out his hands and rolled his shoulders.

"Startin' to my left we have Mr. Carl Weinder, milkin' Miss Daisy who's being held by his son Mr. Ned Weinder. Next, we have Mr. Ted Newberry milkin' Dolores who's being held by his son Mr. Thomas Newberry. In the middle we have a new milker, Mr. Elmer Brewer, on our returning champ, Poppy. Mr. James Murphy will be actin' as holder.

Next is Mr. Randy Koller, milkin' Hayley, held by his brother-in-law, Mr. George Wheaton. And rounding out the line-up, our youngest competitor ever, eight year old Mr. Bud Clark, Jr., milkin' Jenny who's being held by his sister, Miss Mary 'Tiny' Clark."

The crowd gave another round of applause as the milkers took their seats.

"You can do it, Elm!" Alice yelled as the crowd grew silent, starting another round of applause and laughter. Elmer knew his cheeks had to be as red as his hair.

"The goal is to be the first to fill the bucket to the red line. If your cow kicks your bucket, you're disqualified. If your cow kicks you, you're disqualified. If your cow kicks a judge, you're disqualified. And if your cow kicks the bucket, you've got bigger problems than losing a milkin' contest. When the milker gets close to the line, it's up to the holders to yell for the judges. The judges will then determine if the milk is at the red line. If so, we have a winner. If not they just keep on goin'. The judges this afternoon are Mr. Donald Lutter and Mr. Edward Smith, both from Wilson. We appreciate y'all comin' out."

The judges took a bow as the crowd cheered.

"Without further delay... Milkers on your mark... get set... GO!"

Elmer yanked on the udders as fast as he could causing Poppy to release a low moo.

"Not so hard, Elmer. Keep it steady and quick," said James.

Elmer shook his head and adjusted his technique. The roar of the crowd made Pastor Spaulding's play by play hard to hear. Elmer strained to listen.

"Looks like Ted Newberry has got a nice start, followed by Randy Koller. But don't count out Elmer

Brewer whose workin' Poppy at a crazy pace. Carl Weinder and Junior are neck and neck." Dolores let out a loud moo. "Oh, and Ted Newberry is out! Dolores has kicked her bucket!"

Elmer looked up long enough to see Ted throw his hat onto the ground.

"Randy Koller and Elmer Brewer still at a steady pace, Junior's coming from behind. Looks like Carl Weinder's cow, Miss Daisy's, slowin' and yep, she's done! Miss Daisy's down to a trickle, with half a bucket to go. Junior is catching up to Randy Koller, but look at this folks, Elmer Brewer has pulled into an outstandin' lead. His bucket is almost full."

Elmer barely heard the announcement and kept milking; telling himself James knew what to do. As he reached the red line, he heard James yell, "Judges!"

The two men came running as Pastor Spaulding continued, "James Murphy has called for the judges. They're lookin', noddin', and there it is folks! They have placed the blue ribbon on Poppy's harness. Her reign as the best milkin' cow in Knollwood County continues!" Elmer stood up and hugged James. "But hold on, folks, we still have two more ribbons to give away, and it's a close one."

"Judges!" yelled Tiny, a split second before George. The judges looked at Junior's bucket and then Randy Koller's. They huddled for a second before placing the red second place ribbon on Jenny's harness and the white third place ribbon on Hayley's. The crowd went wild.

"There you have it, folks, the youngin's take the top two spots. Ten year old Elmer Brewer is first, eight year old Bud Clark, Jr., is second, and thirty-something Randy Koller is third. Before you go, folks, be sure to grab y'all a glass of fresh milk at the concession stand. It's free, and we'd hate for any of this milk to go to waste. God bless you."

After shaking hands with his fellow competitors, Elmer found James in the crowd.

"You did great, Elmer," said James, patting Elmer on the back. "Couldn't have done it better myself."

Elmer kicked dirt. "I did ok, I guess."

"Ok?" James raised an eyebrow. "Elmer, you beat out some men who've been milkin' all their lives."

Elmer just shook his head and shoved his hands in his pockets.

"Golly jeepers, Elmer." Tiny rushed up to Elmer, bumping James out of the way. "I've never seen nobody milk that fast. You must've practiced, practiced, practiced. That's what my ma always tells me when it comes to my arithmetic, practice, practice, practice. But I hate it. You must love milkin' though, you were so fast."

Elmer's face turned a fresh shade of red.

"You did good too, Tiny," said James. "If you would've called for the judges a second later, y'all would've been third. Nice work, young lady."

"Jeepers, thanks Mr. Murphy. I just knew Junior could do it. I kept lookin' at Mr. Koller's bucket and then ours till I couldn't stand it any longer. I was so afraid Mr. Wheaton was gonna call for 'em first. It's a lot of responsibility bein' a holder. My stomach was doin' flip flops the whole time."

James laughed. "Mine too."

Tiny pulled Elmer to the side. "Elmer, I'm awfully sorry 'bout makin' fun of the whole dogs from wolves thing. I asked my pa about it, and he said you was right. I shouldn't have laughed at you. That was a rotten thing to do while you were helpin' me try to find Jelly."

"It's ok," said Elmer kicking dirt. "I'm sorry I didn't

finish helpin' you find Jelly. Any sign of her?"

Tiny shook her head. "Pa says she's probably long gone by now. I do miss her."

"Maybe you could talk Mr. Murphy into lettin' you have one of his pups?"

Before Tiny could respond, Dovie and Alice came up behind Elmer. "Good job, Elmer!" said Dovie ruffling his hair.

"Wow, my brother, the milkin' champ." Alice smiled as she looked at the three of them. "It's been a wonderful day. First, Mrs. Grant and me get second place in the pie contest and then Elm and Mr. Murphy get first place in the milkin' contest." She clasped her hands together. "Knollwood is the bestest place ever!"

Chapter Fourteen

November 1934

"Evalyn's sure been quiet," Dovie said to James as they played gin.

James discarded a jack of hearts. "Maybe she's finally realized this isn't such a bad place."

"I hope so." Dovie discarded a two of clubs. "Bill's been workin' her so hard. Not that she don't deserve it. I just wish he could get it through her thick skull that they're not goin' anywhere. It'd make it a lot easier on all of us."

"Why, Dovie, does this mean you want them to stay?" James discarded a queen of diamonds. Dovie picked up his card and smiled brightly.

"All I have to say to that is… gin." She laid her hand down.

"Why do I even play with you?" James studied her hand, looking for mistakes. "You always win." He tossed his cards onto the table.

"Not always. Remember last Thanksgiving, you beat me." She winked.

James scratched his head. "I think you let me win so I wouldn't quit playin' with you."

"Guess you'll never know." Dovie kissed her father's

forehead. "Goodnight, Dad."

The next morning, Dovie woke to the sound of a meadowlark calling. Though a chill wafted through the house, it looked to be a nice day for November. She stood, stretched her lower back, and walked over to the wash basin. As she cleaned the sleep from her eyes, she heard the clang of pots and pans. Dressing quickly, she hustled to the kitchen and found Evalyn cracking eggs into a large bowl.

"I must've overslept. I see you've started breakfast. I'll get on the bread for dinner," she said, tying on her apron.

"Already done," said Evalyn, whisking the eggs.

Dovie stared at Evalyn. "My, you've been busier than a beaver building a dam. What can I do?"

Evalyn put down the bowl and looked at Dovie.

"I've been thinkin' a lot 'bout you. I know I've made it hard for us to get along, and I'm sorry 'bout that." She picked up the bowl and finished beating the eggs. "You've been really good to Alice and Elm. I know it couldn't have been easy for you, 'specially since you're still grievin'."

"Well, color me surprised." Dovie sat. "Thanks for your understandin', Evalyn."

"In a weird way, you and I are alike. I lost my parents. They ain't dead, but they might as well be. And though I don't know how they died, I do know you lost your little girl and husband."

"You and I are nothing alike." Dovie felt her hands tremble. "You're nothing but a goathead under a saddle blanket, irritatin' anything that comes near you. You've got some nerve. My family is dead. They haven't left for greener pastures. They're dead. How dare you compare your runaway parents to my late husband and daughter."

Evalyn held her hands up. "I know it's different. It's

just that I can't help but hold onto the thought we could see them again, my parents I mean, if we would just try. Wouldn't you do everything in your power to see your daughter and husband again if you could?" Evalyn poured the eggs into a hot skillet.

Dovie looked at her feet, glad Evalyn had chosen to have this conversation while facing the stove. "Our situations are nothing alike. I should've been with 'em."

Evalyn glanced over her shoulder. "Didn't quite hear you."

"I said," Dovie took a deep breath, "I should've been with 'em. We were all supposed to go to the Valentine's Day Dance together. Every once in a while, I get these headaches that make me sick to my stomach, and I had one on that night."

Dovie got up and stared out the kitchen door. "Helen was so disappointed at the thought of not goin', so Simon decided to take her without me. Dad told 'em he'd stay here and look after me. My ma used to get these headaches too, so he knew the best course of action was to leave a glass of water on the bedside table and let me sleep it off. We still don't know what happened exactly. Must've been a deer or somethin' run in front of the car. Simon lost control at some point because the car was found upside-down just under the bridge. It wasn't until way after midnight that they were found."

Dovie sniffed and quickly wiped away the tears as she continued to stare into the backyard.

"I'm haunted by the thought that they lived through the wreck and died of exposure. I have nightmares about my little girl lyin' there in the cold. If I would've been there, I could've at least made sure she wasn't cold." No longer able to contain her emotions, Dovie's shoulders began to shake as James walked into the kitchen.

"Dovie?" He turned her around and saw the tears. "What in tarnation did you do now, girl?" he spat at Evalyn as he led Dovie back to her room.

"Mr. Murphy, I swear," Evalyn started, but James was already gone. A smirk crossed her face as Bill walked in the back door.

"What's goin' on?" he asked. "Was Mrs. Grant crying? What did you do now?"

"Honestly, Bill, I didn't do anything. Mrs. Grant and I were talkin' 'bout the accident with her husband and kid, and she got to cryin'. Now Mr. Murphy thinks I did somethin' to hurt her, just like you do," Evalyn explained.

"Why did you even bring it up?" asked Bill, twisting his hat.

"I didn't mean to really. I was just sayin' how she and I are alike 'cause we both lost loved ones, though not in the same way. I was tryin' to find some common ground. I was tryin' to get along with her, like you asked me to." Evalyn shook the wooden spoon she'd been using on the eggs at Bill. "So in a way this is your fault. I can't help it if that woman is unstable."

James returned to the kitchen. "It appears I owe you an apology, Evalyn. I shouldn't have jumped to conclusions like that. Dovie explained what happened. She's probably gonna take to her bed for the rest of the day. Just leave her be. When she's ready, she'll come out."

He sat down at the table with Bill. Evalyn slid some scrambled eggs onto his plate. James put his hand on her arm. "I really am sorry."

Evalyn shook her head in acceptance and hollered up the stairs for Alice and Elmer.

Alice came down and skipped, as usual, to the table.

"Where's Mrs. Grant?" she asked, grabbing a biscuit and the jelly jar.

"She's sick today," answered Evalyn, winking at James.

Alice's smile faded. "Is she gonna be ok, Evie?"

"Yes," reassured Bill, "she just needs to rest. You play outside quietly, so you don't bother her."

"Okay, Bill," she said, smile returning. "I want to take Norman to the orchard and look for treasure. Is that ok, Mr. Murphy?"

"Sure, it'll do that fat goose some good to take a walk. Just remember any treasure you find, you have to share with me." James winked at Alice.

"I'll share with everyone." Alice beamed. "I'd share with the whole world, so no one would have to go hungry."

"That's very Christian of you," said James. "I'm sure the whole world would appreciate it."

"Make sure to cross at the bridge, Alice," said Bill. "The creek's low, but the water's too cold to wade through. You'll end up sick in bed like Mrs. Grant."

"Sure thing, Bill. I don't want to walk in wet shoes anyway. Makes my socks all squishy."

Elmer came in from the back door and placed his hat on a peg.

"I thought you was upstairs," said Evalyn. "Where ya been?"

"Trainin' the dogs," he said as he inhaled a biscuit.

"How they doin'?" asked James.

"Good. Freckles flushed some wild turkeys just north of here." Elmer washed his hands. "Pretty decent flock of twenty or more."

"Wild turkeys, huh?" James raised an eyebrow.

"Yes, sir, and there's a big male out there."

"Guess we'll have to schedule a turkey hunt before Thanksgiving." James looked at Bill. "You fellas been huntin'?"

"I have," answered Bill. "Elm never got a chance."

"We'll have to remedy that," said James. "I've got an old gun of my pa's you can use."

He looked at Elmer. "Are you up for it?"

"Yes, sir," said Elmer, mouth full of biscuit.

"I wanna go," said Alice, sitting on her knees.

"Not this year," said James. "Let's teach Elmer and then maybe you can go next year."

Evalyn sat and started eating her own breakfast. "Trust me, Alice, you don't want to go. Remember how you cried when we killed those roosters for the fair?"

"Yeah, but I fed them roosters every day. I don't feed no turkeys."

"Well, we don't have to worry 'bout that now," said Bill. "Finish up, Elm; we've got to fix the fence on the east pasture."

Elmer nodded, gobbled up the rest of his eggs, and grabbed another biscuit as he rushed out the door.

"That boy's gonna eat ya'll out of house and home," said Bill.

James shook his head. "A growin' boy needs his biscuits."

"Well, best get on those fences." Bill grabbed his hat.

James followed. "I'm taggin' along. It's been awhile since I rode Tex. He's gonna start gettin' fat like Norman." He chuckled as he glanced at Alice.

"Norman ain't fat. He's fluffy," she said to Evalyn, "you know, for the winter."

"I'm sure you're right," said Evalyn.

"Evie?" Alice's voice shook with unease.

"Yes, Alice."

"Mrs. Grant ain't sick like Ellie is she?" Alice asked.

Evalyn dropped the tin plates she'd been carrying to the sink. She hadn't thought of their youngest sister in a long time. The babe was born so small and weak, they had no other choice than to take it to Dr. Ivy and leave it in his care.

"I'm surprised you remember Ellie." Evalyn picked up the tins. "You weren't no bigger than a grasshopper yourself."

"She reminded me of them china dolls in the Sears and Roebuck catalog, so pretty, but so fragile." Alice traced the prongs on her fork. "Is Mrs. Grant fragile like Ellie?"

"No, honey. Mrs. Grant will be fine. She's just got a bad headache." Evalyn ruffled Alice's hair. "There's no need to worry."

"Where do you think Ellie is now?" asked Alice, as she dropped her fork in the sink.

Evalyn thought about how to answer her little sister's question. Most likely the little girl had died shortly after being taken into the custody of the doctor.

"I don't know, Alice. I reckon she's some place safe with a nice family and maybe even a pet rabbit."

Alice's eyes lit up. "Imagine that, a pet rabbit." Then she frowned. "You know, with all the rabbits we got 'round here eatin' up the crops, I don't want a pet rabbit. I'd rather have Mr. Norman. He beats a silly ol' rabbit any day. But I sure hope Ellie keeps her pet rabbit safe and inside."

"I'm sure she has a pen for it," said Evalyn.

"Do you want help with the dishes, or can I go outside?" asked Alice.

"Go on and play." Evalyn pulled lightly on Alice's ponytail. "But remember what Bill said, I don't want you comin' in with muddy shoes."

"Thanks, Evie," said Alice, and she ran out the door calling for Norman.

Evalyn watched Alice through the window and felt a sense of pride and responsibility. Her attempt at getting Mrs. Grant on her side hadn't gone exactly as planned. But she knew Mrs. Grant didn't want them here anymore than Evalyn wanted to be here. She hadn't expected her to share so much or to break down like she did, but at least she had put the question in Mrs. Grant's mind. Evalyn knew if given the chance, Mrs. Grant would do everything in her power to get her own family back and get rid of theirs.

Chapter Fifteen

Alice skipped along the trail to the orchard with her apple bucket. She knew it was too late to find fresh apples, but there were other treasures to be found along the way. She sang "You Are My Sunshine" to Norman as they walked.

Norman softly honked out of tune with the song. Approaching the orchard, Alice spotted something shiny in the dirt. Kneeling, she began digging at the object with a stick.

"It could be a gold coin that will lead us to other gold coins," she explained to Norman. "I'm sure there's some outlaw's treasure out here. One he had to bury before the law got him."

Noticing her feathered friend had gone unnaturally quiet, Alice looked up. There, just a few feet away, stood the biggest dog Alice had ever seen. Holding onto the stick and bucket, she slowly stood up. The dog growled and bared its teeth, letting drool drip from its curled lip. Alice watched the saliva drop to the ground and noticed its ribs protruding from its belly. Hair had begun to come out in spots, giving the dog a mangy look.

She spoke in a low, calm voice. "You look awfully hungry, but I guarantee me and Mr. Norman don't taste no good."

Alice weighed her options. If she ran, the wild dog would catch her in no time, but she could scream and pray the mutt got spooked. She looked at Norman who was staring the dog down. Raising his wings, he positioned himself between Alice and the beast.

"OK, Mr. Norman, on the count of three, we make all kinds of ruckus. Maybe Bill will hear." The goose lowered his neck and hissed. "One... two... THREE!"

Alice started screaming and beating the bucket with her digging stick. The dog leapt in the air but was met with a face full of feathers.

"Norman!" screamed Alice. "Bill! Elmer! Help! Mr. Murphy! Somebody help!"

All Alice could see was a mess of white, grey, and brown. She wanted to run for help but was afraid to leave her friend alone. The winter air filled with honks and snarls. A loud yelp echoed through the trees as the dog retreated, chased by Norman honking on his heels.

Bill charged up the hill on his horse, followed by James and Elmer. Sliding down, Bill embraced Alice. "Are you ok? What happened?"

Alice began to sob. "There was a dog. He looked sick, Bill. He was 'bout to attack me, but Mr. Norman stopped him." She looked around. "You gotta help Mr. Norman! He's out there somewhere and he might be hurt!"

"It's okay, Alice. We'll find him," said Bill, as he mounted his horse. "Elm, take Alice back to the house. Mr. Murphy, I believe we have a goose to find."

"And a dog to kill," said James, untying the strap to his rifle.

"I'm not going anywhere without Mr. Norman," Alice cried.

"Be reasonable," said Bill. "You can't come with us. It's too dangerous. You'll be safe at the house. Elm, get her home."

Elmer jumped down to wrestle his little sister into the saddle when Norman came waddling back down the trail.

"Mr. Norman!" yelled Alice as she ran towards her friend. "Oh, he's bleedin'! Mr. Murphy, do somethin'."

James got off his horse and walked to the goose. Norman had a bite on his left wing several inches long. Alice hugged her friend as James cleaned the bite with his handkerchief.

"He's gonna be fine, Alice. Looks worse than it is." James looked at Elmer. "I'll take them both home and put some ointment on Norman's wing. You go with your brother."

"You're still goin'?" Alice's lips quivered.

"Yes, honey," answered Bill. "We've gotta go get that dog. If he's sick, he needs to be put down, so he doesn't hurt anyone else."

Alice nodded, and James offered to give her a boost onto his horse.

"I'm walkin' with Mr. Norman," she said with her head held high. "I owe him my life, so if he's walkin', I'm walkin'."

James shrugged and walked behind her, leading Tex back to the house.

After returning to the farm, Alice watched James apply the thick, grey ointment to Norman's cut.

"Is Mr. Norman gonna be okay?" she asked, as she patted the bird on the head.

"He's a tough ol' bird. He'll be fine," said James, placing the cap back on the medicine.

"Since the dog was sick, does that mean Mr. Norman is

gonna get sick too?" Alice glanced down at her feathered friend with wet eyes.

"Nah, I've never seen a bird with rabies," reassured James.

"Mr. Murphy?" Alice paused. James looked up to see fresh tears building in her emerald eyes.

"What's wrong, Alice?" His eyes softened as Alice hugged herself.

"Would I've gotten sick if the dog had bit me?" she asked.

James nodded his head. "Yes, you would've gotten very sick. But the good Lord made sure Norman was there to protect you. For that I am very thankful."

Alice sat by Norman and picked dead grass off his wing. "Mr. Murphy, why did God take Mrs. Grant's little girl and husband?"

James wiped the ointment off his hands with his handkerchief and sat on his knees. "We don't always understand the plans God has for us."

"Does that mean you don't know?" she asked.

"No, I really don't know. But I have faith that God loves us, and He knows best. Even though it can be hard at times, we have to have faith. Without faith there is no hope. Nobody is meant to stay on this earth forever. Some people just get to visit Jesus sooner than others."

"Don't you miss 'em?" asked Alice, eyes wide.

"Every day. But I know I'll get to see 'em again in Heaven. I just pray for peace, for me and for Dovie," explained James.

"Then I'll pray for that, too," said Alice.

James stood, groaning a little as his knees popped. Alice patted Norman on the head and also stood. Walking towards the house, Alice grabbed James's hand, sending a buzz of both joy and sorrow through his heart.

Evalyn stopped them before they reached the back door. "What happened to the goose? Did the mean ol' thing finally meet his match?"

Alice scowled at her sister. "You should be nice to him. Mr. Norman saved my life. Just ask Mr. Murphy."

Alice stomped into the house.

"What happened?" Evalyn rolled her eyes. "Another one of her stories?"

"Alice and Norman met up with a rabid dog. Norman fought it off before it could bite her." James rubbed his hands through his hair. "Alice isn't known for tellin' fibs, especially about somethin' like this."

"It's just... I never..." Evalyn's hand flew to her mouth as Alice and Dovie came back outside.

"Was it really rabid, Dad?" asked Dovie, standing in the doorway watching the sisters embrace.

"I believe so, but everyone's okay," said James.

"Thanks to Mr. Norman." Alice beamed.

"No more goin' to the orchard alone, you hear," Evalyn scolded, squeezing her sister's shoulders.

"I wasn't alone. I was with Mr. Norman, and I like the orchard," Alice whined.

"There's no need for that anyway," said James. "Your brothers are out there now takin' care of the situation. She's perfectly fine to run around anywhere on the homestead alone."

Evalyn's eyes narrowed. "I'm surprised you can be so careless with my sister's life. You of all people..."

"Well, come in and get some lunch," Dovie interrupted. "With all this excitement, I'm sure y'all must be hungry."

"You go on in, Alice," said James. "I'm gonna check

on the boys. I'll be back in a minute."

James turned back down the orchard path. As soon as he was around the corner, he dropped to his knees and looked to the sky. "Oh, Lord, thank you for protectin' our little Alice today."

His heart ached as he thought about the day he lost his granddaughter. Losing Alice would have been unbearable for everyone, especially Dovie.

Elmer and Bill continued the search for the dog. It didn't take them long to spot the mangy creature. Pulling out his shotgun, Bill shot the animal dead with one shell. Approaching the downed dog, he holstered his weapon.

"Definitely rabid. I don't want to think of what might've happened if Norman hadn't been with Alice." Bill shook the thought away.

Elmer examined the dog. "I think this is Jelly."

Bill raised an eyebrow. "What's jelly?"

"The dog," said Elmer as he shook his head, "I think its Tiny's dog, Jelly. She went missin' a few months ago during one of the dust storms. It's got a red rope collar just like Tiny said."

Elmer slid off his horse and approached the deceased dog.

"You shouldn't touch it," Bill said, reaching out to his brother.

"I know, but I've got to give Tiny something, so she knows what happened to her dog." Elmer put on his gloves before delicately cutting the red collar off the dog's neck.

Bill sighed. "We should bury it then. Some place nice, so Tiny has a place to come visit if she wants to."

"Just north of the orchard," said Elmer, "there's a place where the sun shines through the trees. It always feels warm there."

After burying Jelly, Elmer left Bill at Quail Crossings and took off towards the Clark's farm. He chose to ride the road to Tiny's house instead of using the backcountry path. He used the time to think. He'd never had to tell someone their dog had to be put down due to rabies. He fingered the red collar. Knowing Tiny, she'd probably talk his ear off about how good Jelly was. She'd be ok.

Riding up the drive to the Clark's house, he was met by Bud. "Hey, Elmer, was Tiny expecting you for dinner? She didn't say anything to her ma."

"No, sir," Elmer looked down at the collar.

Bud noticed the collar and inhaled deeply. "Looks like you found Jelly."

"I'm afraid so. Is Tiny around?" Elmer asked.

"I'll go get her," answered Bud. "She's helping her Ma. She really did love that dog. This won't be easy on her. Are you sure you don't want me to tell her?"

Elmer dismounted from his horse. "No, sir. We had to put Jelly down. It's only right I explain what happened."

Bud nodded and went to retrieve his daughter. A few minutes later Tiny barreled out of the house. "Jeepers, Elmer, I can't believe you rode all the way to my house. It's almost dark. My pa never lets me ride after dark…"

"Tiny," Elmer interrupted, "we found Jelly. There's no easy way to say this, but she was rabid. She went after Alice. We had to put her down." He handed her the collar. "I'm really sorry. If only I would've helped you find her that day of the duster …" He trailed off.

Tiny stared the collar. "Is Alice all right?"

"Thanks to Norman. He fought off Jelly, so Alice didn't get bit. I really am sorry, Tiny."

"It ain't your fault," Tiny whispered. "You had to do

what you had to do. I'm just glad Alice is okay and that nobody got hurt."

Elmer could see her bottom lip start to quiver. Before he could stop himself, he reached out and hugged his friend. "I'd bring her back if I could. We buried her just north of the orchard. I can take you there tomorrow to pay your respects if you'd like."

Tiny stepped back from the hug. "I'd like that. I better go inside now and help Ma finish up dinner."

Elmer watched her shuffle into the house before mounting back up. Riding home he felt as if his own dog had died. The look on Tiny's face when he handed her the collar had spoken volumes - she was devastated. Elmer heeled his horse into a trot, he had to get home. He had a dog to train, Tiny's dog.

Chapter Sixteen

"Elm, wake up." Elmer awoke to his big brother shaking him.

"Make sure to dress warm," Bill said, as Elmer rubbed the sleep out of his eyes. "It's cold out there."

Elmer nodded and grabbed for his thick overalls pulling them on over his long johns. They met James at the bottom of the stairs to put on their heavy winter coats and boots. Elmer's breath fogged up the kitchen window as he stared out into the pre-dawn darkness.

"Should I grab Freckles?" he asked James.

James shook his head. "I'm afraid it's too cold for them to pick up a scent, and we don't want to spook the birds. Let's try it without him."

It was his first time hunting, and Elmer was nervous. He'd practiced target shooting with Bill, but this was way different than shooting some tin cans. Thanksgiving dinner was riding on this hunt and their ability to find the flock of turkeys he'd spotted a few weeks earlier. If they couldn't find them, there would be nothing to eat but yams and corn bread. What kind of feast would that be? thought Elmer.

He followed James and Bill into the cold and took the lead to find the place where he had spotted the birds before. He wished they could take one of the dogs, cold or not, he knew Freckles would find the flock without spooking them.

"Remember," said Bill, giving some last minute advice, "always keep the barrel pointed down and away, until you're ready to shoot."

Elmer nodded, double-checked his safety, and tucked the shotgun under his arm.

They advanced north, past the tree break and creek. The winter wind made Elmer's eyes water. He constantly wiped his nose on his sleeve as he worked his way to the secondary boundary of trees. Elmer put up his hand, and they all stopped to listen.

The faint call of turkeys could be heard to their east. They worked their way to a small cluster of sand plum bushes and hunched down. About thirty feet on the other side of the thicket, stood the flock of turkeys, a big male just to the left of the females.

The tom fanned his tail as he strutted around the females. He was a glorious bird, with a twelve inch beard, fattened by the abundance of grasshoppers that plagued the plains. He had to be over twenty pounds, thought Elmer. That bird would feed them for a week.

"Ok, Elmer, you found 'em, you get the tom. Bill, let's see if you and I can get a couple of hens. When you're ready, Elmer," James whispered and took aim at the flock.

Elmer's barrel shook as he raised his gun. Bill placed his hand on his brother's shoulder. "Just take a deep breath," he said softly. "Remember what we practiced."

Elmer inhaled and exhaled slowly and nodded at Bill. Bill nodded back and took aim at the flock. Elmer steadied the shotgun against the fleshy part of his shoulder. He took the shot but jerked his head. The shot had to be high, he thought. The flock scattered into the trees and beyond.

Elmer scanned the clearing, two birds lay motionless

and one was the big tom.

"I got it!" yelled Elmer as he ran to the big male, with James and Bill on his heels.

"Good for you, Elm," said Bill, patting his brother on the back. "Nice shot."

"I thought it was too high." Elmer ran his hand through his hair. "I jerked back when the gun went off."

"Well, lucky shot then," James added as he walked over to retrieve his hen.

"Where's yours?" asked Elmer, looking around for Bill's kill.

"I must be rusty," said Bill. "It's been awhile since I've been huntin'. Let's get these birds back to the house. I can already taste the stuffin'."

"That's all right, Bill. We'll be eatin' for weeks off these two birds. We got to leave some for Christmas." Elmer picked up his tom by the legs and headed toward the house. His mouth watered at the thought of the big bird's leg sitting on his plate.

They returned to the house and set the birds in the old barn, so they could start plucking. "We'll save my bird for some other time. Better go tell Dovie you got a big one and to get the fire goin'," James said to Elmer.

Elmer ran towards the house to spread the good news.

"Thanks for not tellin' him," said Bill.

"I understand the boy needs to feel important," said James, "but if we go huntin' again he's got to learn to keep his eyes open. It'd do him more harm to find out you're the one who got the tom, then lied about it."

"I know," said Bill. "I'll work on it with him. I just wanted him to have this moment."

Elmer ran back into the shed, panting. "They're really excited. This is going to be a great Thanksgiving!"

"Well," said Bill, handing Elmer the turkey, "you shot it, you pluck it. I'll start the milkin'."

Bill leaned towards James and smiled. "There are other benefits for not taking credit, I hate pluckin'."

Elmer happily sat down and started plucking the large bird. He worked steadily for over an hour, making sure the bird was free of all feathers before grabbing it by the legs and taking it to the house.

"My, my," said Dovie, grabbing the turkey from Elmer. "You weren't exaggeratin'. This bird's bigger than a truck."

She took it to the sink and began preparing it for the oven. "We'll all eat like kings, thanks to you, Elmer."

Elmer took off his heavy coat and warmed his frozen fingers over the stove. "I was so nervous. All I could think 'bout was eatin' Thanksgivin' dinner with no turkey, and it would be all my fault." He laughed. "You should've seen the way my barrel was shakin'."

Elmer put out his arm and shook it up and down. "I can't believe I hit anything, much less that big fella."

"I'm sure it takes a lot of practice at huntin' not to be nervous," said Dovie. "I still get nervous every time I have to kill a chicken, though I've done it a thousand times. We would've been just fine had you not gotten the bird, though. Plenty of chickens in the coop. Thanksgiving wouldn't have been ruined."

"Chicken ain't the same as turkey." Elmer sat at the table. "I was thinkin' 'bout restuffin' Mr. Murphy's pillow with the turkey down. He's been so nice to me. Treats me like a real man. Nobody's ever treated me like that, except for Bill." Elmer leaned forward. "I ain't much good at stitchin' though. Will you help me?"

"Sure." Dovie smiled. "That's a wonderful idea. Lord knows he needs a new pillow, stubborn old man won't let me order one for him at the general store."

Elmer sniffed the air. "Smells like home. Nothin' like the smell of Thanksgivin' dinner cookin' to make a man happy to have a home." He inhaled again before rising and walking to the door. "I guess I should go gather the down and get started on the other bird."

Elmer put his coat back on and turned to look at Dovie. "I should've said this sooner than now. I'm sorry I haven't, but thanks."

"For what?" asked Dovie, scrubbing down the bird. "You did the hard part by pluckin'."

"Not for cooking, though I'm thankful for that too, but for helpin' us and lettin' us stay here. There were times I thought we'd never be happy again. Never feel the warmth of a good stove or have our bellies full. Y'all gave us that, and it seems like today's the best day to say thanks."

Dovie turned and looked at Elmer. "You're very welcome. And I'm thankful for all the help you've given Dad. It means a lot to me to know he's got you and your brother to help out."

Elmer nodded a "you're welcome" and walked out the door.

James entered the kitchen and looked curiously at Dovie.

"What's wrong?" he asked.

"Nothin'," she replied turning back to the turkey.

"Then why did you have that look on your face?"

"I think I just had my first conversation with Elmer."

James threw his hand up. "Nonsense, you talk to the boy every day."

"Not like that, Dad." She turned and placed the turkey

in the roasting pan. "A real conversation. Up till now, the boy's only said a few words to me and only when necessary. I think he's beginnin' to think of this place as home."

"Well, then," James ran his hands through his hair, "we definitely have somethin' to be thankful for."

He reached for his coat. "Now that my hands have warmed up, I'm gonna go pluck my turkey."

"No need, Dad. Elmer's doin' it."

"Well, I guess I have two things to be thankful for." He sat at the table. "What do you suppose we should get the lot for Christmas?"

"Should we get them anything?" asked Dovie. "Is that something they're accustomed to?"

"Of course we should." James slapped his leg. "Doesn't matter if they're accustomed to it or not, they'll get used to it."

"Don't you think they'll feel obligated to get us something in return?" Dovie twisted her apron. "You know they can't afford it. I'm not sure we can."

"We'll make do," said James. "You know I always put some money aside for Christmas, and this year I put a little more in that fund just for them."

"I don't know, Dad. Christmas just isn't goin' to be the same without Helen and Simon. I'm not sure I'm feeling much of the Christmas spirit. How 'bout we skip the festivities this year?"

"Now, Dovie Christine Grant, you know better than that. Christmas isn't just about presents and eatin'. It's about comin' closer together to celebrate the birth of Jesus. If that ain't somethin' to be festive about then nothin' is. Besides comin' closer together is just what we all need." James rose. "You don't have to go all out, but you do have to remember why we celebrate Christmas in the first place and put yourself second to those kids who need some upliftin' traditions in their lives."

James put on his heavy coat and sighed. "I didn't mean to sound callous. The first holidays without them are gonna be hard. No one expects you not to grieve their absence. I just pray you can find it in your heart to see a little joy in what we have now."

"I'll try, Dad."

James pushed his plate away. "Dovie you outdid yourself this year. You're gonna have to let out my pants. I do believe I gained fifty pounds."

"Well, no one forced you to eat a third piece of pumpkin pie." Dovie laughed.

"I just couldn't help myself." James placed his palms on the table. "It was wonderful. Did you do somethin' different this year?"

"I sure did," said Dovie, smiling. "I didn't make it."

James scanned the table. "Well, then, who did? I must know who made that pie 'cause let me tell you, it'll be your job for Thanksgivin's to come. It was you, wasn't it Bill?"

Bill grinned and looked at his plate. "No, sir, I can barely cook beans much less a pie. Just ask the kids."

"Must've been Elmer then," said James, looking around the table.

Elmer shook his head. "I cook like Bill."

Everyone laughed causing Elmer's cheeks to flare.

James rubbed his belly. "Well, that just leaves two people."

"It was Evie!" Alice piped up.

"Hush, Alice," snapped Evalyn, "everyone knows it was me. He's just actin' silly."

"That was one fine pie, young lady," said James. "And Lord knows I don't act silly about pie."

As he grabbed her hand, her muscles tensed, and he could tell she was trying hard not to pull away from the gesture.

James looked Evalyn squarely in the eyes. "I'm so thankful you're here." Not letting go of her hand, he looked around the table. "I'm so thankful you all are here. We are truly blessed. I never imagined this table would be full again, especially not with kids. But I'm so glad it is. I look forward to celebratin' many Thanksgivin's to come with you fine folks."

Evalyn slipped her hand away from James's and placed it in her lap. James knew he hadn't won her over yet, but he vowed he would.

Chapter Seventeen

December 1934

December blew in with a strong northerly wind and clouds that promised snow. Bill glanced up at the sky and prayed for more than a dusting. They needed the moisture and lots of it. He was sure there would be few complaints if a blizzard forced the whole town to shut down.

Bill rode to James's side.

"Is she just teasin' us?" Bill asked, pointing up to the sky.

James shook his head. "Not sure. Any other time I would bet on it snowin'."

"I know what you mean." Bill dismounted from his horse, Pronto. "Better tend to the animals. Even if it doesn't snow, it's gonna be a cold one."

The men entered the barn.

"You got the kids squared away for Christmas?" asked James.

Bill took the saddle off Pronto. "You got a Bible right?"

"Of course," said James. "What's that got to do with gettin' the kids presents?"

Grabbing the saddle pad, Bill shook his head. "Ma and

Pa never did believe in givin' presents for Christmas. Thought it was getting' away from what Christmas is really about. We used to get some oranges from our neighbor, but that's it. We just read the Bible. No need to go to a fuss for us."

James shook his head. "It ain't no fuss. It's part of the beauty of Christmas day. Trust me, Bill, you'll never forget the looks on those kids faces when they open their presents come Christmas morning."

Bill thought about it for a moment. He had seen an ad in a magazine once, kids surrounded by colorful wrapping paper, faces beaming as a boy held up a toy fire truck and two girls hugged stuffed teddy bears.

He imagined Alice having toys for the first time and getting Elm that new knife he'd been drooling over in town. He saw Evie twirling around in a new dress.

"I don't know." Bill shook his head. "What if we have to leave one day? Wouldn't it be harder on them to experience a Christmas with gifts, then the next without? I mean you've heard Alice talk about drinkin' straws, and she only got to use one once. I can't image her disappointment at a Christmas without presents after having one with them."

"And just where do you think y'all will be next Christmas?" asked James. "I thought we'd settled this already after Evalyn put Poppy in the schoolhouse. She can't do nothin' that'll make me fire you. Or are you having second thoughts about stayin'?"

"Not at all," said Bill. "I just know in times like these things change. You might not be able to afford to keep me hired on. Nobody knows how long this depression will last. You have to put yourself and Dovie first. I know that."

"Nonsense," said James, "no matter what happens,

we'll get through these tough times together with hard work and prayer. I know you're constantly waitin' for the next bad thing to fall in your tracks, but I'm here to tell you, you've reached the end of the line. You will always have this place to call home, no matter the circumstances. And that goes for your whole family, and I mean each and every one of them."

"Okay," Bill nodded, "let's do it. I'll talk to the kids tonight. Let them know to make something for you and Mrs. Grant."

James flapped a hand at Bill. "No need. We want this day to be special for them."

"I insist," said Bill. "The way I see it, the givin' of Christmas gifts is what it's supposed to be about, not the receivin'."

"Well," said James, running his hand through his hair, "you got me there. I just don't want them to go to too much trouble. Or spend much of your money. Y'all keep that for a rainy day."

"Like we'll see any of those days ever again." Bill laughed.

Dovie had a strong fire going in the den and hated to leave its warmth, but she had to look for it before the kids got home from school. She walked to her bedroom and closed the door tightly behind her. Approaching her small closet, she closed her eyes.

"Dear Lord, give me strength," she prayed.

Working carefully, she pulled out a box shoved behind her stockpile of multicolored quilts. She set the box on the bed and fingered the ribbon that crossed the lid. Inside this one little hat box was all she had left of her lost family. Taking a deep breath, she took off the lavender lid.

The weeks following the funerals were a blur. She vaguely remembered packing up her husband's and child's clothes and taking them to the church for the needy. She had gotten rid of everything so fast, her dad was sure she'd have regrets. She did, but they didn't have anything to do with giving the clothes to charity. Everything she couldn't part with, was in this one small box. If it wasn't in here, she wasn't sure where it would be.

Helen's baby blanket lay on top, a small little quilt covered in embroidered puppies. Dovie had worked on it every free minute during her pregnancy, making sure every stitch was perfect. She paid extra for the softest cotton fabric she could find, so her child would always be surrounded in gentle clouds.

Helen carried the blanket around until she was four and even then it was a fight to get her to relinquish her prized possession.

"Honey, you have to at least let Mommy wash it," Dovie had pleaded.

"No, then it won't smell right," whined Helen.

"Smell right?" Dovie laughed. "Right now the pigs smell better than your blanket. I bet even Norman would run from the stench. Now let Mommy have it, and you'll get it back in a couple of days."

"My blanket don't smell like pigs," said Helen, bottom lip protruding. "It smells like Daddy."

Dovie started to laugh, swallowing it when Helen squinted her eyebrows. "There's no way that blanket smells like your Daddy. You've been draggin' it around the farm for weeks now."

Getting down on her knees, Dovie leaned in to smell the blanket. Her nostrils filled with the smell of grass and hay with a hint of musk. Helen was right, her blanket smelled exactly like Simon.

Dovie sighed. There was no way she was getting the blanket from her daughter's grip now, not that she really wanted too.

"I understand, Helen. I won't take the blanket to the wash, but you have to make me a promise."

Helen eyed her mother. "What's the promise?"

"You keep the blanket upstairs in your room. No more carryin' it around the farm or even downstairs unless it's a really cold day and you're gonna wrap yourself up in it like Mommy does her afghan. Promise?"

"But Mommy, I love my blanket. Not only because it smells like Daddy, but because you made it for me with love. Remember, you told me that. That's why I like to carry it around with me always."

"I know, sweetie," Dovie tucked a wayward strand of hair behind Helen's ear. "I just want to help you keep it safe."

"Okay, Mommy. I promise what you said."

"Good, now run along and gather the eggs. I'll put your blanket upstairs for you."

Helen headed outside, stopped, turned around, and ran to her mom. "I love you, Mommy."

Dovie squeezed her daughter tightly. "I love you too, pumpkin."

She hugged the blanket as she pulled out Simon's brown fedora and giggled at the memory of the first time he had come home with the awkward-looking hat. Most of the men in town wore their cowboy and straw hats. Not Simon, he had worn the fedora proudly, tipping it to everyone he met on the street.

"You look like a fool," she had teased.

"But a stylish fool." He winked. "Does it make me

look like Clark Gable?"

"Now, why would I want a Clark Gable when I have a Simon Grant?" she asked, throwing her arms around him.

Dovie smiled at the memory and put the hat on her head, as she looked again into the box. Tears filled her eyes as she found what she was looking for, sitting next to her mother's worn copy of Pride and Prejudice.

She reached in and grabbed the small cloth doll with red yarn hair and blue button eyes that matched the light blue flowered dress the doll wore. A thin yarn smile told everyone she was the happiest doll in the world.

Placing the blanket back in the box, Dovie stared at the doll, remembering the last Christmas she had shared with her daughter and husband. She had worked tirelessly on the doll after Helen had gone to bed. Her heart swelled with pride as she showed Simon what they would give to their daughter on Christmas morning.

Simon bit his lip as the corners of his mouth twitched.

"What did you do?" she scolded.

"Why, Dovie honey, I don't know what you mean." He tried to erase his smile.

"What I mean is, whenever you have that cat-that-ate-the-canary look on your face, you've done somethin'. Good or bad, it's somethin'."

"I got Helen a horse for Christmas," Simon confessed.

"You did what?" Dovie's shoulders sunk as she looked at the dolly.

"The Bells couldn't afford their geldin' anymore. They'd been tryin' to sell it for weeks, with no takers. Accordin' to George Wheaton, they were gonna give it to the government." Simon paced around the room. "You heard what the government did to all those cattle and horses they bought. They butchered them. He's a good horse, and it seemed like an awful waste of a horse."

"I had to do somethin', so I went and gave 'em a decent offer, and they took it. I hope you don't mind, but I told them we'd bring 'em some milk for their young'un, Paul. He don't look so good. Are you mad?" Simon's soft eyes melted Dovie's heart.

She sighed. "I just wish you would've discussed this with me first."

"Honestly, honey, I didn't think you'd mind. You're always givin' milk and stuff to those worse off."

Dovie crossed her arms. "Simon, I'm not talkin' about the milk. Of course, I'll take the Bells some goods to help 'em out."

"Then what's the problem?"

"Do you really not know?" she asked, dropping her hands to her hips.

"No." Simon shrugged.

Dovie let out a slow breath before she spoke. "Buyin' a horse is a big deal by itself. I know a man's got the right to buy a horse when he sees fit, and I don't have a problem with that. It's buyin' a horse for our daughter for Christmas without askin' me my opinion that's hard to swallow. You saw me workin' on the doll. Who'd you think it was for, Dad?"

She tossed the doll into the chair and walked to the fire, rubbing her arms. Simon followed and hugged Dovie from behind.

"I didn't think 'bout it. I'm sorry. I didn't mean to hurt your feelin's. I just didn't want a good horse put down. Helen's always askin' us for her own pony, so I took the opportunity." He squeezed her tight. "We can give her both."

"No, what you did was right. I'll just give her the doll

for her birthday in March." She turned and hugged Simon back. "Just don't be bringin' her a pig or somethin'."

But Helen never saw her next birthday. Dovie had fully intended for the doll to go into the donation box, but she hadn't had the heart to give it away, even though her daughter had never even seen it.

She knew Alice would love the little doll and it finally felt right. Giving the doll another squeeze, she carefully wrapped it in brown packing paper. Using an old red hair ribbon, she quickly fashioned a beautiful Christmas bow. Sliding the gift under her bed, she removed the fedora from her head and placed it back into the box. She traced the trim with her finger as she whispered, "I miss you, Simon."

Chapter Eighteen

The week before Christmas was full of chores of the gift variety. Dovie had exchanged her father's pillow with an extra from her bed, so Elmer could restuff James's with the turkey down. She had been in town twice to pick up the new shotgun for Elmer and turtle hair clips for Evalyn. When she asked James what Bill needed, he said he had taken care of it but wouldn't tell her what he had bought. She tried not to be upset at her father's secrecy. She just wanted Bill to know how thankful she was that he was helping her dad out, regardless of the hassle the siblings brought.

"Dad, are you gonna cut down a Christmas tree this year?" Dovie asked her father at breakfast.

"I've been doin' a lot of thinkin' 'bout that, and I reckon we better talk about it." He looked around the table. "I like havin' a Christmas tree as much as the next person, but I think we better keep all the trees we got in the ground this year. They keep the soil where it belongs, plus they break up the north wind. Just doesn't seem smart to cut one when we can't replace it."

"No Christmas tree?" Alice sighed. "I was so lookin' forward to having one. I can't remember the last time we had one. I've seen them in other people's houses and in magazines, and they had one at that soup kitchen in Amarillo, but I can't remember the one we had with Ma and Pa." Alice placed her finger on her cheek and looked to the sky as if looking through her brain.

"That's because we never had one," said Evalyn. "We never had any trees close by to cut down. You know Ma and Pa never had the time for that type of nonsense."

"Surely we can spare one tree," said Dovie, eyeing Evalyn before looking at Alice.

"Just a little one," Alice begged.

James shook his head. "Everythin' we've got is helpin' to keep the wheat in the ground. I'm sorry, we just can't this year."

"Are you okay with that, Alice?" asked Bill. "I know you were lookin' forward to it, but you know the farm has to come first."

Alice nodded and played with her oatmeal as the adults changed the subject to the cattle. A smile crept along her lips as she stood.

"What if I don't kill nothin'?" she blurted out.

"What do you mean?" asked James.

"What if I find us a Christmas tree without cuttin' down any trees or pullin' anything out of the ground? You know so the soil stays put."

"That sounds fine to me," said Dovie and then nudged her father. "Don't that sound fine, Dad?"

"Of course," said James, nodding. He poked his spoon at Alice. "You find us somethin' that will work as a tree, and we'll make it look as festive as ever."

Alice clapped her hands. "Oh, goody, I'm gonna find the bestest dead Christmas tree ever!"

Evalyn stifled a laugh, letting out a snort. "Alice, you can be so foolish sometimes. Can you imagine a dead

Christmas tree? Somebody better telegraph Norman Rockwell, he'll want to paint a picture of the all-American farmer's Christmas tree."

Glares meet Evalyn from around the table.

"You just wait," said Alice, planting her hands on her hips. "I'll find us a Christmas tree."

Alice braved the cold every day for the next three days searching for her tree. She started at the brush pile, looking for a suitable branch that might have fallen off during a duster but found none. She came back to the house scratched and shivering, but still determined.

"Alice, it's ok," said Dovie, tending to her scratches. "We'll still make the inside look festive. Maybe we can use that ol' coat rack? My lands, girl, you've got scratches all over your arms, and you're colder than a polar bear's toenails. Is it really worth it?"

"I'm not givin' up," Alice said between chattering teeth.

Her next step was to walk along the tree break and orchard, making sure her hero, Norman, was always by her side. She was still looking for a branch that would make do as a Christmas tree. But again, she came home cold and empty-handed.

Bill tried talking to her next. "Alice, you're gonna catch a cold out there. Maybe you should stay inside unless you're doin' your chores."

Alice crossed her arms and stuck her bottom lip out. "Then Evie gets her way."

"That's better than getting sick," said Bill. "Plus you need to work on your readin' over the break. Wouldn't that be better than runnin' around in the cold?"

Alice shook her head and stomped her foot. "I'm gonna find us a Christmas tree. I have to."

Bill shrugged, "If you wind up in bed Christmas mornin' with a fever, don't blame me."

On the third day, she strolled along the feed shed, and there it was - the biggest tumbleweed she had ever seen, stuck in the corner between the shed and barn.

"Look, Mr. Norman, it's perfect!" she squealed, clapping her mittens together.

Skipping towards her delightful find, she sang "O Christmas Tree" and carefully pulled the dead shrub away from the other tumbleweeds that had collected in the corner. The small thorns pricked her fingers through the mittens, but she continued to smile. When it was finally free of the smaller tumbleweeds, she grabbed her bush by the base and slowly dragged it towards the house.

Bill ran up to help his sister. "What are you doin'?"

"This here's our Christmas tree." She beamed.

Bill raised an eyebrow as he eyed the dead plant. "Well, let's see what you got here." He picked the plant up and stood it on its base. "It's almost as tall as you."

He shook his head and clicked his tongue as he examined the find. Finally, he nodded and let out a low whistle. "Yep, I do believe this will work. Why don't you let me carry it to the house, bein' I've got on my leather gloves? What do you say?"

"Thanks, Bill. I'll go tell Mrs. Grant it's comin'." She skipped to the house, still singing her Christmas carol.

"Mrs. Grant," she yelled as she burst in the back door, "I found it!"

"My, child, you scared the goose pimples out of me," said Dovie, fanning herself with a dish towel. "Now what are you babblin' about?"

"Our Christmas tree!" Alice beamed. "Bill's bringin' it now."

Dovie looked out the window and saw Bill and James examining a tumbleweed.

"You mean that ol' tumbleweed?"

"Yes, ma'am." Alice danced in the doorway.

Dovie tilted her head as if trying to imagine making a tumbleweed into a Christmas tree. Alice had followed through with her vow, and they had promised to decorate it. She was going to make them keep their promise.

"I guess we don't have to worry 'bout waterin' it," said Dovie. "Go tell your brother to bring it into the den. We don't want to set it too close to the fire, but I believe we can find a place."

Alice clapped her mittened hands again and ran back outside.

Dovie hurried to the den to make a spot for the "Christmas tree". She grabbed the stand out of the box of decorations and set it by the sofa. She wasn't sure if it would be small enough to keep the tumbleweed upright, but with some dishtowels it might work.

Bill brought in the weed and set it in the stand. Holding it upright with his leather gloves, he waited as Dovie and James adjusted the stand.

"Okay, let 'er go," said James.

Bill carefully let go of the plant, keeping his arms out to catch it if the stand gave way, but the tree stayed in place.

"We'll leave you ladies to your decoratin'," said James as he turned to Alice. "Mighty fine job, young lady."

"You're cleverer than a coon," said Dovie, admiring the standing tumbleweed.

"I'm gonna go get Evie," said Alice as she ran upstairs. "I wonder what shade of red her face will turn when I tell her that I found us a dead Christmas tree."

Dovie started sorting out the tree decorations. "My,

that girl does have an imagination," she thought.

"We're gonna decorate that?" Evalyn walked into the den and wrinkled her nose.

"Yep," said Alice, undeterred by her sister's face. "Wanna help?"

"We'll have to make a new star. Mine's too heavy for the tumbleweed," said Dovie, eyeballing the top of the shrub.

"I'll do it," said Elmer as he walked into the den. "Do you have any foil?"

"In the cupboard on the left side," answered Dovie as she grabbed a red ribbon. "Shall we get started?"

She tied a beautiful bow on one of the branches being careful to avoid the small thorns. "Just keep with the light ones, so we don't break any branches."

"What do you say, Evie? Are you helpin' to decorate this fine tree or what?" asked Alice, hands on hips.

"We aren't really doin' this are we?" Evalyn stared at Mrs. Grant. "I mean it's a weed, a dead weed. It's embarrassin'."

"The only thing that's embarrassin' is your attitude," said Dovie. "We promised your sister if she found somethin', we'd make it work, and that's what we're gonna do. Now the way I see it, you've got two choices: stay and help in here or go and help in the barn. If you think for one second that you'll be lazin' around upstairs while everyone else is working, you're dumber than a rattlesnake sunnin' on round-up day."

The last thing Evalyn wanted was to get poked by a weed disguised as a Christmas tree. "I'll go make the popcorn," she said, rolling her eyes.

"That's more like it," said Dovie.

Alice is so childish, thought Evalyn as she retreated to

the kitchen, decoratin' a dead weed for Christmas. Ma would be appalled they had a tree at all. She'd always said a Christmas tree was nothing but a waste of firewood.

"Why ya gotta be like that?" asked Elmer startling Evalyn out of her inner rant.

"Like what, Elm?" Evalyn grabbed a large jar of dried corn from the pantry.

"All... I don't know," Elmer scratched his head. "All negative 'bout things. Alice looked for that tree for three days, can't you be a little supportive. Aren't you lookin' forward to celebratin' Christmas like everyone else?"

"Christmas isn't about presents and dead trees, Elmer," scolded Evalyn. "Ma and Pa taught us the true meanin' of Christmas. All this other stuff is just foolishness."

Elmer held up his finished star. "Seems to me the true meanin' of Christmas is about being good to one another cause we're celebratin' the birth of our savior. A savior that loves us more than we love ourselves, even though we don't deserve it. Seems to me if Jesus was down here, he'd love that ol' tumbleweed Christmas tree because it makes Alice happy, not because of the way it looks. Shouldn't you love it for the same reason?"

Elmer took his foil star to the den, leaving Evalyn alone with her thoughts once again. Of course the stupid tumbleweed made Alice happy. Everyone cooed over her like a lost kitten. She could bring in a dead skunk, and they'd all tell her what a fine job she was doing.

Once they got to California, there would be no need for a tumbleweed Christmas tree. California was full of green trees and lush bushes. She was sure her ma would be more than willing to decorate a tall spruce or pine.

"Probably not a tumbleweed in the entire state of California," she said under her breath as she shook the pan of corn kernels over the hot stove. She pictured herself sitting lazily by a sparkling blue pond surrounded with trees and thick grass, not a spot of dry cracked dirt or a tumbleweed in sight.

Chapter Nineteen

Alice woke before the sun rose on Christmas morning and glanced at her sister who was snoring softly beside her. She knew if she woke up Evalyn, she'd be grumpy, and that was no way to start Christmas morning. She could sneak down and take a peek at all the presents but shivered at the thought of walking around the cold house. No one was up to restart the fires, and she had been warned not to mess with the fireplaces. But if Evalyn was up, then she could start the fire, and they could look at the gifts together. The trick was to wake her sister without her knowing Alice had been the one to interrupt her slumber.

Alice yawned loudly, but Evalyn continued to snore. Sighing, she reached over and gently touched the tip of Evalyn's nose. Evalyn snorted, rubbed her hand over her nose, and turned on her side. Alice crossed her arms. There had to be a way to wake up Evalyn. She turned from one side to the other rapidly, bouncing the bed. Evalyn stopped snoring, and Alice quickly snapped her eyes shut and pretended to sleep.

Evalyn rolled over and looked at her sister.

I can't believe she's still sleepin', she thought.

She lay on her back and thought about the last Christmas with her parents. Alice had only been four, so there was no way she could remember the way her parents laughed in delight as they ate Christmas dinner and told stories of their own childhoods. Everyone had been so happy. She wondered where her parents were. Were they still happy they left their kids behind? How had things turned out like this?

"Are you cryin', Evie?" Alice patted her sister's shoulder.

"Now why would I be cryin'?" Evalyn brushed her cheeks. "My eyes are just waterin' cause of all the dust in the air. What in the world are you doin' up before the roosters?"

Alice shrugged and put her finger on her chin. "But if you're awake and I'm awake, what do you say we go downstairs and look at the presents? You can get the fire started, and everyone else will wake up all warm and cozy."

"Oh, I don't know. It's early." Evalyn did an exaggerated stretch. "I could use some extra sleep."

"Come on, Evie. I can't wait any longer! We finally get presents!" Alice bounced up on her knees and put her hands together to beg, "Please, please, please, please...."

"Well... okay. Get your slippers and housecoat on."

Alice jumped off the bed and hurried into her robe and slippers. She looked at Evalyn who was leisurely putting her hair in a ponytail.

"Evalyn!" Alice stomped her foot.

Evalyn turned and smiled. "I'll race you." She ran out the door before Alice had a chance to respond. They ran down the stairs, excited to see their Christmas surprises.

"Sounds like a herd of buffalo runnin' down the stairs," said Dovie as she tended to the fire.

Alice ran to the tumbleweed tree and looked at all the packages wrapped in brown packing paper. She had been disappointed they couldn't buy proper Christmas paper, but now the brown bundles seemed to glow with the yellow reflection of the fire.

"When can we wake Bill?" she turned to Evalyn.

"No need. Heard y'all stompin' down the stairs," said Bill, entering the den followed by Elmer who kept glancing at the presents.

James entered the room and looked at his makeshift family. He smiled at the crowded room and felt warmth that didn't come from the fire. "Well, what are we waitin' for?" he asked.

"Can I pass out the gifts?" asked Alice.

Dovie nodded and then sat in her favorite blue sewing chair. Alice looked at every package carefully and announced each present as she walked it to its receiver. "This one's from Evalyn to Bill."

Once Alice was done, Dovie looked around the room, "Do we take turns or just dig in?"

Everyone looked at each other. Then as if on the count of three, they all ripped into their gifts.

"Jeepers," said Elmer, "a real twelve gauge shotgun! Thanks a lot, Mrs. Grant and Mr. Murphy. Jeepers!"

"Jeepers?" said James, raising an eyebrow at Dovie.

"How nice," said Dovie, "thank you so much for the dishtowels, Evalyn. You did a wonderful job on the needlework."

"It was nothing," answered Evalyn, "and thanks for the hair clips."

"Well, this looks like my old pillow," said James, squishing the familiar form. "I was wonderin' where it got off to."

"It might be your old pillow, but I restuffed it with the turkey down from the Thanksgiving birds, and Mrs. Grant sewed it back up for me. I hope you like it." Elmer turned a familiar shade of red.

"It needed new stuffin'. Thanks, Elmer." James patted the boy on the shoulder. "I like it very much. It was a very thoughtful gift."

"Well, I'll be," said Dovie, raising her hand to her chest, "new wood serving spoons and a cuttin' board. Y'all do excellent work. They are so smooth. Thanks Bill and Elmer."

"Look, Evie, Bill got me a new dress," said Alice. "Isn't it pretty?"

"Yes, but not as pretty as mine." Evalyn smiled. "Thanks, Bill, it's lovely." She held the dress to her body and twirled around. "Those silk stockin's you got me will go perfectly with it, thanks Elm."

"Thanks for the hankies, Alice," said Bill. "When did you get to be so good at embroidery?"

"Evie helped. She drew the initials on with a pencil, and then I embroidered over it. She also cut and hemmed the hankies. So y'all need to thank Evie too."

Everyone giggled as Alice blushed. "Well, if you haven't opened your present from me, guess you know what you're gettin'."

"They're very nice," said Bill.

"Oh, Dad!" Dovie held up a glass picture with hand-painted yellow daisies on it. "It's lovely."

"Had Ali Smith in town paint it for you. Thought you'd like it."

"Like it? I love it," she got up and hugged her father. "It's by far the prettiest thing anyone has ever given me."

"Thank you for the leather gloves, sweetheart," said James, hugging Dovie back.

"Wow, it's a little Mr. Norman," Alice squealed,

holding up a small wooden goose. "He's perfect, thanks Elm."

"And thanks for the overalls, Elm. How did you ever afford 'em?" asked Bill.

"Mr. Murphy paid me for trainin' them dogs. I told him he didn't have to, but he brought up you needin' some overalls and stuff," Elmer said looking at his feet. Next, he unwrapped his gift from Bill. "Wow, a new pocket knife. Thanks, Bill, mine was gettin' kinda dull."

"Well, I'll be," said James. "What a fancy satchel. Tex will be so puffed up with pride we won't be able to get him into the stable. Thanks, Bill."

"Oh, Evie, thanks for the puppy. It's so cute!" cried Alice, hugging her new stuffed animal.

"And for the new shirt," said Bill and Elmer together. They looked at each other and laughed.

"Look, Bill, it's my very own apron," said Alice. "There's somethin' rolled up in it."

She unrolled the apron to find the little doll Dovie had made for Helen. As she looked at the doll, tears started forming in the corners of her eyes. Bill went to his sister.

"What's a matter, Alice?" he asked, wiping the tears off her cheeks.

"It's just that I had to leave my dolly when we left, and I haven't had one since. I really missed havin' a dolly, and this one's so perfect." She looked at her brother and smiled. "These are happy tears, Bill."

Bill smiled and hugged Alice. As he looked at his family, he too started to tear up. Even Evalyn seemed to be having a good time. The last Christmas had been so hard on them. They had eaten dinner in a soup kitchen, surrounded by hacking adults and crying babies. He looked up to the ceiling and silently thanked God for this wonderful

Christmas.

"Dad," Dovie whispered, "where's Bill's gift?"

"Don't worry, honey, I haven't forgot." James winked. "Bill, I just want you to know I really appreciate all the work you and your brood have done for us. I know it hasn't always been easy." He looked at Evalyn. "But I am glad y'all are here, all of y'all."

"Can't thank you enough for your hospitality, Mr. Murphy," said Bill.

"No, we ought to be thankin' you," said Dovie, hoping her Dad was going somewhere with his little speech.

"The thing is, it's just me and Dovie. We have all this land and no one to hand it down to. So the five acres in the southeast corner are yours, no strings attached. Not much for farmin', but you could build a real nice house there. Merry Christmas."

Bill's mouth fell open as James continued. "The rest of the land will remain in our family till we're both gone, then it belongs to you, unless Dovie here has any more children. Point here is that you now have a home of your own. Y'all can live in this house as long as you like with me and Dovie, but that five acres is yours to do with what you please."

"Mr. Murphy, I don't know what to say," said Bill.

"Well, you can start by callin' me James and Mrs. Grant here, Dovie. That goes for all y'all. We're family now."

Bill crossed the room and shook James's hand. "Thank you, Mr. er - James."

Dovie grabbed her father's hand as soon as Bill had let go. "Dad, I need your help in the kitchen. That ol' stove is actin' up, and I need you to look at it."

James gave Bill an apologetic look as he left for the

kitchen. "What's this about, Dovie? There's nothin' wrong with the stove."

"No, there's not. It's your brain that needs fixin'," Dovie whispered.

"What in the devil are you talkin' about?" James ran his fingers through his hair.

"When you said you had Bill's gift covered, I figured you were givin' him a horse or somethin', not part of our livelihood."

James shook his head. "I gave him five acres to build a house on. The ground's not good for farmin', and the livestock can live without an extra five acres to graze. They can put down roots now. Not have to roam from town to town lookin' for the next roof."

"How do you know he won't sell it?" Dovie twisted her dish towel. "You're too trustin', Dad. Sure they've been helpful with chores, but that's no reason to give them land. This farm's been in the Murphy name for decades, and now you've promised it to them."

James laid a hand on his daughter's shoulder. "Dovie, I prayed about this long and hard before I decided. Bill needs a place to call his own for his family. I'm not gonna be around forever, and he can look after the farm once I'm gone. I'm tryin' to look out for you too."

"I can handle the farm just fine on my own," snorted Dovie.

"I know you can, but you shouldn't have to." James hugged his daughter. "Dovie, I want nothin' more than for you to be happy. I want you to find someone that makes you happy, but I understand in all likelihood you're not gonna look at anyone the same way you looked at Simon. I'm not foolish enough to tell you to go find a husband, but I don't want you to be alone after I'm gone. This way I can insure he has a home for his family and that you will always have a family."

Before Dovie could continue the argument, James made his way back into the living room.

"Everything okay with the stove?" asked Bill, glancing at Dovie.

"It will be," James patted Bill on the shoulder. "Nothin' to worry about. Enjoy the day. I'm gonna change for chores."

Bill watched James walk into his room before turning and looking at his family. Alice hugged her dolly with one arm while making her wood Norman waddle across the floor with her other hand. Evalyn was smoothing out her new dress as Elmer examined the blade on his new knife.

"I hate to break this up, but we best get to our chores," Bill announced to his siblings.

He smiled at the groans. "The gifts will still be here when you get done, but what kind of Christmas would it be for the livestock if they don't get anythin' to eat or drink."

Certain everyone was on their way to do their chores, Bill turned around, grabbed his coat, and walked out the door. He headed to the stables and began to brush Pronto. Stopping, he leaned his head against the white and brown paint. Pronto stomped his foot twice and let out a low gruff.

"It's okay, Pronto," said Bill. "These are happy tears."

Chapter Twenty

Alice sat in front of the fire and played with her new toys. Her new doll, now named Molly, was teaching the new stuffed puppy, Beets, and the wooden Mr. Norman how to hunt turkeys.

"Did you have a good Christmas, Alice?" asked Dovie, sitting in her sewing chair surrounded by her presents and brown wrapping paper.

"I sure did." Alice hugged her doll. "It was the bestest Christmas ever, wasn't it Mama Dovie?"

Dovie's mouth dropped. "Mama Dovie?"

"Oh, I hope you don't mind if I call you that. We went to this soup kitchen once, and all these colored girls were callin' this lady Mama Kay. I asked one of them what it was like to have all them sisters. She looked at me all funny, so I explained I heard everyone callin' that lady Mama Kay, so I figured they was all hers. She just laughed at me and said she wasn't none of their mama, but since she took care of all of 'em they call her Mama Kay. Since Mr. Murphy, I mean Mr. James, said we could call y'all by your first names, and since you take care of me, I thought it would be okay." She looked at Dovie expectantly. "Is it okay?"

Dovie swallowed hard. It had been a long time since anyone had called her mama. She felt a familiar sting in her heart as she looked at her hands. What was happening here? Her dad was giving away farm land, and here Alice was trying to make her a mother figure. Was God trying to tell her to move on from her true family?

No, she wasn't going to let her dad give away the family land, and she wasn't going to have a replacement daughter. Glancing up, she caught Alice's big green eyes and fumbled for an excuse. "I don't think your sister would like that. She's looked after you all this time."

"She did it cause she had to; Bill made her. I ain't no dummy. Besides who cares what Evie likes?" answered Alice. "She's an ol' stick in the mud."

"Don't talk ugly 'bout your sister. I'm sure she tried her best. Can't be easy for a young girl to take on a role like that. It's like tellin' a rabbit to guard the garden. It ain't gonna work." Dovie smoothed the front of her dress. "What about your own Ma? She wouldn't like it, I'm sure."

Alice looked up to the ceiling, then shook her head. "Don't expect we'll be seein' her or Pa ever again. Nope, I'd say they're long gone. And since she left, I don't reckon she has much of a say. It's like she gave up on bein' my ma."

Dovie's heart broke at Alice's last sentence. She couldn't image a mother choosing to leave her kids behind for greener pastures, but she did know a thing or two about being left behind. "I guess it would be okay for you to call me Mama Dovie."

As soon as the words slipped out of her mouth, guilt overwhelmed her. Would Helen be upset with this other little girl calling her mother "Mama"? Dovie choked back a sob.

Alice ran up and hugged Dovie.

"I won't call you that if you think it would hurt your

daughter's feelings or if it makes you sad." Alice stated as if reading Dovie's mind. "Nobody should be sad on Christmas, and I'd hate for anyone in heaven to be mad at me. They might tell Jesus, and it's his birthday. Wouldn't want anyone to ruin Jesus's birthday. You think they have party hats in Heaven? I saw some of them in a magazine once."

"I'm sure they do." Dovie smiled. "And no, we wouldn't want you to be in trouble with the big guy, but I don't think Helen would mind." Dovie hugged Alice's back. "She always wanted a sister."

With a final squeeze, Alice hopped down. "Well, I better go do my chores like Bill said, and say hi to Mr. Norman. He gets all mopey if I don't visit him every day." After a quick change, Alice ran out the door, grabbing her coat along the way.

Dovie stared at the fire for a long time after Alice went outside. Her heart hurt, and she wanted nothing more than to curl up in her bed with the doll sitting neatly in the corner with Beets and mini Norman. The first Christmas without her daughter, and she had allowed someone else to call her Mama. She glanced at her bedroom door and then to the kitchen where the sweet potatoes sat on the counter. She stood and wiped her cheeks. Taking a deep breath, she picked up the wrapping paper littering the den and went to the kitchen to start the sweet potatoes. Today was not a day to spend in bed crying. Today was a day for rejoicing.

Alice skipped out of the chicken coop with Mr. Norman waddling by her side. She sang "Silent Night" at the top of her lungs, cradling the eggs close to her chest in a makeshift bowl made of her buttoned coat. She noticed Evalyn sitting in the corner between the shed and the barn.

"Watcha doin', Evie?" she asked.

"Nothin'." Evalyn rolled her eyes. "Leave me alone."

"Why? Are you mad? You shouldn't be mad. It's Christmas. It's the bestest Christmas ever." Alice twirled around causing an egg to fall and break.

"Be careful, Alice!" scolded Evalyn. "Of course I'm mad. Mr. Murphy shouldn't have given Bill that land. Now we'll never get out of here."

"Why would we want to? I like it here. Mama Dovie said I could mash the taters later…"

"Mama Dovie?" Evalyn leapt to her feet. Alice took two quick steps back, causing three more eggs to fall and break.

"Now look at what you've done!" Evalyn yelled. "You can't do anythin' right. You're nothin' but a baby!"

"Well, you're a big meanie!" Alice started to cry. "You made me break the eggs."

"If you wouldn't have tried to run away like a little sissy then the eggs wouldn't have fallen." Evalyn placed her hands on her hips. "That's why Ma never let you do anythin', 'cause you'd ruin it."

"That ain't true, Evie," Alice stuttered. "I was too little to help. I didn't ruin nothin'."

"You're the reason they left," yelled Evalyn. "You ruin everythin'. If it weren't for you, they'd still be here, and we'd be a happy family."

"Take it back, Evie," Alice cried harder, causing her to drop a couple more eggs.

"See what I mean? You ain't good at anythin'. You're just worthless." Evalyn raised a hand to Alice.

Norman jumped in front of Alice and bit Evalyn hard on the belly. Evalyn screamed, and Bill came running from the barn.

"What's goin' on?" he asked, looking at his two sisters.

"That bird bit me!" Evalyn rubbed her stomach.

"Only cause you was goin' to hit me," Alice wailed.

Bill's eyes grew large. He turned to Alice. "Honey, you go on in the house and give them eggs to Dovie."

"I didn't mean to break the eggs, Bill. Honest." Alice sniffed. "Evalyn made me drop 'em."

"It's okay." Bill playfully pulled on Alice's braid and forced a smile. "Nobody's mad at you. Go on inside, you hear?"

Alice nodded her head and walked toward the house, carefully cradling the rest of her eggs. Norman followed, letting out a low hiss as he passed Evalyn.

"I demand that bird be killed." Evalyn stomped her foot. "I think I'm bleedin'."

Bill waited till Alice was in the house before he turned back to Evalyn.

"In the barn. Now!" He grabbed her arm and dragged her towards the barn. Once inside he turned and began to pace. "How dare you? Have you already forgotten?"

"What are you talkin' 'bout, Bill?" Evalyn continued to rub her belly, checking her blouse for signs of blood.

He stopped pacing, and his mouth fell open as he looked at Evalyn. He closed the three steps separating them. "You know as well as I do that Ma used to hit Alice for no good reason."

"I know no such thing." Evalyn crossed her arms.

"Come on, Evalyn!" Bill yelled. "You ain't stupid. We both know Ma wasn't right after Alice was born."

"Alice needed a firm hand, that's all." She leaned against Poppy's stall. "She called that woman, Mama Dovie. She is no mother to us. She has no right to that title."

"That's none of your concern," growled Bill. "That's

between Alice and Dovie. Why do you even care?"

"Because she ain't our Ma!" cried Evalyn.

Bill's face turned red. "She's the closest thing Alice has ever had to a real mother."

"What about me?" Evalyn planted her hands on her hips. "I've been the one to mend her clothes and tend to her scrapes. I'm the closest thing Alice's got to a mother, not Mrs. Grant... Me!"

Bill shook his head. "No, you've always acted like an older sister with the burden of takin' care of her little sister. Always complainin' and huffin' about going to California. Had you been actin' like a mother, you wouldn't have put grasshoppers in Dovie's beans or placed Poppy in the schoolhouse because bein' here is what's best for Alice, and you've done all you can to get me fired. A real mother would never raise her hand to her child or deny what really happened with our Ma. I'm done with this conversation, but I'll tell you this just once. If you ever raise a hand to Alice, or even to Elm, ever again I'll..." He kicked the stable door and stormed out of the barn unable to finish his sentence.

He walked toward the southeast corner, trying to cool off. Evalyn had turned happy tears into fits of frustration all before Christmas dinner.

"How can she deny everythin' that's happened? Why can't she see how good we have it here? Why is it so hard for her to believe our parents were not good people? For cryin' out loud, they abandoned us!" he yelled to the sky.

He kicked a dry cow patty and paced the pasture. How was he going to deal with Evalyn? Her actions today could not be ignored, and the extra chores had done nothing to curb her behavior. Bill fell to his knees and picked at the dead grass. He heard horses behind him and looked to see James riding up on Tex, leading Pronto.

"Let's go take a look at the land, shall we?" said James.

Standing, Bill took Pronto's reins and hopped up into the saddle. They headed to the southeast corner in silence. Bill couldn't erase Evalyn's smug look from his mind. He shook his head trying to think of what to do next.

"Wanna talk 'bout it?" asked James.

"Don't know if it'll do any good," Bill said. "Can't figure out what to do with Evalyn. Her attitude has gotten out of control. She almost hit Alice today."

James stopped Tex and looked at Bill who stopped Pronto.

"Did you say she almost hit Alice?" James ran his hand through his hair.

"Yep, Norman bit her before she got a chance."

"Remind me to give that bird some extra feed this evenin'." James clicked his tongue, causing Tex to move forward again. They rode in silence, both pondering the situation.

"Any suggestions?" asked Bill.

"I think it's safe to say Evalyn will think twice about raisin' a hand to Alice again with Norman around, and we'll make sure she doesn't do anythin' like that in the house."

Bill nodded.

"As for Evalyn's attitude," continued James, "I don't think there's anythin' we can do but keep givin' her extra chores and keepin' her from extra school activities. She's got to make up her mind this here is it and decide to make the best of it."

"I wish there was somethin' else we could do," said Bill.

"Well, there is," answered James. "We can pray."

Chapter Twenty-one

January 1935

"Come on, Evalyn!" hollered Dovie from the back door. "It's time to make bread."

Evalyn yanked a cold stiff towel off the laundry line. "Be right there!"

She hitched the laundry basket up on her hip and walked towards the house. "Cinderella, it's time to make the bread," she mumbled under her breath. "Cinderella, go get the laundry off the line. Nag, nag, nag... that's all that woman ever does. You'd think she'd have somethin' better to do than get on people all day. Especially people who work all day for free. I'm nothin' but a modern day slave."

Sitting the basket by the kitchen stove to warm the towels, she began to gather the ingredients for the bread. Since Christmas, she had done every chore imaginable, and no one would talk to her unless it was to give her an order. She hadn't intended to hit Alice, only scare her. Now everyone was acting like she raised a hand to Jesus himself. They were all over-reacting to the situation. After all she was the one that got bit by that crazy bird. Alice walked away with nothing more than her feeling's bruised. It was Evalyn with the real wound.

A chair scraped across the floor, startling Evalyn from her thoughts. She turned to see Dovie sitting at the table with her hands folded.

"I've already apologized and explained what happened with Alice a dozen times," Evalyn said, measuring the flour and rolling her eyes. "I really don't need another lecture. I've heard it from Bill, and Elm won't even look at me. Besides Alice is fine..."

"I don't want to talk about Alice," Dovie interrupted.

Evalyn stopped and raised an eyebrow at Dovie.

Dovie took a slow breath. "I want to talk about you and the conversation we had a while ago. The one where you asked me about gettin' my family back?"

Evalyn nodded and turned back to her mixing bowl. "Well?"

"The answer is yes," Dove sighed. "I would move Heaven and Earth to get them back. But you see, our situations are not the same and not just 'cause my kin are dead."

Evalyn continued to concentrate on the bread so Dovie continued.

"I was left by my family, a lot like you were. I felt abandoned, angry, and lonely, like a part of my heart was ripped from my chest, as I reckon you did. At that point I had two choices: be consumed by the anger and loneliness or be consumed by the love that surrounded me from my family and friends. I chose the latter. I made up my mind to love and appreciate what I have left. Even though my heart was broken and to this day it aches."

Dovie stood and walked to the back door.

"That's the difference between us," she continued. "I wouldn't hurt my Dad for anythin', and it seems you're goin' out of your way to hurt your family."

As Dovie left, Evalyn slammed her hands on the bowl. How dare Dovie act like she knew what Evalyn was going through. She was never abandoned by her parents, left to find food for younger siblings when she had none herself. Besides she wasn't tryin' to hurt anybody. She just wanted them to see the truth. Bill was wrong. Ma and Pa were good people, and if only they would go to California and find them, everything would be like it was. No, it would be better.

She let out a low scream of frustration and pushed the bowl away, knocking over the salt. Whipping the towel from her apron she began to brush the salt into a pile. Looking out the window, she saw Alice run up to Dovie.

"Mama Dovie! Mama Dovie!" Evalyn mocked, scooping up the salt and throwing it into the bread mix. "Let's see how Mama Dovie likes her bread now."

That evening the family gathered around the table for a dinner of vegetable stew and bread. James blessed the meal, and they all dug into their soup. It had been a long day of moving cattle, and the men were famished.

Evalyn watched as James grabbed his bread. He was talking to Bill about a stubborn bull, and the bread became animated with his conversation. Evalyn willed him to eat it. Finally, story over, James folded his bread in half and dunked it deep into his stew. Taking a huge bite, his nose scrunched.

"What's wrong, Dad?" asked Dovie as she took a bite of her own bread. Grabbing her napkin, she spit the salty bite into it.

She looked at Evalyn who was staring at her bowl, trying to mask a smirk.

"You might want to put the bread down," Dovie said to Bill, who was about to take a bite. "It's saltier than Poppy's salt lick."

Bill laid his bread on the plate and took a bite of stew instead. "Any of those biscuits left from breakfast?"

"Good idea, Bill," said Dovie. Turning she grabbed the tin of cold biscuits off the counter. "We'll just give this bread to the chickens tomorrow and make another loaf."

Evalyn looked around the room. Everyone continued eating as if nothing had happened. What kind of game were they playing? Were they just waiting for one person to start the lecture?

"How's the calf?" asked James.

"Seems to be holdin' his own," said Bill. "Poppy's got plenty of milk. I think he's gonna make it, even with the bottle feedin'. Too bad Poppy's being picky about him drinkin' from her teat. Would've saved us a lot of work."

Alice giggled. "I like feedin' the calf. He gets all slobbery. Then he looks at me with his big brown eyes, like I'm his mama or somethin'. It's so cute."

"Good to hear, 'cause you'll be doin' a lot of it." said Dovie. "I'll go to town tomorrow and pick up a couple more feedin' bottles."

Evalyn felt her head would explode. "Come on," she thought, "yell at me! Get mad! Do somethin'. Don't just sit there like a bunch of dumb bunnies talkin' about cows!"

Bill turned to Evalyn. "Finally," she muttered raising her head high, ready to take the tongue lashing.

He opened his mouth to speak and then turned to Alice. "Got a job for you, Alice."

"Oh, goody!" Alice clapped her hands. "Do I get to bottle feed the piglets too?"

Bill laughed. "No, thankfully we don't have to do that. Their mommy's doin' her job, but it's just as big of a job."

Alice's eyes grew wide. "Bigger than feedin' a whole

mess of piglets?"

"Yep, you're gonna supervise Evalyn makin' another loaf of bread." He looked at Evalyn. "Since she doesn't seem to know how to get the recipe right."

"What does "supverise" mean?" Alice asked.

"Super-vise," corrected Dovie. "What do you think it means?"

Alice tilted her head. "That I have to watch her?"

"Yep," Bill shook his head. "You're gonna watch and make sure she does it right."

Alice clapped her hands again. "That is bigger than feedin' piglets."

Bill turned to Evalyn. "Evie, you're gonna need to make bread tomorrow."

Evalyn groaned and pushed her stew away, causing it to slop over the sides. Laying her head on the table, she tried to ignore the farm talk.

Evalyn got up early the next morning. There was no way she was going to have her brat of a little sister supervise her making the bread. Alice was the whole reason she was in this mess in the first place. She tiptoed out of the room, careful not to wake her younger sister.

Shivering, she added another log to the wood-burning stove. It was going to be another cold, gloomy January day. Gingerly, she got out the ingredients for the bread, trying not to make a sound. The last thing she wanted was to wake Dovie and get another "you're ruining your family" lecture. Evalyn knew when she added the salt yesterday, she was going to have to make more bread. Having to remake it didn't bother her nearly as much as their reaction, or rather, the lack of reaction.

Why hadn't they thrown a fit? After all, she had ruined

a perfectly good loaf of bread during a time when everyone was short of food. A twinge of guilt ran through her as she remembered the pictures in the newspaper of all those unfortunate people standing in the bread lines. It wasn't long ago they had been standing in those lines and eating in soup kitchens. The bread was never salty there. Just the opposite, it rarely had any taste. But it didn't matter. Sometimes that bread was all they'd get to eat all day.

"Evie!" yelled Alice.

"Shhhh!" said Evalyn, turning to see her little sister standing on the stairs rubbing her eyes.

"You were supposed to let me supe...- watch." Alice stomped her foot.

Evalyn wiped her hands on her apron. "I guess you should've gotten up earlier then."

"No fair!" Alice turned to run up the stairs. "I'm tellin', Bill."

"Stop, you little monster." Evalyn rolled her eyes. If Alice went upstairs and told Bill, he'd just make her start over. "I ain't finished. You can supervise the rest of this loaf and all of the next one."

Alice turned back around and skipped down the stairs. Pulling up a chair, she stood on it, carefully watching Evalyn's every move.

"Why do you keep getting in trouble?" Alice asked.

Evalyn ignored her.

"I mean you put grasshoppers in Mama Dovie's famous beans." Evalyn cringed at "Mama Dovie". She still hadn't gotten used to hearing her little sister call that woman mama. Alice continued to click off Evalyn's misdeeds. "Then you put poor Poppy in the schoolhouse after Bill let you go to the fair. It was like the minute you got out of trouble, you had to go get right back into it. It always makes Bill feel bad. What did he ever do to you?"

"What do you mean, Alice?" Evalyn brushed the flour off her hands. "You know Bill hasn't done anythin' to me."

Alice shrugged. "Then why you tryin' to get him into trouble too?"

Evalyn sighed and grabbed the salt. "You're bein' foolish, Alice. Just like Bill is. You really think we'll all live here happily ever after, like in one of your story books?"

"Make sure you go easy this time." Alice pointed at the salt. "I don't see why we can't all be happy here. I like it at Quail Crossin's. It's got an orchard that's great for explorin', and a pond that Mr. James says we can swim in come summer when it's hot. There's the baby cow and piglets. Oh, and don't forget Mr. Norman..."

"Because this ain't our home," Evalyn snapped.

Alice looked deep into her sister's eyes as she laid a hand on Evalyn's shoulder. "But it could be, Evie. If you just gave it a chance, it really could be."

Alice jumped off the chair and slid it back to the table.

"Hey," said Evalyn, "you still have to supervise me, remember? I'm not done."

"I trust you, Evie," Alice said, and grabbing her coat she bounced out the door calling for Mr. Norman.

"This will never be our home," Evalyn whispered. She pictured what her life would be like if she stayed in a town like Knollwood. She'd be married probably before she graduated from high school and start having kids by the dozens. If she was really lucky, they might hire her on as a teacher, or she might be able to work at the general store. But more than likely she'd be stuck on a farm just like Quail Crossings. She'd become Dovie.

She shook the thought away. There was no way she

was getting trapped in this poor excuse for civilization. She would make it to California. Even if they didn't find their parents, she would be a Hollywood star, and they would never have to make their own bread again, much less stand in a bread line.

Chapter Twenty-two

Bill slowed as he approached the white car sitting near the ditch of the dusty road. Pulling alongside the stranded vehicle, he muttered an oath when he saw the driver was Charlotte. Without waiting for permission, she opened the door and plopped herself next to Bill.

"I'm so glad you came along. I thought I was gonna freeze to death." She rubbed her hands together. "Not really dressed for a hike to the nearest farm." She showed Bill her new pair of beige high heels.

"What's wrong with your car?" Bill asked, paying no notice to the shoes.

"I don't know anythin' about those silly machines," Charlotte said, blowing on her fingers.

"What are you doin' way out here?" Bill scanned the horizon.

"My ma thinks it's a good idea for me to learn how to drive, so I was practicin'," explained Charlotte. "Thought I'd drop by Quail Crossings and see what you were doin'."

"I'm workin', just like every other day." He sighed. "Well, let me take a quick look at it." Bill got out of the truck and hopped into her car. He looked at the gauges and shook his head.

Getting back in the truck, he looked at Charlotte.

"Didn't your pa show you how to fuel her up?"

"Oh." Charlotte covered her mouth with her hand. "Didn't think about that. He usually makes sure it's full, so I don't have to worry about it."

Bill chuckled. "Don't worry about it. I'll take you home."

"That's mighty nice of you, Bill. Are you sure it's not too far out of your way?"

"It's really not a problem," answered Bill. "You're just lucky I came along."

"Don't I know it." Bill caught Charlotte's smirk out of the corner of his eye, but shrugged it off.

As they drove, Charlotte inched closer and closer to Bill. He tried to scoot away but soon met the door.

"You know, Bill, I was awfully disappointed we didn't get to dance at the fair hoedown." Charlotte produced a pout.

"Tell you the truth, Charlotte," Bill said. "I'm not much of a dancer. Would you mind movin' over a bit? You're makin' it kinda hard to shift."

Charlotte ignored him and stayed put. "Still, it would've been nice. There's not much to dancin'. I'm sure I could've taught you. I'm a great dancer." Her thigh now touched his. "It's all about havin' the right partner."

"Seriously, would you mind movin' a bit, Charlotte?" Bill wiped his forehead. "I've got to shift."

Charlotte curled her legs up in the seat and leaned into Bill.

"Is that better?" She traced her finger along his jaw, causing Bill to flinch.

Charlotte laughed. "My, you look so serious. Do I make you uncomfortable?" Her hand moved from his jaw, down his neck, and continued along his chest. Bill grabbed her arm and slammed on the brakes, causing the truck to stall.

Charlotte giggled again and smashed her lips against his.

Bill pushed her away. "Stop it, Charlotte!"

"It's okay, Bill, you don't have to be a gentleman with me." She winked and leaned in for another kiss.

He caught her by her shoulders. "Look, Charlotte, you're a very pretty girl, and any fella would be lucky to have you…"

"You could have me," she interrupted, jerking his hands away and kissing him again.

Bill pushed her away for a second time. "I'm sorry, Charlotte, this isn't gonna work. You've been awfully nice to me and my family since we moved here, and I really appreciate it, but I don't think of you like that."

She started to take off her coat. "I will help you see me that way."

"Stop that!" Bill yelled, looking around the deserted road in case anyone was watching. "Put your coat back on." He put the truck in gear and started it. "What kind of man do you take me for?"

She yanked his arm, causing the truck to stall again. "Oh, Bill, I just want you to see that I'll make a good wife. I can help you raise your siblings, and we can have a few kids of our own. It'll be wonderful, Bill, just you wait. I'll cook you delightful dinners and keep your house so clean you'll be able to eat off the floors. We'll be so happy together. I'll make sure all your needs are met."

He didn't answer but started the truck for the third time and headed towards her house. Her eyes narrowed. "Bill, you need to think about what you're doin' here. My pa and Mr. Murphy are good friends. One word from me and you're back in the bread line. Is that what you want for your family?"

He pulled into her drive and stopped the truck. "I guess I'll have to take that chance."

"You're messin' with the wrong girl, Bill Brewer." Charlotte narrowed her eyes. "You have no idea what I could do to your family."

"Let's get one thing straight, Charlotte. You can threaten me, but you leave my family out of this. James isn't gonna fire me because I was honest with you. You're wastin' your time tryin' to play games with me. They won't work. Now you'll want to put your coat back on. It's mighty cold out there." He leaned over her and opened the passenger side door. "Do you need me to explain things about the car to your pa?"

"I'm quite capable of gettin' fuel in the car, thank you very much!" She got out and slammed the door, making the glass rattle.

Bill waited until she was safely inside before starting the truck again. George Wheaton ran out to stop him. Bill sucked in a breath and wondered what Charlotte had told him.

"Hey, Bill," said George, opening the truck door. "Charlotte said somethin' was wrong with the car?"

"She ran out of gas over near Quail Crossings," explained Bill. "I just happened to be comin' back from town when I saw her."

"What in tarnation was she doin' over there?" George asked himself. "Bill, would you mind takin' me back to the car? It's a mighty cold ride on a horse, and my grain truck ain't runnin' right."

"Sure," said Bill, finally releasing his breath.

"Thanks," said George, "just let me get the gas can. I'll

be right back."

George walked around the house as Charlotte came back to the truck.

"I'm so sorry, Bill," she said, batting her eyelashes. "I should've known you'd be appalled by my aggressive behavior. You want a lady, and what I did wasn't very lady-like. I do hope you won't tell my pa about my proposition. He would be so crushed, and my reputation would be ruined."

"It's okay, Charlotte. I'd like to forget the whole ordeal. Your reputation is safe. Just please don't do anythin' like that again." He furrowed his brows at her. "Most men wouldn't be such a gentleman."

"Oh, I know," said a wide-eyed Charlotte. "When Lou Anne suggested I throw myself at you, I thought she had gone mad. But she insisted that's what you wanted."

Bill picked at the steering wheel. "Lou Anne told you to act that way?"

"Yes, she said that's the way she got Jon to notice her."

Bill looked at the gauges. "Please, don't lie to me, Charlotte."

Charlotte sat down. "I'm not, Bill. How well do you know Lou Anne? She told me she was gonna kiss you on the hayride even though she's seein' Jon. Becky Green told me she saw Jon and Lou Anne behind the hay barn at the hoedown pawin' all over each other. I have to believe her. I mean why would Becky lie?"

Bill thought of the way Jon kissed Lou Anne's cheek. He had taken her look to be one of shock, but maybe she was flirting.

She touched his shoulder. "I can tell you really like her, but she's not interested in you, Bill, and I am. Just keep that in mind."

George jogged back to the truck. "Sorry to take so long. One of the boys must've been playin' in my shed again. It took me a while to find my gas can." He set the can in the back of Bill's truck and looked at his daughter. "Are you comin'?"

She shook her head and slid out of the seat. "I told Mother I'd cook dinner."

"Are you makin' your chicken noodles?" George asked Charlotte and then looked at Bill. "This girl makes the best chicken noodles. Makes my stomach growl just thinkin' about 'em."

"What else?" she said as she kissed her dad's cheek, then looked at Bill. "Think about what I said."

Charlotte walked back toward the house as George got in.

"What was that all about?" he asked.

"I'm not sure yet," answered Bill as he pulled out of the drive and headed back to the stranded car.

Elmer pulled his collar tighter around his neck, letting out a low whistle as he approached Tiny's house. One of Button's pups came barreling through the sand plum bushes, tongue hanging out, ready for the next command. Elmer motioned for the dog to run ahead into the drive as he trotted behind on the horse. He caught sight of Tiny coming out of the chicken coop just beyond the drive.

He let out two more whistles, and the dog ran up to Tiny and sat. Tiny giggled as she rubbed the dog's head. "Jeepers, Elmer, what a smart dog. I've always wanted a smart dog like this. I tried to train Jelly a few times, but she never listened, and I got bored. Always ended up quittin' and lettin' Jelly do whatever she wanted. Probably should've worked harder with her, so she wouldn't have left and got sick." She looked at the ground. The dog gave her hand a quick lick, causing a smile to widen across her face. "Did you train him?"

"Her," corrected Elmer as he dismounted, "and yep, I trained them all, but she's one of the smartest."

"What are y'all doin' way over here?" Tiny asked. "It's colder than an Eskimo's nose today. Mama made me come out here to feed the chickens, but I sure didn't want to. Can't put on enough layers for weather like this. Jeepers, it's like bein' under ice. I can't imagine ridin' a horse all the way here. Brrr!"

"I wanted to bring her to you," he pointed at the dog.

Tiny tilted her head. "To me?"

"I talked it over with Mr. Murphy," explained Elmer. "And he talked to your pa. They said it was all right for you to have one of Button's pups since Jelly, well..." Elmer ran his hands through his hair. "Well, since Jelly ain't here anymore."

"Jeepers!" squealed Tiny, "Do you mean it? You're not pullin' my leg? That wouldn't be too nice, and it don't seem like the kind of thing you'd do, but really, you mean it? She's really mine?"

"Yep." Elmer smiled.

"Oh, my goodness, I never thought I'd get another dog ever. Maybe if some stray had found its way here, but never in a million years did I think my pa would let me have another dog. After Jelly left, he went on and on about how much calmer the chickens were. I think he was tryin' to make me feel better, but it didn't really work, but Pa does that from time to time. Oh, Elmer, I just..."

Tiny threw her arms around Elmer, the force causing him to step back. "Thank you so much." She released him from her death grip and leaned into the dog. "Does she have a name? I mean if you've been callin' her somethin', I don't want to confuse her. She's so smart and callin' her by a new name might put a kink in the wrench."

"I've been callin' her Lady," Elmer said. "But you can call her whatever you want. She's a smart cookie; she'll catch on to her new name."

"Lady's a perfect name. Jeepers, everythin' about her is perfect," said Tiny, running her hands down the dog's spotted back. She looked up and winked at Elmer. "Just like you."

Chapter Twenty-three

Elmer felt like he'd been run over by a herd of cattle. His body ached, and he couldn't get warm, no matter how many layers he put on. He grabbed the milk bucket and headed towards Poppy. He just wanted to get his chores done, go lay by the fire, and take a long nap. Norman jumped in front of him, honking and hissing.

"Get away from me, you stupid bird." Elmer swung the bucket at the crazed goose.

Norman dodged the bucket, raised his wings, and continued to block Elmer's way to the stall.

"Please, Norman, let me through. Sorry I called you a stupid bird," Elmer pleaded, "I just want to get my chores done." Norman stood his ground. Elmer had had enough; he swung the milk bucket harder at the beast and felt himself fall toward the ground. The barn spun, so he closed his eyes and let the darkness take over.

"Mr. Norman, what's all the ruckus about?" Alice pushed the barn door open and saw her brother lying on the ground, with Norman dancing and honking around him.

"Somebody help," she screamed, running towards her brother. "Elm's hurt!"

James ran in behind her and saw Elmer's still body on the barn floor. He picked up the boy and ran towards the house.

"Dovie, get some cold towels." He said, busting through the back door. "This boy's burnin' up."

He placed Elmer on the sofa and covered him with the blue and white checkered quilt. Dovie hurried in with a bowl of water and some towels as Alice stood in the doorway crying.

"Alice, honey, he's gonna be fine." James moved out of Dovie's way and grabbed Alice's hand. "Let's you and I go feed the chickens."

"But I want to stay with Elm," Alice cried. "Is he okay?"

"He's gonna be fine," assured James. "We just need to let Dovie work, okie dokie? Anyhow we better check on ol' Norman. I bet he's scared too."

Alice gave a tentative nod and allowed James to lead her to the door, as she continually looked over her shoulder. "Please, Jesus, help my brother," she whispered.

Dovie felt Elmer's forehead with the back of her hand before covering it with a damp cloth.

"Evalyn!" She pulled the quilt off the back of the sofa and began undressing him. "Get down here! I need your help."

Evalyn trudged down the stairs, her normal pace since having to do so many extra chores. "What is it now?" she asked, staring at her fingernails as she leaned on the door jamb.

"Evalyn, look at me," ordered Dovie.

Evalyn rolled her eyes before glancing at Dovie. Her eyes shifted to the couch. "Oh, my goodness, Elm!" she screamed running to her brother's side.

"He's gonna be all right," said Dovie. "I need you to fix some chicken broth, okay?"

Evalyn was too busy crying on her brother's shoulder to answer.

"Evalyn!" Dovie snapped. "Cryin' like a leaky faucet ain't gonna help. Go fix that broth now. I'm gonna need your help, and if you make yourself sick too, you'll be no good to me or Elmer." She grabbed Evalyn's chin. "Understand?"

Evalyn knocked Dovie's hand away, nodded, and ran to the kitchen to start the broth.

Elmer heard his sister's cry and Dovie's strict demands through a heavy fog that engulfed his brain. He tried desperately to tell Evalyn he was fine. He tried to sit up, but was met with Dovie's hands, pushing him back down on the sofa.

"You're all right, Elmer," she cooed. "Just lie back and let us take care of you."

Elmer wanted to protest that he didn't need to be taken care of. That was Alice and to an extent Evalyn, but not him. He was a man, and there were chores to be done. He thought about making another attempt, shrugging Dovie off, and getting up, but he felt weaker than a newborn pup.

"Gotta milk Poppy," he mumbled.

Dovie ignored him and continued pressing a wet cloth on his forehead. Someone else entered the room. Elmer tried to make out who it was, but lacked focus.

"How is he?" asked Bill.

"He's got a high fever," answered Dovie.

"Do you think it's the same as what Tiny's got? I heard in town today that she's real sick."

Elmer bolted up. "What's wrong with Tiny?"

His head spun as it had in the barn, and he didn't need Dovie to tell him to lie back down.

"Could be, Bill," said Dovie. "Go to the Clark's and

see if they'll bring Tiny here and take care of Alice for a little while. We don't want her and little Ruth gettin' sick."

"Tiny?" Elmer tried asking again.

"You're both gonna be fine," reassured Bill. "I'm gonna go get her right now."

It wasn't long before Bill came back, cradling the fragile girl in his arms. Dovie had moved her mattress onto the floor in the front room by the fire and motioned for Bill to put Tiny on it. She was surprised to see Lou Anne Garber follow him into the living room, carrying a small bundle.

"Little Charles is sick. We went to the Clark's, after hearin' 'bout Tiny. Ma didn't want Joan or Clare to be exposed. She thinks it's influenza."

"I'm afraid she's right. How old is Charles now?" Dovie put a cool washcloth on Tiny's head and motioned for Lou Anne to put Charles next to Tiny.

Lou Anne put Charles down. "He's two. I was told to stay and help."

"Evalyn's makin' chicken broth. We'll need some help tryin' to get them to eat." Dovie felt Charles's forehead. "Dad went to town to get some medicine from Johnson's Drug and to call the doctor in Tucket."

"Do you think he'll come?" Bill paced the room.

"He'll try, just depends on how busy he is." Dovie looked at Bill. "How did Alice take stayin' with the Clarks?"

"Not well." He ran his fingers through his hair, reminding Dovie of James. "She thinks we're sendin' her away because Elm is worse off than we said." He fingered his hat. "She thinks she'll never see him again."

"Why don't you go take a walk or somethin'? Clear your head." Lou Anne put her hand on Bill's shoulder.

"We'll take good care of Elmer."

"She's right," said Dovie, "Poppy needs to be milked, and we'll need the milk later on. Why don't you go take care of that, okay?"

Bill nodded and slowly put his hat back on. He touched Elmer's cheek before heading out to finish the job Elmer couldn't.

Lou Anne watched him walk out the door. "He sure loves his family."

Dovie nodded. "Besides Dad, I've never seen a man so devoted."

Evalyn walked in carrying three bowls of chicken broth on a wooden tray. "Soup's done. I've let it cool. I think it's just right to try now."

Grabbing a bowl, Dovie headed towards Charles. "Evalyn, you see if you can get Elmer to eat some." She nodded at Tiny. "Lou Anne, try with her."

The three coaxed and cooed to their patients for the next hour, only managing to get a few bites down each person. James stomped his boots on the back stoop before entering the kitchen. Clearing his throat, he entered the front room. "The doc won't be comin'. They've got quite an epidemic in Tucket. He said this should help." He held up a bottle of green liquid. "They won't like it much. He said it tastes rotten. You got any of that honey left, Dovie?"

Dovie nodded and hurried into the kitchen, grabbing the honey and three spoons. It was an old trick her ma had used, chasing the medicine with the sweet honey.

James handed Dovie the bottle on her way back into the front room. "David Garber was in the store and told me 'bout Charles. The doc says that medicine's too strong for him. He can't take it."

Dovie stared at her Dad. "He doesn't want us to give it

to him? Are you sure, Dad?"

"I'm sure. The doc said the medicine will do more harm than good for Charles. Could cause him to have fits."

"And what did my pa say?" asked Lou Anne. "Is my ma comin'?"

"He said he'd tell your ma, and if she wanted to do somethin' different then he'd bring her over, but for now you're to stay here until you hear otherwise."

Lou Anne sucked in a breath and looked at Dovie. "What does that mean for Charles?"

"It means we have our work cut out for us. It'll be important to keep him eatin' the broth."

Lou Anne released a slow sigh. "Will he die?"

Dovie put her arms around the young woman's shoulders. "We will do everythin' we can to prevent that from happenin'. He's a strong little boy, and I believe he'll pull through. You have to believe it too, Lou Anne. Don't ever give up hope." She gave Lou Anne a tight squeeze. "He's sleepin' now, so why don't you go outside and get some fresh air."

Lou Anne grabbed her scarf and coat and walked outside towards the barn. She shivered as she sat on a hay stack. Swallowing hard she tried desperately to stop the tears that already ran down her cheeks.

"They'll be okay."

Lou Anne looked up to see Bill in the doorway.

"James got the medicine from town. The kids will be up and runnin' in no time," Bill explained.

Lou Anne let out a loud sob. "Charles can't take the medicine. He's too little. Doc says it will do more harm than good."

Bill approached Lou Anne and kneeled before her. "Dovie's a smart lady. She'll do everythin' in her power to make sure he lives. And you'll be there to love on him and make him feel secure even though he's not at home."

"Mrs. Grant knows more than anyone we have no power when it comes to life and death," Lou Anne cried. "I don't know what I'll do if he dies. I don't want to imagine a life without that little boy."

Bill moved to Lou Anne's side and wrapped his arms around her. He longed to find the words that would take her tears away. He wished he had the power to make sure she never cried again.

Elmer stared at the ceiling, trying to figure out how he'd gotten into the den and why the sofa he was laying on had been pushed closer to the fire. He was thankful for the warmth as he shivered under the quilt. The last thing he remembered was walking out the back door to milk Poppy.

Hearing muffled voices in the kitchen, he leaned up on his elbow. Evalyn was pacing in the doorway ranting something about hick doctors, while Dovie and Lou Anne Garber sat slumped at the table, uneaten sandwiches sitting before them. Lou Anne Garber? What was she doing here?

Elmer laid back and rubbed his temples. Flashes of the afternoon came into focus; Norman blocking his path, Dovie pressing a cool rag against his forehead, Evalyn crying, and Tiny... there was something about Tiny.

A soft moan came from beside the sofa. Elmer turned on his side and peered down. A mattress had been laid on the floor, leaving only a small path in front of the sofa. A small little boy sucked his thumb near the fire, sweat beading on his forehead.

Another moan brought Elmer's eyes to the form closest to him. It was Tiny. Eyes closed, she wiped her forehead with the back of her hand, then pulled the covers close to her chin before turning her back to Elmer.

Without thinking, Elmer slid off the sofa. He grabbed the basin at the end of the mattress and pulled out a fresh rag. He gently draped the cool cloth on Tiny's forehead before curling up beside her. Putting one arm over her he heard her whisper, "Please don't leave me."

He couldn't help but whisper back, "Never."

Chapter Twenty-four

Two days and nights went by with very little sleep. Bill and James paced in the kitchen while the three women tried to keep their sick family members cool and full of fluids. As dawn began to crest over the prairie on the third day, James made coffee and scrambled some eggs.

"Bill, we have to take care of the farm. I understand it's gonna be hard to work knowin' these young'uns are in here, but it'll be better if we keep busy and out of the women's way."

"It's my job," Bill said softly.

"What?" asked James.

"It's my job to keep them safe, and I've failed." Bill slumped into a chair. "Elmer's fightin' for his life, Alice is scared to death at the neighbors, and Evie... well don't even get me started on her. I've failed them all."

James made a tsking noise. "Now, Bill Brewer, I'm ashamed of you."

Bill looked up confused.

"Here you are throwin' yourself a big ol' pity party while those kids are in there ill. You know better than anyone if there was a way to keep them safe from illness and from being scared, you'd do it. You're a great brother to these kids and they're lucky to have you. If you think you're gonna sit there, feelin' all down on yourself and get a compliment from me, you're sorely mistaken." James winked at Bill. "Now come on. Mopin' around won't help anybody. Them kids are in good hands."

He stuck his head in the den. "Dovie, I made some fresh coffee and eggs. You ladies should try to eat something this mornin'. We can't have y'all gettin' sick too."

Dovie nodded and looked at Lou Anne lying beside her brother. Evalyn lay on the couch, her hand resting on Elmer's shoulder as he lay next to Tiny. All were sleeping. Knowing her dad was right, she went into the kitchen to get some breakfast before the others woke up. Placing her head on her hand, she picked at the eggs. Didn't seem like it was that long ago she was trying to help her mother fight off the same illness. A battle they hadn't won. In the end, her mother went peacefully in her sleep. Thankfully there had been no fits or visions. Dovie had heard of some people so delusional with fever they ran into blizzards thinking it to be summer. Still to lose her mother, peacefully or not, had been devastating - at the time the most devastating thing she had ever encountered, that is until she lost her daughter and husband.

"Oh my, Mrs. Grant, come quick," Lou Anne shouted from the front room, snapping Dovie out of her thoughts. "Charles is burnin' up. He's so hot. What do we do?"

Dovie didn't answer, but swooped the boy up and rushed him back into the kitchen. Placing him in the dish wash tub, Dovie looked to Lou Anne. "Start pumpin'. He's not gonna like this, but it's all we can do."

Charles screamed as the cold water surrounded him. Lou Anne pumped frantically as she sobbed. "Oh, God, don't let him die. Please, God. How will I tell my ma if he dies?"

"Either get control of yourself or leave," Dovie snapped. "You're scarin' him. It's only gonna make things worse carryin' on like a hen with a fox in the coop."

Lou Anne stiffened as gentle hands pushed her away from the pump. Bill stood in her place, pumping the cold January water onto Charles, while Lou Anne rubbed her hands in worry.

Dovie nodded to Bill. "That's plenty. Come here and hold Charles upright, Lou Anne. Talk to him; let him know it's gonna to be okay. He needs his big sister right now."

Lou Anne placed her hands under Charles's arms. "It's okay, Bubba. Sissy's here. I know it's cold, but you'll feel better soon," she cooed to the scared toddler.

Dovie grabbed the kettle off the stove, added a little bit of hot water to the bath, and started singing "Amazing Grace". Lou Anne joined in before looking at Bill, her eyes red from crying. A silent thank you filled the room as Bill gave a quick nod before leaving the women.

James watched Bill return to the barn and went about feeding the chickens. He was worried about the women and what would happen to all of them if the women got sick.

The chickens were quiet when he entered the coop, as if they knew something was going on. He tossed the feed and thought of the way Alice talked to them. She had made friends of all the animals on the farm. Norman had pouted at the pond since Alice left. James almost felt sorry for the grumpy old bird.

Making his way out of the chicken house, he thought of Bill on that first day at the farm. He was trying so hard to keep it all together as he concentrated on fixing that little wire on the coop. James's mind turned to Evalyn and the way she had smiled shyly when he complimented her pumpkin pie at Thanksgiving.

Next he thought of Elmer and pictured him training the pups, only to have his mind turn to the sick boy on the mattress, with his arm wrapped around his friend. James felt the sting in his heart instantly. He knew influenza liked the old and the young, having lost his wife to it just five short years ago.

Storing the eggs, he walked slowly towards the orchard. He needed a moment with God, and nature was where he felt closest to Him. The north wind hurt his ears, but he knew the trees would soon make it bearable. Finally, he spotted the small wooden bench he had made for his lovely wife, Sylvia. She loved sitting in the orchard watching the birds pick at the apples.

He sat and looked up at the gray sky. "Hello, Lord, it's me your old friend, James. I know I ask you for a lot, sometimes for things I don't need, but think I do. I'm askin', no I'm beggin' you to forget all those needless things and concentrate all your healin' power on Elmer and those children in there. Those are good kids, your lambs, and I know it's up to you to decide when to call 'em home, but please God not now, not this time." James wiped away his tears with the small hanky Alice had given him for Christmas. "Thanks, Lord, for listenin'. I ask these things in your name. Amen."

As James was saying his prayer, Dovie handed Charles over to Lou Anne. "It seems like his fever broke," she said. "You can take him back to the front room. See if you can't get him to eat some more broth."

She had spent the last hour giving Charles cool baths and wrapped her water wrinkled hands in a warm towel. "I think he's gonna be okay."

"Thank you so much, Mrs. Grant," said Lou Anne, hugging her brother. "I'm sorry I lost control earlier."

"It's okay, dear. Death is scary when it's beating on the door of a loved one."

Bill walked in the back door, removed his hat, and stared at the two women.

"How's he doin'?" he asked, pointing his hat at Charles.

"Much better now," said Lou Anne. "Thank you for your help, Bill. I lost my senses for a bit. I appreciate you were there to help me while I found them."

"Lou Anne, I'll always be there for you," Bill looked into her hazel eyes. "That is if you'll let me."

"I'll give you two a moment," said Dovie, taking Charles and making her way back to the front room.

"Bill, I just can't." She turned away from him. "Don't ask me why."

"Are you seeing Jon Gates?"

Lou Anne didn't answer.

"Just tell me the truth," begged Bill. "If you're seein' him, I'll leave you alone and never talk about it again. But one way or another, you have to tell me. I feel like I'm Harry Houdini on a high wire with no rope."

Turning to facing him again, Lou Anne shook her head no.

"Why did you lie to me?" Bill asked. "Does this have anythin' to do with Charlotte?"

Lou Anne rolled her eyes and threw her hands up in the air. "It has everythin' to do with Charlotte. She's made up her mind you're the one for her. Trust me she'll do anythin' to make sure you pick her."

"But I don't want her, Lou Anne." Bill slammed his

hat on the table and grabbed Lou Anne's shoulders. "I want you. Since the first day we met, I've felt we've had somethin' special. I know you feel it too. That day on the hayride and in the barn the other day, I could see it in your eyes. Just give me a chance, Lou Anne. I just know we can make each other happy."

Lou Anne opened her mouth to speak but was interrupted by Tiny's voice in the front room. It had been days since either Elmer or Tiny had tried to speak. She rushed to see what was going on.

"Can I have some water?" Tiny asked.

Lou Anne smiled as Evalyn gently lifted a glass to Tiny's mouth. Dovie walked to Elmer and felt his forehead. Still too warm, she feared he'd be the next to need a cold bath. She took the rag that covered his forehead and dunked it in water, wrung it out, and placed it back on the boy's head.

"How's he doin'?" asked Bill.

"Still has a fever." Dovie played with Elmer's hair before walking to Bill. "But I'm hopin' it'll break tonight."

Bill looked at Tiny. "The medicine seems to be workin' for her."

"Yeah, gives me hope for Elmer." She patted Bill's arm.

"Dovie, why don't you go lay down?" Bill asked. "You look tired. Tiny's doin' better, and I can look after Elm for a bit."

Dovie grabbed a biscuit from the tin on the floor and nodded. "You're right; I should. I'll be in Dad's room if anyone needs me."

She walked towards James's room and noticed Elmer was awake.

"How do you feel?" She searched his face for an

answer.

"Hungry." Elmer whispered as he tried to sit up a little.

Dovie smiled. She knew the worst was over. "All right then, let's get this boy some soup."

"Jeepers, Elmer, you don't look so good," Tiny said weakly. "I bet we got that influenza my ma's always going on about." She turned and looked at Charles before looking back at Elmer. "Sure is scary, that influenza." She reached out and grabbed his hand. "But I don't feel so scared since you're here."

Elmer smiled at Tiny and squeezed her hand. "You're gonna be just fine, Tiny."

Tiny's eyes grew wide. "People die from influenza all the time. It wasn't that long ago Mr. Murphy's wife passed from it. I was little, but I remember goin' to the funeral with my grandpa. It was so sad. It was the first time I'd seen a man cry. When I asked my grandpa why Mr. Murphy was cryin', Grandpa said it was because he was so full of grief he had to let some of it out, or he'd explode from sadness. The cryin' was the way the grief got out."

Elmer pursed his lips together. He couldn't imagine seeing James that sad. A man like him should never feel sad. He's too good to people, Elmer thought.

"I saw him cry one other time when they laid little Helen and Mr. Grant to rest. It rained so hard that day, Ma said it was like Jesus himself was cryin'. I wonder if my pa will cry if I die from this influenza."

"That's not somethin' you need to think about," said Elmer.

"How do you know?" asked Tiny.

"Like I said, you're gonna be fine," said Elmer. "I'll see to it personally."

Chapter Twenty-five

February flurries whipped through Dovie's hair as she sat on the little hill that held her husband and child. She traced Helen's etched name on the small stone tablet.

"I miss you, honey." She had no sooner said the words when tears started to fall. "One year ago today, you and your daddy left me for Heaven. I've been so lonely ever since."

She played with the heavy denim quilt covering her legs.

"Of course, I've had your grandpa with me." She blotted her cheeks with a handkerchief Alice had embroidered for her. "He tries real hard to keep me company, and I'm sure you know 'bout the young'uns stayin' with us now. I hope you don't mind little Alice playin' with your doll. She loves it so. I know you would've loved it too. I reckon you and her would've been like two peas in a pod, if you were still here. Gettin' into all sorts of trouble with Norman. Probably keepin' your daddy on his toes, tryin' to keep y'all out of stuff in the barn."

At the mention of her husband she turned and looked at Simon's stone. "I really miss talkin' to you, Simon. When somethin' happens, you're the first person I want to tell, and when I realize I can't, I don't feel like tellin' nobody. I got second at this year's pie contest." Dovie rolled her eyes at herself. "I tell you like you don't already know. Like you're not watchin' our every move from above. It just helps to tell you, to share with you. Gives me back a little bit of what we had."

"There was a bit of a scare last month with some of the local children when a bout of influenza made the rounds. The Garber baby, Charles, and Tiny and Elmer all got real sick. They're all doin' good now, thanks be to God. Hopefully, the fever didn't affect little Charles's mind. I'm just so glad Alice didn't get it. Don't know if her fragile body could've handled it after all they've been through with their parents leavin'. I just can't understand parents who up and leave their children like that. We could've never abandoned Helen; she's even got one of us in Heaven. I hate that you're both gone, but I'm glad y'all have each other." She shook her head as fresh tears threatened and changed the subject.

"Elmer's doin' much better, though he's tired most of the time. You should see Dad. Ever since Elmer's fever broke, he just walks around singin' 'Thank you, Jesus.' Poor Elmer though, he's still a bit weak, and I swear that boy had ants in his pants till Dad brought home a radio. Can you believe it, a radio? Everybody scrimpin' and savin', and he goes out and gets a radio. Says it's to hear the president's speeches and to keep in contact with the world. I think he just likes to listen to the fiddle player they have on in the evenings. Dad said our ol' wind charger has more than enough energy to keep it goin' along with the lights, and he was right."

"Elmer listens to that thing all blessed day, but his

favorite is the Jack Armstrong show. Lives for adventure that boy does. Wouldn't know it by how quiet he is." She giggled. "Speakin' of adventure, he got a valentine card from Tiny this mornin' and turned three shades of red when I handed it to him. What a sight. They did spend an awful lot of time together while sick, playin' cards and listenin' to the radio. She still comes over most Saturdays after her chores, so he can catch her up on all of Jack's adventures. I think she'd rather hear Elmer tell the stories than listen to them on the radio anyhow."

"I remember the first valentine you gave to me. Don't think we were much older than Elmer and Tiny. It was on pale blue paper. I remember because it was the first time I'd seen paper that was blue. I believe it was your mother's good stationary. I wonder if she ever noticed a piece was missin'?" Dovie folded her hands under the quilt.

"Oh, and you should've seen Alice ice skatin' on the pond with Norman, yesterday. Yes, our crazy ol' goose and Alice are friends. She calls him, Mr. Norman. Dad stood on the bank and watched them all nervous like, even though he knew the pond was frozen solid. It's real low on account of the drought, so it didn't take much. They had themselves a good ol' time. Hearin' that girl giggle reminds me a lot of you, Helen." She looked back at her daughter's stone.

"The older girl, Evalyn - her siblings call her Evie - she's a handful. Though I'll be the first to admit she was a mighty big help when the kids got ill. I feel bad for the poor girl. She really wants to see her folks again. Can't say I blame her. She once asked me if I could get back to y'all wouldn't I do everything I could? Of course the answer is yes, and I almost told her how close I came to doin' the one thing I could think of to get me where y'all are. If I wasn't so scared of goin' to Hell, I would've in a heartbeat. But an eternity without y'all is a lot longer than a lifetime."

She took in a deep breath to steady her nerves.

"The older brother, Bill, has asked Lou Anne Garber to the Valentine Dance tonight. They'd make a cute couple, but she seems to be holdin' back for some reason. She only agreed to go with him if he invited Charlotte Wheaten too. Maybe she's nervous 'bout goin' on a date. Can't say I'm not nervous 'bout him drivin' into town. Brings back some bad memories for me. I know it's silly. The snow isn't goin' to amount to much, and he's a grown man. Of course, so were you."

She gasped as fresh tears streamed down her chapped cheeks.

"I always told you that you drove too fast. How could you swerve for a silly ol' deer? You should've just hit the mangy ol' critter. We could've gotten a new car. I can't get a new you or Helen. Didn't you think what leavin' would do to me? You left me all alone, Simon Grant. How am I supposed to do this without you? I never wanted to imagine a world without you and Helen, and now here I am livin' in one."

She cried hard into her hands, wept like she had done on the first day in her world without them. Standing, she kissed the top of Simon's headstone.

"I never could stay mad at you." She smiled. "I just miss you both so much, and I'm angry 'bout not havin' you in my life anymore. But I'm not angry at you. Fact is I don't know who to be angry at. Guess I'll just be mad at the deer. Tell you the truth, I want those kids to like me." She folded the blanket. "Even Evalyn. They've warmed my heart a little, and I think in time it'll warm even more."

Dovie returned to Quail Crossings as Bill was getting ready for the dance. He wore an old navy blue suit of

James's and a new starched white shirt. Evalyn had trimmed up his sideburns and given him a nice close shave.

"My, oh my, Bill," exclaimed Dovie. "You look better than the preacher during Easter morning services."

"Thanks. Do you think Lou Anne will like it?" Bill pulled on his jacket and straightened the wrinkles out.

"If she doesn't, she's blind as a mole." Dovie bit her lip. "Bill, do me a favor."

"Anythin'," he said, fumbling with his tie. "As long as it don't get me dirty. Took me an hour in the tub to stop smellin' like Poppy." He winked at her.

"Here let me," she said, tying his tie. "Just be careful tonight on the roads. I know they ain't slick, and you're a good driver. It's just you never know what critter might..."

He put his hands on her shoulders to stop her. "I understand it's a hard day for you. I promise to be careful. The last thing I would want to do is hurt you anymore on this already tryin' day."

She nodded grateful thanks as Alice came running into the kitchen and bounced into her brother's arms. "Tell me again 'bout askin' Lou Anne to the dance."

"Alice, I've told you a thousand times. It ain't that interestin' of a story."

"Sure it is, Bill," Alice said seriously. "One day your kids will want to know how their parents got together, and I have to be able to explain it to 'em, like a good aunt."

"Aren't you gettin' a little ahead of yourself, Alice," said Dovie. "It's their first date."

"Exactly!" said Alice, "It's part of their story, and I have to get it all right. It's my job."

"Okay," Bill said as he put Alice down, "but then I have to go so I won't be late pickin' up Lou Anne." Alice nodded as she sat at the kitchen table and placed her chin on both hands.

"Well," started Bill, "as you know we went to church last Sunday, like we do every Sunday. After services, you and Elm came home with Dovie and James, and I stayed behind with Evie so she could attend the youth meetin'. It was a fairly nice day, so I decided to walk around outside for a bit. When I went outside, I saw Lou Anne sittin' on a swing. As I approached, she looked up at me with her honey eyes, and I just knew I had to ask her to the dance. But I was all nervous, so I talked about other things instead, till I could work up my nerve."

"I can't believe you were nervous, Bill," said Alice. "You always act so calm."

"Well, Alice, sometimes I act calm, but there's nothin' but storm clouds inside."

"You too? I thought only my tummy acted like storm clouds."

"Oh, honey," said Dovie, "we all get storm clouds in our bellies from time to time."

"So what did you say?" Alice asked Bill.

"Well, first we talked about the weather and how nice it was for a February afternoon. Then we talked about why she was skippin' the youth meetin'. You see she was supposed to be in the sanctuary with all the other high schoolers, but since…"

"No, what did you say about the dance?" Alice said dramatically. "I don't care about the weather or the youth meetin'!"

Bill smiled. "Well, I said, 'Lou Anne, I'd sure like to take you to the Valentine's dance next Saturday, if that's okay with you?' and she looked at me and smiled. I had my hands shoved way down in my pockets, scared to take 'em out cause they was so sweaty. I just knew she was gonna say no and say she was going with that Jon Gates, guy." Alice wrinkled her nose. "But she didn't," continued Bill. "She said she'd love to go with me, but before she could say yes, I had to do two things for her. Well, at that point I would've walked to the moon and back for her, so it was easy for me to say 'anythin' you want, Lou Anne.'"

"What were the two things?" Alice bounced up on her knees.

"First, I had to push her on the swing. She said it'd been ages since anyone had made her fly on a swing. That was easy enough, so I pushed, and she just laughed and laughed. Then the kids started comin' out from the youth meetin'. So I asked her what the second thing was, and she said I had to invite Charlotte and Peter to join us. Said her pa wouldn't allow her to go alone, and it had to be a group thing."

"That's a shame," said Alice tsking her lips.

"Nah," said Bill, "it would've been a shame if she had said no."

Chapter Twenty-six

Bill could hardly stop himself from smiling as he drove to pick up Lou Anne. Pulling in front of her house, his heart did a somersault. He couldn't wait to see her. Putting on his hat, he grabbed the milk and eggs Dovie had asked him to bring and made his way to the front door. He wished he had some flowers to give Lou Anne instead of food for the family, but in February, flowers were hard to come by, and food was greatly appreciated, no matter the season.

Hannah answered the door and gave Bill a nice big smile.

"Lou Anne, Bill's here," she yelled towards the back of the house. "Please come in and have a seat. You know us women, always runnin' late."

Bill held out the eggs and milk. "Dovie asked me to bring you these."

Hannah took the items. "She's such a generous soul." She looked down. "How's she doin' today?"

"She seems to be handlin' it okay."

"Well, let her know I'm prayin' for her and James. Lord knows what I would done if I'd lost Charles." She hurried into the kitchen, putting the items away. "Probably take to my bed and never come out again. Dovie Grant is a stronger woman than I am, that's for sure."

Bill sat fidgeting with his hat. "How is Charles doin'?"

"Oh, he's doin' good, thanks for askin'." Hannah returned to the living room and sat in an old rocker. "He sleeps a lot, but his appetite is good. The doc saw him last week and thinks he'll make a full recovery, bless the Lord."

"Good to hear," said Bill.

"Hello, Bill." Lou Anne glided into the room wearing a lovely pink dress with a white coat hanging over her arm.

"Wow, you look amazing," Bill stuttered as he stood. Shaking his head, he grabbed her coat. "Let me help you with that."

Lou Anne blushed and turned so Bill could help her with her coat.

"The dance ends at ten. I'll have her back no later than 10:30," Bill said to Hannah. "Is that okay?"

"That'll be fine." Hannah stood and hugged her daughter. "You two go have fun. Just be careful not to wake Charles or your father when you come in."

Bill opened the front door for Lou Anne and then hurried to help her into the truck. "This really isn't necessary, Bill. You're gonna be mighty tired openin' doors for both me and Charlotte all night."

"I think Peter will be more than happy to open Charlotte's doors," said Bill.

"She doesn't want Peter to open her doors. She wants you. You know that as well as I do," said Lou Anne, sliding into the truck.

"Well, it's high time she learns she can't always get what she wants." Bill winked at her.

"Bill, don't cause trouble with her. You wouldn't believe what she's capable of." Lou Anne stared out into the distance.

Bill leaned in close. "So why don't you tell me? You

were gonna tell me somethin' at the house when Tiny interrupted. Don't think I forgot."

"It's nothin', Bill." Lou Anne smoothed out her coat. "Let's just go pick up Charlotte and Peter and forget about everythin'-- the kids bein' sick, who wants who -- everythin'. I just want to have fun and dance the night away without a care in the world."

Bill nodded. "We can do that."

Smiling, Bill turned away from Lou Anne's house and headed towards Charlotte's. He pulled up to the house and reached for his door handle. Lou Anne put her hand on his arm. "Why don't you let me go get her? That way there's no confusion."

"Okay," said Bill, leaning back. "I'll keep the motor runnin'."

Lou Anne hopped out of the truck and walked slowly to Charlotte's door. She took a deep breath as she knocked. Kathleen answered with a wide smile.

"Hello, Lou Anne," she said. "It's so nice to see you."

"Thank you, Mrs. Wheaton. It's nice to see you, too, is Charlotte ready?"

"Just about, I think. Why don't you go check on her? You know where her room is." Kathleen gestured up the stairs.

Lou Anne took the stairs two at a time. Now that she was in the house, she wanted to get the confrontation over with. She knew Charlotte would be upset to see her instead of Bill. She gave three solid raps on the door.

"Mom, tell Bill I'll be right down," Charlotte said through the door.

"It's me, Lou Anne. Can I come in?"

The room was quiet for a moment before the door was yanked open.

"Where's Bill? Is he okay?" asked Charlotte.

"He's fine," said Lou Anne, entering the room Charlotte shared with her sister. "He's in the truck."

Charlotte looked at her sister, Harriet, who was laying on her bed reading. "Take a hike, Harry."

Harriet rolled her eyes. "This is my room, too and don't call me Harry. You know I hate that."

"Leave now, or I start callin' you Harry at school," Charlotte raised an eyebrow. "Bet your lover boy, Mark, would love to have a new nickname for you."

"Fine," Harriet huffed before stomping out the door.

Charlotte watched Harriet continue down the stairs before glaring at Lou Anne. "Why didn't he come to the door? It's the respectable thing to do, double date or not. I knew it was a mistake lettin' you and Peter tag along. But I just can't say no to Bill, if you know what I mean." A devilish smile sang across her face.

"Because this isn't a date," Lou Anne said softly.

"Of course it is, silly. You're goin' with Peter and I'm goin' with Bill," said Charlotte.

"No," said Lou Anne, "we're goin' as a group, just to have fun. I came up here instead of Bill so there wouldn't be any misunderstandin'." Lou Anne swallowed hard. "Charlotte, we used to be friends, and I miss that. I miss you. Can't we just go out and have fun without lettin' boys come between us?"

"Lou Anne, it's Valentine's day. You're supposed to be with the man you love on Valentine's Day." She released an ornery smile. "Besides, Bill's no boy."

"You don't love Bill." Lou Anne sat on the bed as Charlotte put on her shoes.

"No, but I will, and Pa told me Mr. Murphy gave Bill some land for Christmas. They're gonna help him build a proper house for his family. How many other boys 'round here have a house and land?"

"None I suppose," said Lou Anne.

"So remember our deal. I get Bill, and Bill keeps his job and the land. You steal Bill from me, and my pa will have a little talk with Mr. Murphy and Bill will get nothin'." Charlotte stood and adjusted her dress. "I'd hate to see that young family back on the streets, livin' out of that tiny truck. Especially little Alice, it just breaks my heart to think of her cold and hungry. Not to mention that other boy."

"Elmer?" Lou Anne raised an eyebrow.

"Yes, Elmer. He'd probably die. I don't mean to sound harsh, but he's still weak from the influenza. Yep, it would be a terrible shame to get Bill fired. But a girl's got to do, what a girl's got to do." Charlotte looked at Lou Anne, daring her to speak. "You ready?"

Lou Anne nodded, and the two made their way out to the truck, where Charlotte slid next to Bill. Lou Anne shrugged at Bill and got in. Charlotte talked the whole way to Peter's house, and Bill let out a thankful sigh when he saw Peter waiting for them on the front step.

Twenty minutes later, Bill pulled up to the dance barn and hurried to open the door for Lou Anne. To his surprise, Charlotte slid behind him and held out her hand for help getting out of the truck. By the time he had helped her out, Peter had already helped Lou Anne out on the passenger side. They could hear a fast fiddle playing accompanied by clapping inside the large building.

Charlotte reached out for Bill's arm and was instantly met by Peter's.

"Please allow me to escort you into the dance," he said winking at Bill. "You don't mind, do you, Bill?"

"No, not at all," said Bill, holding his hands up.

Charlotte glared at Lou Anne as Bill took Lou Anne's arm. "Ah, Bill's just being nice, Peter. Why don't you go in with Lou Anne?"

"I know you're just tryin' to spare Bill's feelings, Miss Charlotte, but I think Lou Anne is more than capable of walkin' young Bill into the dance. Come on now, they're playin' our song." Peter tightened his grip on Charlotte's arm and headed toward the barn.

"We don't have a song," Charlotte grumbled.

"Well, then, we best remedy that," said Peter as he dragged her further away from Bill and Lou Anne.

"Shall we?" Bill asked Lou Anne.

Lou Anne smiled and nodded yes, as they followed Charlotte and Peter.

"What was that all about?" Lou Anne asked.

"I don't know what you're talkin' about," said Bill with a smile.

"I saw Peter wink at you. Are you up to somethin'?"

"You have your secrets, Lou Anne, and I have mine. You want to have fun tonight, and I'm here to ensure you do just that."

"And what about Charlotte?" Lou Anne asked as they walked into the barn.

"What about her?" Bill pointed to the dance floor. "See, Peter's already sweepin' her off her feet."

Lou Anne looked at Charlotte who was being spun around by an energetic Peter. Every time she tried to walk off the dance floor, Peter would swing her back. Lou Anne glanced up at Bill. He smiled triumphantly.

"This wasn't part of the deal," said Lou Anne. "She's gonna be mad."

"I don't really care if Charlotte's mad, and the deal stated I had to invite them to come with us, which I did.

You didn't say nothin' 'bout puttin' it in Peter's head that Charlotte's interested in him, or that she likes a strong man who takes charge. I'm sure it doesn't hurt I gave him two dollars to keep her busy."

"Bill, you're so ornery." Lou Anne tried not to laugh. "She's gonna skin you alive if she finds out."

"If she finds out," said Bill, pulling Lou Anne towards the dance floor. "Come on, let's dance."

Bill led Lou Anne to the dance floor before twirling her into his arms. His heart beat faster than the fiddler's two step. Lou Anne followed his every move, and together they flowed across the dance floor.

Lou Anne's continuous smile confirmed she was having as much fun as he was. Now if he could only get her to open up and tell him what she was going to say at Quail Crossings while the kids were sick. After they started getting better, they hadn't had a moment to slip away and continue the conversation.

As the fiddler finished his jig, a young red-headed woman with her hair pinned up in tight curls, took the stage. "We're gonna take it down a notch, so grab your girl and hold her tight," she purred.

Lou Anne looked to the edge of the dance floor. Charlotte had escaped Peter and was leering in their direction. "We should probably go check on Peter and Charlotte," said Lou Anne.

Bill pulled her in close. "I'm sure they're fine. Besides I grew up to be a gentleman."

Lou Anne giggled. "What's that got to do with anythin'?"

"Well, when a lady tells you to do somethin', you do it. And that lady up there on stage said I should grab my girl and hold her tight."

"Bill, we've been through this. I'm not your girl."

Bill sighed. "Well, then just let me pretend a little while longer. Can you do that?"

Lou Anne nodded and leaned into Bill's shoulder. She wanted nothing more than to be Bill's girl. Deep in her heart she knew Mr. Murphy wouldn't fire Bill on the word of Charlotte or even Mr. Wheaton. But Bill's family meant the world to him and taking care of them was his top priority. She loved him too much to jeopardize what they had going for them at Quail Crossings.

Her heart jumped at the words in her head. Love? Did she really love a man she barely knew? He pulled her in tighter, making her heart flutter and arms tingle. His arms were exactly where she was supposed to be, and she did indeed love Bill Brewer.

She blinked back tears. There was only one thing to do, enjoy the night, and then never see him again. She could stand the pain of losing him, even to Charlotte, as long as it meant he and his family were safe.

"Are you okay, Lou Anne?" Bill pulled away, and examined her face as the lady finished her romantic melody. "It looks like you're gonna cry."

"Just a little sawdust in my eyes," Lou Anne lied as the fiddler started back up. "Spin me around, Bill. Spin me around like it's the last dance we'll ever have."

Chapter Twenty-seven

Lou Anne made her way to a small wood table while Bill went to find them something to drink. Her stomach soared with happy butterflies, and her jaw hurt from laughing so much. Bill was everything she had hoped for, romantic, charming, and a wonderful dancer.

He held her close during all the slow songs and spun her around wildly during all the fast jigs, never once missing a beat. Peter had held up his end of the bargain, and Charlotte hadn't bothered them once.

Sitting, she rested her head on her hand and let herself daydream about a future with Bill. Lost in thought, she didn't see Charlotte come up behind her. Charlotte knocked her arm out from under her head, causing Lou Anne to lurch forward. She barely caught herself before falling to the floor. Charlotte swung around to face her.

"What are you doin'?" Charlotte snarled. "I thought we had a deal?"

"Everyone's havin' a good time, Charlotte," said Lou Anne. "Why don't you just go with it, and let this infatuation with Bill go. At least for tonight, tomorrow he's all yours."

"Cause it's Valentine's Day, and I want Bill! I told you that, Lou Anne, and you didn't listen. Now Bill's gonna get fired. Is that what you want?" scolded Charlotte.

Lou Anne played back the evening. The way she felt while in Bill's arms, the way he said her name, just flowed over her like warm molasses. It was all right, no just right; it was perfect. It was love. She loved Bill. Every ounce of her knew he loved her too. He hadn't said it, but his actions proved it. She was not going to lose something so special, especially not to a brat like Charlotte Wheaton.

"I honestly don't think Mr. Murphy's gonna fire Bill, no matter what your pa says." Lou Anne stood. "I like Bill, and I've been lettin' you bully me around for long enough. Bill has made it clear as day he doesn't want to be with you. Pull yourself together, Charlotte. You look desperate."

Charlotte's eyes narrowed. "Desperate, huh? Think I was desperate when I spooked them horses? Just wait! I'll show you what real desperation looks like."

"So it was you?"

Charlotte spun around to see Bill staring at her, holding two tin mugs of punch.

"It's not what it sounds like," said Charlotte.

"It sounds like you made them horses spook, causin' the wagon to topple over." Bill narrowed his eyes. "You could've killed Elmer! You were lucky Lou Anne only had a twisted ankle."

"She deserved more!" shouted Charlotte. "I was aimin' for her, tryin' to keep her from kissin' my man."

"I have never been your man," said Bill.

Charlotte threw herself into Bill's arms, making him drop the tin mugs. "But you could be. I would make you so happy, Bill. Lou Anne don't know nothin' 'bout makin' a man happy. My pa has money. Think of what you'll inherit if you chose me."

"Your pa would be ashamed." Bill unwrapped

Charlotte from around his waist.

"What's all this standin' 'round?" asked Peter, coming up behind Charlotte and grabbing her hand. "We should be dancin'."

"Peter, do you think you can find a ride home for you and Charlotte?" asked Bill.

Peter nodded. "Sure, my brother's here. He'll give us a ride. Also I saw Charlotte's folks dancin' just a few minutes ago, so I'm sure we can manage. I see my brother. I'll go ask him real quick."

"Thanks. I'll let Mr. Wheaton know," said Bill, as Peter made his way through the crowd.

"What are you gonna tell my pa?" asked Charlotte, folding her arms around herself.

Bill stared hard at her.

"We'll tell him I'm not feelin' well," said Lou Anne, laying a soft hand on Bill's arm. "And Bill's drivin' me home."

"You're not gonna tell him 'bout the hayride?" asked Charlotte.

"It's not our story to tell," said Bill, taking Lou Anne's hand. "Just leave us be, Charlotte, or we'll have no choice."

He led Lou Anne away before Charlotte could say any more.

After a quick chat with George and Kathleen, Bill and Lou Anne walked slowly to his truck. Bill loved the feeling of Lou Anne's soft hand intertwined with his. He never wanted to let it go. It was a perfect fit.

As Bill helped Lou Anne into the truck, she laid her hand on his cheek. "Thank you for that."

"You're gonna have to help me understand," Bill said. "You have more right to be mad at Charlotte than anybody."

Lou Anne shrugged. "She used to be my friend. If word got 'round she caused those horses to spook, then no one in this town would have anythin' to do with her. Funny as it sounds, I want her to be happy."

"Well, she thinks she'd be happiest with me." Bill smiled.

"Well, I think you'd be happiest with me." Lou Anne leaned forward and kissed Bill lightly on the lips. "Now take me home before you ruin my reputation," she said dramatically.

Evalyn cringed as Bill whistled while he got dressed for morning chores. He hadn't stopped talking about how fantastic the dance had been and how Lou Anne was everything he hoped for. She, of course, hadn't been allowed to go to the dance because of her "attitude". All Evalyn could do was roll her eyes and pray it was a phase. She still hoped they'd go to California, and Bill being smitten with Lou Anne was only going to make it harder.

"Could you please stop that racket?" whined Evalyn.

"Ah, Evie, you're just jealous," Bill sang.

"Maybe I am, but there's a new rule, no whistlin' before breakfast." She headed downstairs.

"Look, Evie," said Alice, holding up a biscuit. "Mama Dovie said we could use the honey her friend mailed her from Armadillo."

Evalyn's ears burned at the words "Mama Dovie".

"It's Amarillo, Alice," scolded Evalyn. Placing her hands on her hips, she looked around for Dovie. "And it ain't ours to eat."

"Come on, Evie, don't be so sour," protested Alice.

"Mama Dovie said it was all right."

"Yes, it really is fine." Dovie entered the kitchen. "As you know, my friend sent me quite a bit for Christmas. I haven't even finished what she sent last year. She knows I like it in my tea."

Dovie met Evalyn's stare. "You know y'all can have whatever you want in this house. I've never told you no. Alice just happened to find it in the back of the pantry this mornin' and asked if she could have some."

She looked back at Alice. "Go on. Eat up, dear."

Evalyn stomped her foot. "Alice, if you take one bite of that honey, we won't be sisters anymore."

"Evalyn, you're bein' more unfair than a fox in a hen house. It's okay, Alice, eat the honey," Dovie encouraged.

Alice stared at the two women and smiled.

"What if I eat one side with honey and one side without? That way you'll both be happy."

"Sounds like a splendid idea," said Dovie, suddenly realizing how silly she must look arguing over honey. Things had been goin' so well with Evalyn since the influenza scare. Why had she suddenly become so hostile again? thought Dovie. She couldn't win for losing.

"Do you feel all right, Evie?" asked Dovie.

"Don't call me, Evie," Evalyn snapped. "Only my family calls me that, and you ain't family."

Alice looked at Dovie and shrugged. "Don't worry 'bout it, Mama Dovie." Alice took a big bite of the honeyed biscuit. "She's crankier than a mule chewing bees."

Evalyn grabbed her coat and headed into the cold February morning, slamming the door behind her.

Elmer watched his sister storm out of the house, squeal at the sky, and then stomp off in the direction of the barn.

He shook his head. She made absolutely no sense to him. Here they were with a warm house, honest work, and good food in their bellies, and she was acting like they were being tortured by giant mutant ants.

Putting the slop bucket back in the shed, Elmer headed out to the orchard with Freckles. He knew James was ready to sell the dogs, but so far they had no takers. He really wanted to show people what his dogs could do, but understood a dog was more of a luxury than a necessity now-a-days. Freckles stuck close to his right side, waiting for a command, but Elmer wasn't in the mood to train today. He was in the mood for an adventure.

He slid the shotgun under his arm and started walking southeast from the orchard. He wished he had a shoulder holster like Jack Armstrong. A good adventurer always had his hands free in case he had to wrestle a tiger or bear, or to catch a damsel in distress as she hung from a towering cliff.

He thought of Tiny as his damsel and quickly pushed the thought away. Tiny would never be a damsel in distress. If she was hanging from a towering cliff, she'd just scramble up the side like it was nothing instead of waiting for some man to catch her. That was one of the reasons he liked Tiny. She was fearless and didn't mind getting dirty when the occasion called for it.

Elmer heard the soft grunt of a feral pig as Freckles went on point. "Easy boy," he whispered and held up one hand. The dog released his point, nose twitching. Crouching in a draw, Elmer crawled on his belly until he had the creature in his sites. She was nice and plump, but it wasn't fat that lined her belly. Elmer could tell from taking care of the pigs at Quail Crossings that this sow was pregnant.

Freckles inched forward, and Elmer held up his hand. "Not this time, pal. Just wouldn't be right." Freckles let out a low gruff, but relaxed his posture.

As the pig rooted off in the opposite direction, Elmer threw his arm out, and Freckles took off running after the pig. Elmer knew Freckles wouldn't get the sow, but he sure would have fun trying. He rolled over on his back and took in the vast sky. Even with an overcast of clouds, the sky seemed to go on forever. Elmer wondered if it ever ended. He wondered if the folks in big cities like New York ever saw the sky in its eternity. He wondered if his parents ever looked at the California sky and thought about them. He pushed that thought away too. He doubted his parents gave any of them a second thought. Unlike Evie, he had no delusions. He knew their parents had left them for their own selfish reasons.

Elmer heard a rustle behind him and rolled over onto his belly expecting to see the Freckles again, but came face to face with a large boar, twice the size of the sow. The pig grunted and stomped a foot. Elmer had heard of feral pig attacks before and didn't want to have any part of that. He lay very still and thought about what Jack Armstrong would do.

He tightened his grip on the shotgun and slowly released the safety. The pig grunted again and bared its ugly teeth. Elmer knew he'd have just one shot, and if he missed, the boar would be on him like flies to chicken poop.

Raising the gun, he took a deep breath and willed his eyes to stay open this time. He took one more deep breath and pulled the trigger just as the boar barreled down on him. Elmer fought the instinct to cover his ears after the ear splitting shot. The boar fell to the ground.

Still holding the gun, Elmer got to his shaky feet, ears ringing. The pig didn't move. He kicked it with his boot and again the boar lay still. Thrusting the gun over his head, Elmer let out a triumphant cry. Tonight they'd be feasting on ham.

Chapter Twenty-eight

March 1935

James scratched his head. How in tarnation did his hoe end up in the pond? He had tried to pull the tool out with a rope, but the rope kept slipping off. He was going to have to wade in and get it.

Pulling on his waders, he looked at the sky. Blue had taken over the grey of winter. He searched the horizon for rain clouds, finding none. His pond was less than six feet deep now and getting lower every day. He shook his head and stepped into the muddy water. His foot sunk to his ankle, but he maintained his balance. Taking another careful step, his hand skimmed the cold water, making him shiver.

"One more step ought to do it," he said to himself, taking his last careful step.

Leaning over, he reached for the hoe, catching a flash of white over his right shoulder. He tried to straighten, but it was too late. Norman launched, aiming right for James's behind, and sending him face first into the freezing water.

James coughed as he surfaced. "You ugly ol' bird!" He slapped the water with his hand. "I have half a mind to cook you."

He shook his finger at Norman who was swimming

triumphantly a few feet away. "You'd probably taste like an ol' boot."

James turned and retrieved the hoe. He was going to find out how this hoe ended up in the pond, and someone else was going to feel what it was like to swim in March.

Making his way to the house, he threw the hoe into the shed and walked to the kitchen.

"Dovie!" he cried out.

Dovie entered the kitchen and choked back a giggle. "A little chilly for a swim, ain't it, Dad?"

"Hardy, har," said James, still dripping on the floor.

Dovie tried to look serious. "Well, what on earth happened then? You're wetter than a beaver building a dam."

"Norman, that's what." He held up his hand as the water dripped off his sleeve.

Dovie laughed so hard, she snorted.

"Well, don't just stand there laughin' like a billy goat," growled James. "Get me a towel, will ya, before I catch my death."

Dovie hurried to get her dad a towel as Alice entered the room.

"Mr. James, how'd you get so wet?" Alice asked.

"Your Mr. Norman, that's how. Someone threw my hoe in the pond, and I was tryin' to get it out when that goose of yours attacked me. Probably Evalyn again, tryin' to get out of breaking ground for the garden. I swear if that girl would spend more time just doin' the work and less time thinkin' of ways to get out of it, she'd be done already."

Alice's face turned red, and she looked at her feet. "Mr. James, it wasn't Evie. It was me. I was tryin' to pull some of the weeds 'round the pond, so Mr. Norman would have more room to swim, but I lost my grip on the hoe. I meant to tell you about it, but Norman and I got to playin' hide-and-go-seek, and I forgot. I'm sorry." She looked at him and pouted her lips. "Are you mad at me?"

James felt his anger fading fast as he shivered. "Alice, a farmer's tools are very important. I'm gonna have to make a new handle and re-sharpen the blade."

Dovie arrived with the towel and looked at Alice. "Why, Alice, you look like someone kicked your puppy. What'd I miss?"

James grabbed the towel. "Come to find out, Alice is the one who put the hoe in the pond. The hoe I was tryin' to get out when Norman knocked me in." He dried his head. "What do you think your punishment should be, Alice?"

She looked at Dovie and then again at James. "Maybe I should do the dishes by myself for the next week."

"Sounds fair," said James, and he crouched to look Alice in the eyes. "You owned up to the wrong and that's worth somethin'. Always tell the truth, Alice. It's worth more than gold." He pulled on her pigtail. "I'd say since you told the truth and decided a fair punishment, we'll lessen it to three days of dish duty." He held out his hand. "How's that sound?"

"Okie dokie." Alice smiled as she shook James's hand. "If you want, I'll help you mend the hoe."

"Okie dokie." James smiled as he headed to his room to change.

Bill poked his head in the back door. "Is James in here?"

"Yeah, he went to his room to change," answered Dovie.

"Change?" Bill raised an eyebrow.

"Don't ask." Dovie laughed.

Bill smirked. "Norman?"

Dovie laughed even harder, and Bill nodded. "It's always Norman or Evalyn. What'd he do this time?"

Dovie wiped away tears. "Norman gave Dad a surprise bath in the pond."

Bill chuckled. "Speaking of baths, would it be too much trouble to heat me up some water? I've got a date with Lou Anne tonight. That's why I was lookin' for James, to see if I could call it quits a bit early and wash some of this farm filth off. Hate to take her to Annette's smelling like a pig pen."

"You two sure are spendin' a lot of time together." Now it was Dovie's turn to raise an eyebrow. "Is it serious?"

"I sure hope so." Bill blushed.

Dovie nodded. "The water will be ready by the time you finish in the barn, Romeo."

"Thanks a lot, Miss Dovie." Bill tipped his hat.

Later that evening Alice stood on a stool Bill had made her and washed dishes while Dovie sat in the kitchen keeping her company.

"How long do you think Bill will be gone?" Alice asked, watching the soapy water drip from her fingers.

"Oh, I'm sure he'll have Lou Anne home by nine, so he'll be here a little after then," answered Dovie. "Why?"

"Just wonderin' if I'll still be awake. I want him to tell me 'bout Lou Anne."

"So I guess that means you like her?" Dovie smiled.

Alice sighed. "She's ever so nice and pretty. But it's the way she makes Bill smile. I haven't seen him smile like that in a coon's age."

"That's a very nice thing to say," said Dovie. There was a long pause before Dovie continued. "I'm very proud of you, Alice."

"What for?" Alice scrubbed the biscuit pan. "What I said 'bout Bill and Lou Anne or puttin' Mr. James's hoe in the pond?"

Dovie shook her head. "Neither, I'm proud of you for tellin' the truth and for not complainin' about doin' the dishes."

"I kinda like doin' dishes," Alice plopped some silverware into the soapy water. "Makes me feel all grown up."

"Just makes me feel old." Dovie laughed. "So are you lookin' forward to Saturday?"

"What's Saturday?" asked Alice.

"Didn't anyone tell you?"

Alice shook her head no.

"I can't believe nobody told you. I figured Evalyn would've been howlin' it to the moon since she gets to go some place other than school." Dovie made a tsking noise. "Well, Saturday we're all goin' to town."

"Why?" asked Alice. "We never go to town on Saturdays."

"Well, the market starts Saturday," explained Dovie. "We'll take in eggs, cream, milk, butter, and some of the chickens to trade and sell to the other folks in town."

"That sounds like fun." Alice watched a bubble pop in-between her fingers.

"That's not all." Dovie got up and leaned on the counter. "Have you ever been roller skatin'?"

"Roller skatin'!" Alice squealed, dropping the fork she'd just been washing back into the murky water. "We get to roller skate?"

"Sure do." Dovie shook her head. "The whole town does. You know what else?"

"What?" asked Alice, her dishes forgotten in the sink.

"They're gonna throw pennies off the top of the post office."

"Really!" Alice's eyes grew wide.

"Yes, and all you kids can go and grab 'em. It's just for y'all."

Alice clapped her soapy hands. "What fun!" Then she frowned. "Mama Dovie, I ain't got no skates."

"You can use Helen's. I think they're in the barn somewhere. If those don't fit, we can rent you some."

"Can we go look now?" Alice hopped off her stool.

Dovie sat back down. "'Fraid not, it's darker than a bear's den in January out there. Besides you've got to finish your dish duty. We'll find them tomorrow."

"First thing?" asked Alice.

"First thing," assured Dovie.

The next morning before breakfast, Dovie and Alice climbed up to the loft. Alice played hopscotch in the outline of the loft's big rolling window.

"Helen had a special hidin' place for her skates. Clever as a fox she was." Dovie brushed her hands on her dress. "She didn't think I knew about it." She winked at Alice. "Let's play hot and cold and see if you can find 'em."

Alice giggled and started walking around the loft.

"Burr," said Dovie, pretending to shiver, "you're freezin'."

Alice walked towards the north wall.

"Gettin' a little warmer." Alice kept walking. "Warmer."

Alice stared at a stack of old square hay bales and started to look in-between the squares.

"Lordy, you're on fire," laughed Dovie, fanning herself.

Alice crawled in the middle of the stack. "The middle's

hollow. It's like a playhouse in here!"

"Helen would spend hours up here, playin' house and makin' up stories to tell her dolls." Dovie played with a piece of hay. "She thought we didn't know where her hidin' place was, but Dad found her up here sleepin' one afternoon."

"There's a box in here." Alice pulled out a dusty brown box and opened it. "It's the skates, and they ain't rusted one bit." She spun the wheel.

"Mama Dovie?"

"Yes."

"Does it hurt your feelings when I play with Helen's stuff?"

Dovie stared out the window. "Well, I miss Helen every day, so it hurts some to know she won't be usin' those skates ever again or hidin' up here durin' the heat of the summer." She turned to Alice. "But no, it don't hurt to see you playin' with her things. I'm just happy they ain't goin' to waste."

Alice smiled. "This is the bestest playhouse ever."

"Now, keep in mind if Dad needs the hay, then we'll have no choice but to use it, and your playhouse will be gone."

"That's okay, them cows are too skinny anyway," said Alice. "My pa used to say, if our cows got any skinnier we'd be able to see through 'em. I don't wanna see through Poppy."

"Do you miss your pa?" Dovie pulled another piece of hay from the bail and wrapped it around her finger.

"Nah, I like it better here." Alice crawled out of the hole. "I'm gonna get Lil' Norman and Beets." She tilted her head as she looked at the ladder. "Bet I can't get Mr. Norman up here."

"No, probably not." Dovie dropped the hay strand and stood.

"Mama Dovie?" Alice turned before heading down the ladder. "Could you not tell Evie 'bout this place? She might claim it as her own and not let me up here. You know how she likes to be alone." Alice rolled her eyes as she said the last part.

Dovie put her arm around Alice. "It'll be our little secret."

Evalyn watched Dovie and Alice return to the house from the barn in giggles. "What was so funny about a barn? Probably laughing at Poppy's spots. These hicks are so easily entertained," she thought.

Just before the stoop, Alice wrapped Dovie in a big hug. Evalyn was surprised to see Dovie return the gesture. Dovie was not only getting used to having them around, she looked like she was enjoying herself while hugging her sister.

Evalyn let out a low growl. First Elmer constantly hanging out with that ever annoying chatty Tiny. Then Bill all smitten with doe-eyed Lou Anne and now Alice was hugging Dovie. How was she going to convince her family to go to California and look for their parents if everyone was getting so cozy? She had to find a way. They'd been at this flea infested farm too long.

Chapter Twenty-nine

James helped Alice oil her skates before heading out to the market. They were putting up the supplies when Bill called for a family gathering.

"Bill, if you're just gonna lecture us on how to behave, save it." Evalyn crossed her arms. "We all know you're talkin' to me, and I'm sick of not bein' able to do anything."

Bill playfully tugged her ponytail. "Good to hear, smarty pants, but that's not why I gathered you up."

He reached into his pocket and brought out three shiny nickels. "Okay, each of you gets five cents to spend on whatever you want. Ice cream, soda pop, candy - whatever." He handed the coins out. "James and Dovie have agreed to cover the cost of skate rentals if you want to roller skate, so don't worry 'bout that. They appreciate all the hard work y'all have done 'round the farm."

"Don't forget they'll be throwin' pennies off the post office too." James said, with a wink.

Evalyn looked at her nickel. "If I can just get five more cents, then I can buy that fingernail polish at Johnson's Drug. It's called Hollywood Red." She held out her hand and imagined the fancy color on her nails.

Main Street was lined with people setting out their

goods on the backs of their trucks. Husbands and wives took turns walking the truck line, while the other watched for possible trades and sells. It was the first big town event since the Valentine's Day dance, and people were smiling the hard winter of isolation away.

A group of young boys huddled around the post office, desperate to get a good spot for the penny toss. Teenagers lingered, trying to look like they weren't interested, but hoping to catch a few of their own.

As the trucks parked, Evalyn and Alice hurried to find Harriet and Joan, while Elmer leaned against the truck.

"Aren't those your classmates over there?" asked Bill, pointing to the group of huddled boys.

"Yep," said Elmer, kicking a rock under the truck next to him.

"You don't have to stay," said Bill. "Dovie, James, and I can handle it."

"I'd rather help, if you don't mind." Elmer grabbed a carton of chickens and set it on the street.

Bill nodded. He knew Elmer had been through more than those other boys could imagine. It was hard to relate to others your age when you had to grow up so fast.

"Hi ya, Elm." Tiny skipped to the truck. "Jeepers, are those all your chickens? That's a lot of chickens. Didn't Mr. Murphy give us some chickens back in September? And here y'all are with more chickens than pebbles on the street."

Bill was surprised to see Elmer smile.

"Yeah, I guess we got a good flock." Elmer ran his hands through his hair and reminded Bill of James. "Helps if you've got more than one rooster. We got 'bout five now."

"Did you know they're gonna throw pennies off the

roof of the post office?" asked Tiny. "They do it every Saturday. Last time I caught six whole cents, can you believe it? Got a whole gob of candy with it."

"Maybe this year we can put our money together and get more candy or share a milkshake or somethin'," Elmer suggested.

"Jeepers, that's a mighty fine idea, Elmer Brewer." She grabbed Elmer's hand. "Let's go get a good spot. I just can't wait; it's so excitin'. You know I've always wanted to try one of them root beer floats. My dad buys us each a scoop of vanilla ice cream in the summer, but he never lets me get a root beer float. They look so yummy. Jeepers, I can just imagine it meltin' in my mouth."

Elmer looked at Bill, who waved his hand to tell him to go have fun. He had just gotten everything arranged when he noticed James standing on top of the post office. "Gather 'round, all you kids. It's time for the penny toss!"

Before Bill could blink, the front of the post office was crowded with kids. Three men stood with James on top. Bill recognized them as George Wheaton, Bud Clark, and Pastor Spaulding.

Kids on the road yelled, "Me, me, me!" and "Over here!" He noticed Evalyn slowly making her way to the middle of the crowd, ignoring the other teens standing in the back. Alice and Joan were standing next to Tiny and Elmer, a little to the left of the chaos in the middle.

Pennies flew from the roof and someone yelled "Ouch!" while someone else yelled "Hey, I got one." Bill laughed as kids rolled and dove for the coins. The toss lasted only a few minutes, and soon Alice made her way back to the truck.

"Well, how'd you do?" Bill leaned on the lowered tailgate.

"I got two cents!" declared Alice. "Elm, Tiny, and Joan went on to the store. I thought I'd wait for Evie - see if she wants an ice cream."

Evalyn walked up behind Alice counting the coins in her hand. "Bill, I'm a couple of cents short, can I borrow it from you?"

Bill held up his hands. "Sorry, Evie, if I give you two more cents then it wouldn't be fair to the others."

Evalyn turned toward her sister. "How 'bout you Alice, can I borrow two cents?"

Alice's forehead wrinkled in thought. "If I give you my two cents, will you let me use your nail polish?"

"Alice, you're too little to use fingernail polish," scolded Evalyn. "You'd just waste it."

"Then nope, you can't have my two cents." Alice looked at Bill. "I'm goin' to the store now."

"Bill, make her share," Evalyn whined.

"Evie, it's her money to do with what she pleases." He smirked at her. "Besides I didn't hear you sharin' your fancy Hollywood Red fingernail polish. Just save your money till next week, I'm sure you'll get your two cents then."

An old woman approached asking about the eggs, and Evalyn knew the conversation was over. She shuffled her feet as she made her way to Harriet.

"Well, did he give you the two cents?" she asked.

"No, guess we'll just have to wait till next week." Evalyn looked at her friend. "You know it would've helped if you would've tried to get a couple of pennies too."

"Oh, Evie," Harriet gasped. "You know I couldn't. Mark was watchin'. What would he think if I was pickin' pennies off the ground with all those children? I have a reputation to uphold."

"But it was okay for me?" Evalyn stared at her friend with wide eyes.

"Well, Evie, you're new to the market," explained Harriet. "You can get away with it by not knowin' any better. But you best not do it next week. One time can be explained, twice and you look like a baby. I hope Bill gives you five cents next week too or you're out of luck."

Evalyn turned from her friend and started to walk towards the store.

"Where you goin', Evie? All the kids are in the store now. Let's wait till they're done."

Evalyn didn't answer but kept walking. Dovie stopped her before she entered the store and slipped something into her hand, winked, and then walked away. Evalyn opened her palm and saw two shiny pennies. She turned to thank Dovie, but couldn't find her in the crowd. Letting out a little giggle, she entered the store.

Johnson's Drug was a place you could get anything from ice cream to cough syrup, with a mix of toys and cosmetics thrown in. They had the best selection of penny candy in the county, and the kids blocked the aisle with mouths watering and coins burning holes in their pockets.

Evalyn walked over to the nail polish. She picked up the bottle of Hollywood Red and hugged it in her palm. Alice approached her with a peppermint stick in her mouth.

"Thought you didn't have enough money for it," she mumbled through the candy.

"A friend gave me what I needed." She turned and hugged Alice. "I feel bad for what I said before. You're too young to paint your own nails, but how 'bout I do your nails for you every once in a while."

Alice beamed. "Really, Evie? That would be so much fun." She looked at the ice cream counter. "Do you have any money left?"

"No, I only have enough for the polish." Evalyn turned to walk to the counter, the coins sweaty in her palm.

Alice grabbed her sleeve. "How 'bout I buy you an ice cream?"

"Thanks, Alice." Grabbing her sister's hand, they walked to the counter. "I'd like that."

Bill was packing up the truck as Elmer approached. "I know y'all are goin' skatin'. Would it be okay if I go to the park with Tiny and some of the other kids?"

Bill nodded. "That's fine, but be back at the truck by dark."

As Elmer ran off, Lou Anne approached Bill. "So are you roller skatin' or goin' to the park?" she teased.

He swept her up into a big hug. "Well, Lou Anne, I haven't seen you all day. Where have you been?"

"Babysittin', as usual. Ma's been watchin' the goods while I've been handlin' Charles."

"Your pa didn't come in?" Bill asked as he arranged a bag of potatoes.

Lou Anne lowered her head. "My pa doesn't do well in public."

Bill titled his head. "I don't understand."

"Ah, Bill." She slapped him playfully on the shoulder. "I've finally got away from my family, and all you wanna talk 'bout is my pa. We've barely had a chance to spend any time together, me with my studies and you with work. Let's forget 'bout it all and go skatin' like little kids."

"All right then," he smiled. "Let's go be kids."

"I'll go get my skates from the truck and meet you at the rink." She gave him a peck on the cheek and hurried off.

Bill rubbed his cheek and made his way through the crowd to the big slab of cement that was used for the hoedown during the county fair. It was a great place to skate, and he could see Alice inching along the outside, ready to roll into the dirt if she got to going too fast. Looking towards the park, he could see Elmer and Tiny sitting on the swings talking.

"Here, got you some skates," said Evalyn. "James was over there payin' for mine, so we went ahead and got you some. I'm gonna go help Alice."

Bill bent and tried to figure out how to attach the metal objects to his boots.

"You'll have to go in your socks, silly," said Charlotte, sitting beside him. "Your heel's gonna get in the way."

Bill looked at her. "What do you want, Charlotte?"

"Just to tell you I'm not mad at you for leavin' me at the Valentine's Day dance with Peter." She grabbed his hand. "I could never stay mad at you, Bill Brewer. I love you, and I know you love me too, or you would've told my pa about the hayride."

Bill yanked his hand away. "I don't love you, and you don't love me - you don't even know me. I have feelings for Lou Anne and that ain't gonna change. The only reason I didn't tell your pa, is 'cause Lou Anne asked me not to. It'd serve you right if he'd thrown you over his knee and paddled you right there in the middle of the dance floor."

"I just don't know what you see in that ol' cow, Lou Anne." Charlotte crossed her arms.

"Don't talk 'bout her like that." Bill's jaw tightened.

"She doesn't know the first thing 'bout what to do with a man." She batted her eyelids and leaned in close. "Don't you want to be with a real woman?"

"Get control of yourself, Charlotte." He pushed her away, grabbed his skates, and stood. "She's more of a woman than you'll ever be."

Chapter Thirty

Bill and Lou Anne approached the skating rink with caution. Bill swung his arms around wildly as he fell forward trying to catch his balance. "Maybe you should skate, and I'll watch." He laughed.

"Come on, scaredy cat." Lou Anne pulled him onto the slab. She was light on her feet, making circles around him while he bobbed and weaved trying not to fall. Turning around, she began to skate backwards.

"Here let me help," she said, reaching out to take his hands. As their fingertips touched, Charlotte rammed into her causing Lou Anne to tumble to the cement, followed by Bill who tried to catch her fall.

"Oh, I'm so sorry," Charlotte mocked, raising a hand to her mouth to cover her smile. "I didn't see you there. I can be so clumsy sometimes. Oops."

Lou Anne flinched as Charlotte skated off. Standing, she skated slowly to the dirt with Bill wobbling right behind her. Sitting on the ground, Lou Anne fought tears as she looked at her scraped knee. She let out a low groan as she examined her stocking and dug her fingernails into the dirt. Charlotte was getting even more out of control. Lou Anne hadn't thought that to be possible.

"Are you okay?" Bill fell to his knees beside her.

Taking out his bandana, he placed it gently on the bloody wound. "That Charlotte needs a good whippin'. I've got half a mind to tell her pa about the hayride."

"No, Bill, it really doesn't hurt that much." She forced her voice not to shake. "Besides, I honestly don't think it would do any good. It might even cause more problems. I'm fine really."

"You don't have to be brave around me." He brushed her hair away from her eyes.

"I'm more mad I tore my new stockings. I just got 'em at Christmas. Now I'll have to go back to wearin' my ol' pair. My mother worked hard to scrounge up enough money for them. She'll be so disappointed."

"We'll get you a new pair," said Bill. "Besides it doesn't matter to me what you wear. You'd look more beautiful wearing a potato sack than Charlotte Wheaten ever could. The important thing is you're okay. That was a mighty hard spill."

"Honestly, Bill, I'm fine," she looked up at him. "But I don't feel like skatin' anymore."

"Me either." Bill tied his bandana around her knee. "Do you feel like goin' to the park? We could sit on the picnic table and just talk." He started unbuckling her skate.

"That sounds nice."

Bill and Lou Anne put on their shoes and made their way to the wooden picnic table under a big cottonwood.

Evalyn rested on a bench near the water bucket watching Alice skate when Harriet approached her.

"I know you're mad at me," Harriet said.

Evalyn stuck her nose up. "You made me look like a fool. You could've told me before I made myself look like a child. I thought you were my friend."

"I am your friend." Harriet sat. "And I wanted to, but you were so hell bent on gettin' the nail polish. I didn't think anythin' would stop you. You're like that, Evalyn. Once you get an idea in your head, the Devil himself wouldn't be able to do a damn thing to stop you."

Evalyn's eyes widened at Harriet's language.

"Oh, don't be such a prude, Evie." Harriet sat up a little taller. "Everyone speaks like that in Hollywood. It's only these Bible thumpers, so afraid they'll go to Hell that they won't even think those words, much less say them. I don't even think Hell exists."

Evalyn looked up to the sky and said a little prayer for Harriet before quickly changing the subject. "I got it by the way."

"Got what?" asked Harriet.

"Hollywood Red." A small smile crept to the corner of Evalyn's mouth.

Harriet squealed as Evalyn pulled the vibrant bottle from her pocket. "How?"

"Mrs. Grant gave me the two cents."

Harriet rolled her eyes. "Sounds just like her, forever the do-gooder. I guess she expects you to be nice to her now."

"Probably," said Evalyn, "but if it weren't for her, we wouldn't have the polish. If I'm nice to her, maybe she'll give us money for more shades."

"Don't fall for it, Evie. She's just tryin' to buy your love or somethin'. Why else would she give you the two cents after everythin' you've done to get your brother fired?" Harriet crossed her arms and raised an eyebrow.

Evalyn glanced at Dovie sitting on the other side of the rink. Just why had Dovie helped her out? Harriet was right. It didn't make sense. Dovie Grant was definitely up to something.

"Don't you just love the park this time of year?" Tiny kicked the dirt under the swing as she twisted toward Elmer and gazed into the sky.

"Sure, it's nice." He noticed the goose bumps on her arms. "Are you cold?"

"A little." She rubbed her arms. "I've been colder than Jack Frost since we was sick. I just can't seem to get warm anymore. Jeepers, I can't wait for July. Man, it was so hot last July I could feel myself meltin'. My ma fried an egg in a cast iron skillet that had been sitting in the sun for an hour, just to prove to Pa that she could. You should've seen the look on Pa's face. Said we didn't need to use the stove no more. From now on we'd just cook in the driveway."

"Here, take my jacket." Elmer took off his brown coat and covered Tiny's shoulders.

"Then you'll be cold, silly. There's nothin' worse than being cold. You can always cool down when you're hot. You know, go jump in a stock tank or run through the crick. But when you're cold, to the bone cold, forget about it. You could wrap yourself in a million blankets and never get warm. Aren't you cold all the time from bein' sick too?"

"Nah, I'm fine," he said sitting back down on the swing.

"There's your brother." Tiny pointed toward the picnic table. "Looks like Lou Anne hurt her knee or somethin'." She got up. "I bet she hurt it skatin'. That's why I never go. I went once with my ma, and I wasn't out there two seconds before I fell right on my face and busted my favorite tooth. Thankfully it was just my baby tooth, and it fell out a few months later. Jeepers, could you imagine chippin' one of your grown up teeth? Let's go find out what happened to

Lou Anne."

Elmer grabbed her arm and pulled her back to the swing. "I think they want to be alone."

"Jeepers, why on earth would anyone want to be alone? I hate bein' alone. What's the fun if you don't got no one to talk to?" asked Tiny. "It's always like that at the house. I mean I could talk to my brother or baby sister, but what's the point? That's why I'm glad we're friends. Jeepers, Elm, you get me like nobody else. Come on, I'm sure they won't mind."

"Well, sometimes it's nice bein' alone with just one special person. Someone you can talk to 'bout anythin'," said Elmer, releasing his light grip on her arm. "I'd rather talk to you than a whole mess of people."

"Jeepers." Tiny blushed. "You're right, Elm. I didn't think of that. I feel the same way when I'm talkin' to you. I don't really want nobody else around. My ma always asks me if I've got anythin' other than you to talk 'bout. She says I talk 'bout you all the time. You'd think Elmer Brewer was the only other person in the world." She sat back down in her swing. "Do you think they're boyfriend and girlfriend?"

Elmer shrugged. "I guess so. They've been on quite a few dates now. He really likes her, and they're walkin' in the park alone."

"We're in the park alone." Tiny looked at Elmer under her lashes. "And we hang out just the two of us all the time, which is kinda like a date."

"Yeah, but they're holdin' hands," answered Elmer.

Tiny grabbed his hand. "Now we're holdin' hands. Does that make us boyfriend and girlfriend?"

"Well there's only one way to tell." Elmer kicked dirt and gazed at the sunset.

"How so?" Tiny asked.

Elmer looked over at Tiny. "I guess I have to kiss you. That's what boyfriends and girlfriends do, right? It's really the only way to tell."

Tiny's cheeks glowed red as she swung to meet Elmer's gaze. "Jeepers, I guess you better get to it then."

Elmer turned his swing to face Tiny. Closing his eyes, he leaned in and gently brushed his lips with hers. Pulling back he looked at the sky. "Yep, I think we're boyfriend and girlfriend."

For the first time in her young life, Tiny was speechless.

Lou Anne winced as Bill lifted her to the top of the table.

"Did I hurt your knee?" he asked, looking at the bandana.

"No." She shook her head. "It wasn't you."

He hopped up next to her. "I don't mean to pry, but I saw the look on your face a second ago, and I think it's more than that knee. Maybe the doc needs to take a look. I once busted a rib breakin' a stallion, and let me tell you it was no picnic. Like I said before, you took a mighty hard spill."

"It's really nothin'," she insisted before playfully slapping his arm. "I'm tougher than I look, mister."

He grabbed her hand. "Lou Anne, I know it's somethin'."

She took in a deep breath. "I couldn't keep Charles quiet the other day and Pa... well Pa lost his temper. It happens from time to time. He don't mean it. He's just not in his right head. I should've just taken Charles outside is all, and then there wouldn't have been a problem. I know better."

Bill tightened his grip on the picnic table. "Are you tellin' me your pa hits you?"

She studied his face, trying to decide how to continue. "My pa likes his drink, and sometimes it causes him to be ill-tempered. It doesn't happen all the time, and I can tell he's sorry afterwards."

Bill released Lou Anne's hand, jumped off the picnic table, and started pacing. "If I ever see your pa..." Bill placed his hands on his head and took a deep breath, willing himself to calm down. "I knew somethin' was wrong since I hadn't met your pa yet. I just thought maybe you didn't think he'd approve of us, or maybe you're embarrassed by me."

"Oh, no, Bill." Lou Anne jumped down and grabbed his hands. "I am proud to walk by your side. Please don't ever think anything less."

He wrapped both arms tenderly around Lou Anne as she wrapped her arms around his neck.

"I can't stand the thought of him hurtin' you," he said, looking at the ground. "Of you ever bein' in pain, especially at the hands of another person. He should be jailed for layin' a finger on you. You don't have to put up with that, you know. We could go to the sheriff tonight and have him arrested. You're practically a grown woman, it ain't right."

"Bill, you can't tell anyone, especially not the sheriff. I know it's hard to believe, but we need my pa to survive. Why do you think my ma puts up with it? You know better than most what it's like out there. Without Pa, we'd be livin' in the bread line, just like y'all were before Mr. Murphy hired you."

"I would take care of you, all of you." He leaned his forehead against hers and closed his eyes.

She moved her hands to his cheeks and forced him to

look at her. "I'm okay, Bill. Actually, when I'm with you, I'm more than okay."

Bill reached up and brushed the hair off her delicate forehead.

He kissed her gently. "I am so in love with you."

Chapter Thirty-one

April 1935

Evalyn stared at her bright red nails and smiled. So far she hadn't let Harriet have one drop of the fancy polish. The nerve of her, saying she couldn't be seen grabbing pennies, but she sure wanted to grab the nail polish. She had been furious when Evalyn refused to let her take the polish home after the market. Evalyn shrugged; maybe next time Harriet would be more willing to pitch in.

For the life of her, Evalyn couldn't figure out why Dovie had given her the two cents though. It seemed Dovie had been trying to get on her good side since February. It was obvious she enjoyed having Alice around. Why wouldn't she? She'd lost her own daughter, and now here was a replacement to fill the void.

Evalyn shook her head. There seemed to be more to it than that. At first Dovie hadn't wanted them around at all, not even Alice. Evalyn tried to play on that, getting into trouble every chance she could, but Dovie never even threatened to kick them out after any of the incidences. She had expected a good tongue lashing after the grasshopper beans, but Dovie didn't say a word, unless it was to tell her to do some chore.

She had taken this all very well considering. Evalyn thought of what it would be like to lose Alice or Elmer. Even the thought of Bill not being in her life anymore brought tears to her eyes, no matter how annoying they were. How could their parents leave them, when there were so many parents grieving over children they would never get back?

She should be more thankful they had a place to sleep and food on the table. James and Dovie had been so kind, and Alice was happier than she had been in a long time.

Thinking of Alice, Evalyn smiled. She'd had a lot of fun with Alice at the first market. Every market since, they put their pennies together and bought ice cream cones. Evalyn talked of adding Pink Passion to her polish collection, and Alice promised to help her buy it. Grabbing her Hollywood Red, she went to find her little sister. She had a promise of her own to keep. Maybe California could wait until after she graduated. It wasn't that far off, and then she would have time to practice her acting. Ma and Pa probably wouldn't want her in the picture shows even if she did find them.

Making her way across the backyard, she could hear Dovie and Alice talking in the kitchen. The day was warm and spring-like, so the big wood winter door was left open, leaving only the screen door between Evalyn and their conversation. Curious, she sat on the front stoop to listen.

"Before you know it, you're gonna be makin' these pies by yourself," said Dovie.

"You think?" Alice giggled. "I'm so glad Ma and Pa are gone. I like it here with y'all a lot better than at home with them."

There was silence. Evalyn leaned closer to the screen.

"You don't mean that," said Dovie. "Of course you're

havin' fun now, but I'm sure if they were here, you'd have fun with them."

"Nope, my ma was as mean as a badger in winter, and Pa, well Pa just didn't love me."

Evalyn clamped a hand over her mouth to stifle her gasp.

"I'm sure he did, honey." She heard Dovie say.

"Then why did he let my ma be so mean to me?" asked Alice. "Nope, I don't care if I ever see either one of them again."

Tears flooded Evalyn's eyes as she ran toward the pond.

Later that evening Bill sat at the kitchen table and drummed his fingers, while Dovie washed the dishes.

"Bill, if you got ants in your pants, you can dry." To her surprise, he got up and grabbed a dish towel. "You are aware I was just kiddin' with you?"

"Yeah, I'm not bored, just thinkin'." He held up the dish towel. "And I can do that just as easily while dryin'."

"You wanna talk 'bout it?" asked Dovie.

"Well, I'm drawin' up plans for the house, and I'm thinkin' 'bout makin' it three bedrooms instead of two."

"I can understand you wantin' a room of your own." She handed him a plate.

"That's just it, I don't. I want to share it with Lou Anne."

Dovie dropped the bowl she'd been washing in the soapy water. "Well, I'll be a biscuit in a basket of flowers. Bill are you sayin' you want to propose to Lou Anne?"

"Yes, ma'am, I think I do. But I'm not sure if it's the right time. She'll be graduatin' this year, it's just..." Bill furrowed his brow. "Well, we've only been seein' each other a short while. I don't want to scare her off or make the wrong decision."

"Tell me how she makes you feel." Dovie turned back to her dishes.

Color flushed Bill's cheeks. "Well, when I'm with her, it's like my whole heart is full. I want to do whatever I can to make her happy, to see her only cry tears of joy, and to pamper her like a princess. When we're apart all I can think about is excuses to see her again, and when we're together it feels like all time has stopped, and it's just us in the world."

"Have you talked to her pa?" asked Dovie.

"He's a hard man to pen down." Bill furrowed his brow.

"Well, rumor has it, he has coffee every Monday mornin' at Annette's while waitin' for his feed order to be loaded."

Bill kissed Dovie on the cheek. "You're a life saver."

"Bill, just promise me one thing." Dovie twisted the dish rag in the sink.

"Anything."

Dovie looked him straight in the eyes. "No matter what that man says, you marry her."

Bill grinned. "If she'll have me, that's one promise I'll most definitely keep."

Bright and early Monday morning Bill sat in Annette's with James, drinking coffee. They had been there since she'd opened, not wanting to miss Lou Anne's father. They'd had a nice breakfast and were talking about the new litter of piglets when David Garber entered the café.

David nodded a hello to James and sat at the counter. "Annette, I'll have my usual."

Bill left his hat with James and approached David. "Excuse me, Mr. Garber."

David looked Bill up and down. "I ain't got no work for you." He turned his back to Bill and concentrated on the menu written above the counter.

"Mr. Garber, I ain't lookin' for work," answered Bill.

"Well, I don't hand out charity either," David gruffed.

"Mr. Garber, I work for Mr. Murphy." He pointed to James who waved.

"What do you want then?" David stuffed a wad of chew beneath his lower lip.

"I've grown rather fond of your daughter, Lou Anne," Bill stated.

David raised an eyebrow. "Oh, you have, have you?"

"Yes, I'd like to ask her to be my wife, and I'd like your blessin' before I ask her for her hand."

David gestured to the stool beside him. "Sit down, kid." He spit in a rusty tin can. "You got a lot of nerve comin' in here and springin' this on me. Lou Anne's needed at home. Who's gonna help her ma take care of the baby and other young'uns?"

"Well, sir, Mr. Murphy's given me a place on his farm to build a house. So we'll still be in the county. I'm sure she'll help out when her ma needs her."

David spit again. "Any husband worth his salt ain't gonna let his wife run off home all the time."

"Lou Anne will be free to do what she pleases." Bill closed his fist, and then opened it, careful to keep his temper.

"There's your first mistake, son, a wife needs to know her place. If you don't know that, then you ought not be gettin' married." David looked away. "Not to my stubborn eldest anyway."

"Is that what all those bruises are?" Bill's jaw tightened. "You puttin' Lou Anne in her place?"

"You better watch yourself, kid." David's upper lip twitched as he stood. "Don't tell me how to raise my young'uns."

"Don't call me kid." Bill rose, staring David down. James was behind him in an instant. "I'm gonna ask Lou Anne with or without your blessin', and I swear to God if I find so much as a scratch on her head, you'll be lookin' around wonderin' if lightnin' struck anybody else." Bill took another step closer to David. "Do we understand each other, Mr. Garber?"

David shook his head and sat. "Fine, take the brat. She's nothin' but lip anyway." He spat in his can.

Bill walked to the booth and grabbed his hat. He turned to James who still stood by David. "You comin'?"

"Go ahead, Bill. I'll be right there," assured James. "Take a walk and cool off. I'll meet you at the truck in a bit."

Bill walked out as James sat by David.

"Bill's a good man, David. Your daughter's lucky to have him, and he feels the same way 'bout her. He works hard for his family, and I know he'll do the same for Lou Anne." He leaned in real close to David who returned his stare to the menu. "Just so we're clear, David, if I see a bruise on any of those kids or Hannah, I'll be lettin' the sheriff know the whereabouts of your little stash."

"It ain't illegal to drink no more," snapped David.

"No, sir, it ain't. But that moonshine you make is still illegal. You keep your hands off them kids, and we don't have a problem. I don't mind a man drinkin', or even makin' his own hooch. But when it comes to hittin' those smaller than him, that I do mind, David. I mind it very much."

Evalyn groaned as she saw Dovie approach. What did

she want? Evalyn was in no mood to talk. Her ears turned red as she recalled Dovie and Alice's conversation about her parents. They were never mean. Strict, yes, and maybe a little heavy-handed when it came to punishment, but what kid didn't deserve a whipping every once and a while?

Dovie sat beside Evalyn under the old cottonwood by the pond. "This is my favorite place to fish. I just love how the wind blows through the trees, showering me with leaves."

Evalyn stared at the water, so Dovie continued. "I saw you run from the stoop the other day when Alice was talkin' 'bout your parents."

"Alice is a child who doesn't know what she's talkin' 'bout." Evalyn flipped her ponytail over her shoulder.

"I understand it must be hard to hear bad things 'bout your parents. I wouldn't let someone say somethin' ugly about Dad even if it was true." She smoothed out her dress. "Here's the thing. After you ran off, I told Alice I'm sure your parents loved her, even if their actions were confusin'. That bein' said, Evalyn, I think maybe you miss them so much that you've blocked out the bad things. I'm not sayin' you should dwell on 'em, but at least learn from 'em."

Evalyn picked up a stick and started stripping its bark.

"Evalyn, look at me, please."

Evalyn sighed and dropped the stick. She looked at Dovie, trying to hide the sadness and anger she could feel building behind her eyes.

"Bottom line," said Dovie, grabbing Evalyn's hand, "is I'm glad y'all are here. All of you. You know I wasn't happy when y'all showed up at my door, but y'all have filled my heart with joy again, and for that I can't thank you enough." Dovie patted Evalyn's hand before standing and brushing off her backside.

Evalyn picked up the stick and continued pulling at its bark as Dovie headed to her laundry line.

Dovie squinted at the line. Something was wrong. She counted the clothing hanging on the line. A pair of her unmentionables was missing. Picking up her step, she hoped it had just fallen on the ground. She recounted the remaining underwear on the line and confirmed one pair was gone, and it wasn't on the ground.

"Norman!" she screamed. "You nasty ol' bird. You better come out now, or I'll hunt you down and tear you to bits like a fox does a chicken."

Behind her, the ornery goose honked and ran, the missing pair of panties in his mouth.

"Norman, you get back here! Those are mine!" Dovie took off after the bird. "You're gonna be dinner if you don't drop those drawers."

Norman's laughing honk filled the air as Dovie chased him around the barn.

Chapter Thirty-two

James watched as Elmer directed the dogs to flush the tree line. Only three of Pancake's litter remained, and they were all sharp as a tack. A covey of quail took flight, and James shot two birds down. They nearly had enough quail for supper. Dovie would be pleased. One of her favorite meals was slow cooked quail wrapped in bacon.

Elmer whistled, and the dogs returned. Max and Babe carried the two birds. Freckles wagged his tail behind them. Elmer held out his hand, and the dogs dropped the birds, walked behind him, and sat.

"I'm proud of you, Elm. These are some fine huntin' dogs. I thought Max was gonna be deterred by that porcupine, but he stayed the course. Mighty fine job." He scratched Max behind the ear. "I think we'll take two of them to market next week, see if we can sell 'em."

"Two?" Elmer cocked his head at James.

"Yeah, we won't sell the one you pick to keep."

"Really?" Elmer beamed. "But you've already got Pancake and Button."

"This will be your dog, Elmer. You're a man now," said James. "And a man should have a dog. You've taken care of these pups as well as helped your brother on the farm. You deserve it. Besides you'll need a dog when you get moved into your own place, and…"

Before James could finish, Elmer wrapped his arms around him. James hugged him back. This was the first time he'd seen Elmer show any affection to anyone since the move, including his family.

"Thank you, thank you so much." He bent and rubbed Freckles's head. "Did you hear that, Freckles? You're mine now. I can't wait to tell Tiny. Come on, dogs." He gestured to the dogs, and they ran off in search of more quail.

Alice stared at the old gnarled tree. Turning her head to the side, she held her breath and listened for the noise again.

"What in the world are you doin' out here?"

Alice screamed. "Oh, Mama Dovie, you scared me."

"I could tell by the way you squealed like a piglet after the tit. What's goin' on?"

Glancing back at the tree, Alice shook her head. "That tree ain't right."

"Nonsense, it's just an old cottonwood tree. Been here for years."

"But, Mama Dovie," Alice whispered, "the tree is crying."

"The tree is crying?" Dovie raised an eyebrow.

"Yes, just listen."

As both stood quietly, a soft cry came from the upper branches. "Did you hear it, Mama Dovie? Did you hear it?"

Dovie swallowed a laugh. "Silly girl, it's just a mournin' dove." She walked up to the tree and looked into the branches. "There." Dovie pointed.

Alice's eyes followed Dovie's finger up. There sat a small grayish bird cooing softly to the sky. "She sounds so sad."

"Well, that's how she got her name. Someone thought

it sounded like a woman cryin' as if she was in mournin', hence mournin' dove," Dovie explained.

"How'd you get your name, Mama Dovie?" Alice asked.

Dovie smiled. "Well, while my mom was havin' me, she kept sayin' she could see a white dove. Dad looked all around for that dove, thinkin' one had gotten into the house somehow. The lady helpin' Mom said she was just sick with pain, and there wasn't no bird in the house. But Mom kept insistin' she was seeing a dove. The lady was about to send for the doctor, thinkin' Mom was goin' into fits, when I plopped right out without warnin'. The minute the lady set me in Mom's arms, a white dove landed on the windowsill. Mom said it was a sign and a blessin' from God and named me Dovie." She chuckled. "At least that's the way my mom used to tell the story. Dad says he never saw the dove Mom was talkin' about, but it was such a beautiful thing there was no way he was gonna argue with it. So he let her name me after that bird."

"Well, I like it," said Alice, "and I like the story. Do you miss your Ma?"

"Of course, I do," said Dovie, "but I know she's up there lookin' down on me just like Simon and Helen. Come on, let's go home now. Your brother will be back from his date with Lou Anne soon."

Alice nodded her head and started back to the house with Dovie. She turned to take one last look at the tree and gasped as a white dove settled on a branch and then quickly flew off before she could show Dovie.

"Whatcha lookin' at now?" asked Dovie.

"Just feelin' God's warmth," said Alice.

Dovie smiled and grabbed Alice's hand as they headed back to the house.

Bill kept wiping his sweaty hands on his jeans and hoped Lou Anne hadn't noticed he was sweating through his shirt.

"You all right, Bill?" asked Lou Anne, laying a hand on his arm. "You look nervous. It's not Charlotte again is it?"

"No, honestly, I couldn't be better." He smiled and pulled into the park.

"I thought we were goin' to Johnson's for ice cream." Lou Anne asked looking around the park. "Is there an ice cream social I don't know about?"

"Let's go sit at our table for a minute." Bill gestured to their picnic table under the big cottonwood tree. "Then we'll go to Johnson's."

"Fine, but you owe me a float, mister," Lou Anne teased.

Bill nodded and took Lou Anne's hand as they strolled to their spot. He hoisted her up on the table, as he always did. Her eyes sparkled. He noticed they were more gold than brown today -- a good sign.

He took both her hands in his. "Lou Anne, I know we've only known each other a short time, but I can't imagine spendin' a minute of my life without you. You make my heart do flip flops, and your very touch sends lightnin' down my body."

She tried to say something, but he held up a hand.

"Let me get through this, okay? I got some stuff I want to say -- that I have to say," Bill explained, grabbing her hand again.

She nodded, and he continued. "You're on my mind all the time. I dream about you when I sleep, and I constantly think about you when I'm awake. I'm never as happy as I am with you. You've always been kind to Evie and Elm, and Alice adores you. In my heart you're already a part of the family, and if you let me I'd like to make it official."

He got on one knee and fished something out of his breast pocket. It was a small gold ring with delicate roses engraved around the band. "Lou Anne Garber, would you do me the honor of bein' my wife?"

Tears formed in her eyes, and she choked out a weak, "Yes."

Placing the ring on her left ring finger, he picked her up and twirled her around.

"You've made me the happiest man alive, Lou Anne, and I'm gonna spend the rest of my life makin' sure you're the happiest woman alive," he said, planting a sloppy kiss on her.

Lou Anne giggled. "I already am the happiest woman alive."

She held up her hand and looked at the ring.

"I know it ain't much," said Bill, "but it was my grandma's. My ma gave it to me before they left. Told me to sell it if we got desperate. I don't think I could've ever sold it. My grandma was a kind woman who showed us a lot of love. You remind me of her. I think she'd be glad you're the one wearin' it now."

"It's perfect, Bill. I love it." She wrapped her arms around his neck. "And I love you."

Bill put her back on the table and then hopped up beside her. She grabbed his hand as she leaned against his shoulder. "Bill, I don't want to ruin the moment, but I have to ask."

"Nothin' could ruin this moment." He smiled at her. "Ask anythin' you want."

She paused a moment trying to find the right words.

"Did you ask my pa for his blessin'? Not that it would make a difference. I would say yes even if you didn't. It's just he's been actin' strange lately." She leaned up and looked at Bill. "Like the other day, Charles threw oatmeal at him, and we all held our breath thinkin' Charles was about to get a whoopin' none of us would be able to stop. Pa's face got an awful shade of red, and Ma flung herself over Charles, but all Pa did was wipe off the oatmeal and kept eatin' like it never happened."

Bill tried not to laugh as he pictured David Garber with oatmeal on his face. As far as Bill was concerned, the man deserved a lot more than a face full of oatmeal, but he'd take it. Good for little Charles.

"I did ask your pa," Bill said and then shrugged. "And he gave me a blessin' of sorts. Then I left. James stayed behind and had a couple of words with him. He didn't tell me what he said, but knowin' James, I bet he's the one you need to thank."

"Well, then let's go thank him," said Lou Anne.

"Right now?" Bill wrapped his arms around Lou Anne and nuzzled her cheek. "I thought we could celebrate here a little more."

"Oh, you silly boy." She pushed him away and smiled. "Don't you know when a woman's gonna get married to the man she loves, she wants to tell the world?"

She jumped off the table. "We'll start with your family, and then go over and see mine. You'll have dinner with us, of course." She pulled him off the table and yanked him toward the truck.

"Are you sure your pa won't mind?" he asked. "When I said he gave me his blessing, it wasn't on the friendliest of terms. I'm not sure he'll welcome me with open arms."

"He'll be fine," Lou Anne assured him. "My ma will

make sure of it. She's gonna be so happy. I think she's got a bit of a crush on you too." Lou Anne winked at him.

Bill blushed. "Okay, it's settled then." said Bill, "but at least let me buy you that float I promised."

Ten minutes later they pulled up to Johnson's and sat at one of the small tables in the back next to the soda fountain and ice cream counter. Lou Anne stirred her float while Bill tried to get his thick malt through the straw. Giving up, he grabbed a spoon and was about to take a huge bite when Charlotte waltzed up to the table.

"On a little date I see." Charlotte stuck her finger in Bill's malt and licked it off. "Pity I don't have anyone to buy me a malt." She pouted her lips.

"Maybe you should ask Peter." Bill pointed at Peter who lingered behind Charlotte. "I bet he'd buy you your own malt, so you don't have to stick your dirty fingers in mine."

She glanced at Peter, shrugged, and then concentrated on Lou Anne. "An ice cream float. Oh, Lou Anne, don't you know that's gonna go straight to your hips. I'd hate to see you amblin' around like an ol' heifer."

"That's so kind of you to be worried 'bout little ol' me. What would I do without a friend like you?" Lou Anne set her spoon down and leaned in toward Charlotte. "Turns out this isn't any ordinary float. It's a celebration float." She thrust out her left hand and gazed at Bill. "Bill has asked me to marry him, and I've accepted." She looked back at Charlotte. "So fortunate we should run into you. You're the first one I wanted to tell."

Charlotte stared opened-mouthed.

Bill reached up and grabbed Lou Anne's extended hand. "I do believe this is the part where you say 'congratulations'."

"Well, I never…" Charlotte stomped her foot and looked at Bill. "You're makin' a huge mistake, Bill. Hopefully you'll open up your eyes before you take your vows. When you do, I'll be waitin'." She looked at Lou Anne. "Didn't know you could be such a hussy? I can only imagine what you had to do to get that ring on your finger. Enjoy your moment. It won't last long."

Bill stood to defend Lou Anne, but Charlotte waved him off. "Oh, sit down, we're leavin'. I've lost my appetite."

Charlotte stomped out the door as Bill glared at her. Peter turned, gave a big thumbs up, and followed Charlotte.

"I don't know how he puts up with her." Bill sat and took a bite of his malt.

"Well, he just knows one day she'll come to her senses," Lou Anne smiled. "I believe they call it optimism."

"Seems more delusional to me." Bill looked at Lou Anne, and they both laughed.

Chapter Thirty-three

April 14, 1935 - Morning

Alice tucked her body in the corner of her straw playhouse, trying to make sure she was hidden from the opening.

"Alice, I know you're up here. I saw you climb up the ladder." Alice could see Evalyn looking around the loft, hands on hips. "I'm not leavin' till you come out. I need to talk to you."

Evalyn plopped down on a loose pile of hay and starting weaving pieces of straw. "If you come out, I'll give you this bracelet I'm makin'."

Alice sighed. The bracelet would be nice, and she knew Evalyn wouldn't leave since there wasn't another way out of the loft. "Close your eyes, and I'll come out."

"Just come out, Alice. I know you're in the hay bales. There's no other place to hide."

Alice poked out her head and Evalyn smiled. "Clever hidin' place. Too bad you won't be usin' it much longer."

Alice eyed her sister suspiciously. "It's mine, Evie. Please don't take it."

"I'm not gonna take it, silly." Evalyn continued to braid. "It's just we're not gonna be around here much longer."

"Our house is close enough. Mr. James said I could come over and visit Mr. Norman whenever I wanted. He won't mind if I play up here too."

"We're not gonna be at that house either."

Alice placed her hands on her hips. "Then why's Bill workin' so hard on it?"

"So he can live in it with Lou Anne." Evie shrugged.

"And us." Alice pouted her lips. "He's already showed me where our room's gonna be."

Evalyn shook her head. "No, I'm gonna take us to California to be with Ma and Pa. Got a letter from them yesterday, and they want us to come to California and live with them."

Evalyn pulled out a sheet of off-white paper and gave it to Alice.

"You know I can't read good yet. Just tell me what it says." Alice plopped down beside Evie and handed the paper back.

"Well," said Evalyn, taking the paper, "it says they've been missin' us somethin' terrible. They are very sorry they left us, and they love us with all their hearts. They made some money at the fruit farms and bought a nice house, where we'll both get our own rooms." She pointed to one paragraph. "And here is where Ma says how sorry she is that she didn't treat you like the princess you are."

"Did she really say that?" Tears clouded Alice's eyes.

"Yes, Alice, you know they always loved us." She wrapped an arm around Alice. "Even when they was mad. Parents just get mad sometimes and say and do things they don't mean. It don't mean they don't love us."

"But they left us." Alice sniffed. "If they loved us, they would've taken us too."

"She says right here." Evalyn pointed to another paragraph. "They were afraid to take us 'cause they didn't know anythin' about California. They were scared it was all a lie, and we'd be worse off. They trusted Bill to take care of us here, where he could get work farmin'."

"I don't wanna leave Bill, and what 'bout Elm? Is he comin' or stayin' here? I love Mama Dovie and Mr. James. Besides I can't leave Mr. Norman." Tears flowed freely down Alice's cheeks. She hugged her knees. "Why can't Ma and Pa come and stay here?"

"Elm will be stayin' here with Bill, so he can help Mr. Murphy and earn some money, and I told you they already bought a house there, so they can't move here. What kind of work would they do here? It's not like Mr. Murphy can support our entire family." Evalyn squeezed her sister tighter. "I know it'll be hard at first, but I'll teach you how to write everybody letters. Now there are a few things we need to do before we leave. First we can't tell anybody."

"Why not? That don't make sense." Alice shoved Evalyn off. "We can't just sneak off like Ma and Pa. That ain't right."

"'Cause Bill might decide to go with us instead of finishin' the house. Lou Anne might decide she don't want to move to California and leave her family behind. It'll break Bill's heart to have to choose between us and Lou Anne. It would make him very sad." Evalyn continued to braid the straw. "And Elm would just tell Bill. You know he would."

"Won't they be sad we're gone?" asked Alice, pouting her lips. "I don't want them to be sad."

"Of course they will. But it's time for Bill to start a family of his own, and Elm will be here to support him," explained Evalyn. "And you need to stop calling Mrs.

Grant, 'Mama Dovie'. What if you say that in front of Ma? She'll hate you for it."

"I don't care!" Alice stood. "I don't care 'bout her or Pa and I ain't leavin' here. I'll stay here with Mr. Norman. If Elm can stay, then so can I!" She ran to the ladder. "You can't make me leave, and I know they want me here. I just know it!" She shook her finger at her older sister. "You write them back and tell them we ain't comin'." She flew down the ladder and ran towards the house.

Alice burst in the kitchen door and ran into Dovie's arms. "Please, Mama Dovie, don't make me go. I'll be a good girl and pull weeds in the garden and do the dishes every day. Just let me stay. I don't wanna go. I want to stay here with you and Mr. Norman."

"Heavens child, what are you talkin' 'bout?" Dovie hugged Alice back. "You ain't gonna be but a mile or so from here. You can come over and visit whenever you want. Norman'll just follow you over there and probably stay. There's no need for tears, Alice. You'll like your new place."

"That's not it. Evie got a letter from Ma and Pa, said they want us to go to California to be with them. I don't wanna go." Alice said into Dovie's apron.

Dovie let go of Alice and bent to look into her eyes. "When did she get this letter?"

"Yesterday." Alice rubbed her eyes. "She says Bill and Elm are stayin', but I have to go with her to live with Ma and Pa. Please let me stay, Mama Dovie, please!"

Dovie shook her head. There had been no mail yesterday. "Everything's gonna be all right. Nobody's goin' to California."

"But Evie said," protested Alice.

"You just let me deal with Evalyn," Dovie said sternly.

"Now go wash your face and remember what we learned in church this mornin'."

"God is always with me and will give me strength even when I feel weak?"

Dovie nodded. "Yes, just like the first time you had to go into the cellar. You know, when you sang "Jesus Loves Me", and God protected you and gave you enough courage to keep goin' down those steps. When you got to the bottom, it wasn't scary at all." She hugged Alice again. "Now go on. Wash your face and then lie down for a bit. I'll call you for lunch."

Alice washed her face in the kitchen sink and started upstairs. "I love you, Mama Dovie."

"I love you too, Alice," said Dovie, watching Alice make her way upstairs to lie down.

Dovie grabbed the dish towel on the counter and started wringing it in knots. Why would Evalyn tell Alice those dreadful lies? Looking out the window, she saw Evalyn strolling toward the house. It was time to get answers.

Evalyn stepped into the kitchen, twirling the straw jewelry around her finger. "Where's Alice? I have this bracelet I promised her."

"She's upstairs restin' after you got her all worked up." Dovie shook the towel at Evalyn. "You want to tell me why you lied to your little sister? She's worked herself into quite a state."

"I can only imagine what that child's sayin' now. You know how Alice gets. My, that girl does have an imagination." She rolled her eyes. "Always tellin' stories."

"Did you tell her your parents want y'all to go to California?" Dovie raised an eyebrow. "Or is Alice makin' that up? She was beside herself in tears. Why would you lie to her like that?"

Evalyn shrugged. "Who says it's a lie?"

"I do." Dovie crossed her arms. "I know you didn't get a letter in the mail yesterday or any day before that."

"Maybe it was mailed to Harriet, and she gave it to me at church this mornin'. Did you think of that?" Evalyn glared at Dovie. "Ever think maybe I didn't want Bill to know I was in contact with our parents?"

Dovie inhaled deeply. "Evalyn, we both know you have no idea where your parents are. There is no way you could've found out in the time you've been here. It's not possible. You don't even know where to start."

"You don't know that," snarled Evalyn.

"Okay, then let me see the letter." Dovie willed her voice to remain calm. "I'd like to know where you're plannin' on takin' Alice. I'm sure Bill would like to know too."

"Why would I share anythin' with you?" snarled Evalyn. "You'll just twist everythin' to make me look like I'm in the wrong. You're never fair to me. You get a kick out of every time I'm punished. Nothin' like havin' your own personal slave around to do your biddin'."

"Just stop, Evalyn!" Dovie slammed her fist on the counter. "You've been nothin' but a liar and a thorn in our sides since you got here. We've tried very hard to make things right with you, but you just won't have it. What will it take for you to see that they left y'all, and that you've got a good thing here?"

"A good thing? This place is nothin' but chickens and dust!" Evalyn yelled. "You don't know what they think. They love us, and I know they miss us. We're their children! I think you don't want Alice to leave 'cause then it's like losin' your kid all over again. She's not your daughter and she never will be!"

Dovie gasped. "You little heathen. You know darn well that's not how I see it. Nothin' could take the place of my little girl – nothin'. You just can't stand to see your family happy. You don't deserve them…"

"Stop!" Alice stood on the stairs crying. "Stop fightin', please!"

Evalyn grabbed Alice's arm and pulled her towards Dovie. "We'll end this right now." She leaned down and looked at Alice. "You have to decide. It's either me or her. You can't have us both."

Alice looked from her sister to Dovie.

"If you pick her," Evalyn said, "you'll never see me again. Is that what you want?"

"No, I don't want to pick." She pulled her arm free of Evalyn's grasp and ran outside.

"Alice, wait!" Evalyn started after her, but Dovie grabbed her arm.

"Let her go. This isn't her fight. She'll come back when she's ready. I hope you're happy with yourself."

"Me?" Evalyn jerked her arm away and pointed at Dovie. "You're the one that started it. She'll come with me to California. You'll see she doesn't love you more than me."

"Is that what you're worried 'bout?" Dovie threw her hands in the air. "Alice is your sister. She loves you unconditionally. Not that you deserve it. Y'all fight, that's what sisters do. Even so, you had no right to try and make her choose between us. She doesn't have to. She can have us both, if you let her."

"Of course she loves you more," Evalyn snapped. "You're always takin' her side when somethin' happens. You've been tryin' to win her over since day one."

"Oh, grow up, Evalyn," said Dovie, turning back to her potatoes.

Chapter Thirty-four

April 14, 1935 - Black Sunday

"I can't remember the last time it was this still. Day's almost as beautiful as you are." Bill adjusted a pipe on the windmill and winked at Lou Anne who was sitting on the fence swinging her legs back and forth.

Lou Anne blushed. "Oh, Bill, stop. Not in front of Mr. Murphy."

James laughed. "Lou Anne, as far as I'm concerned, we're your family now, so you can call me James. And don't worry, I used to tell my wife how beautiful she was all the time, in front of God and everybody."

"Still," said Lou Anne, "some things are not meant for an audience."

Bill grinned. "Oh, so you prefer to be alone. Maybe we can convince James to go help Elm in the barn."

He looked over expecting to see James laughing at him, but instead caught him looking into the sky.

"What is it?" Bill turned his head, and Lou Anne jumped off the fence to gaze up.

Birds of all kinds were flying south in a mass exodus. A flock of Canadian geese honked out a warning. Bill looked to the north and saw a mountain of black clouds billowing over the trees.

"Is it rain?" he asked James.

"You don't think it's a duster, do you?" asked Lou Anne. "Not somethin' that large. It must be rain clouds. The drought is over. Hallelujah!" She clapped her hands.

"I don't know. Either way, we best get everyone to shelter." James hurried towards the house as Bill gathered up the tools.

"You better go inside, Lou Anne." Bill said. "It looks pretty nasty."

Lou Anne bent to help with the tools. "I'll go with you."

Bill nodded as he bent to grab a pipe wrench and was zapped by a large charge of static electricity. "It's a duster!" he yelled at James.

The last thing Bill saw was Lou Anne being slammed to the ground as a wall of dark clouds swallowed her.

James nodded at Bill and looked toward the barn where Elmer was cleaning the stalls. "Elm, get to the house now! Where's Alice?"

"Inside I think," said Elmer, running towards the house. "I'll double check with Ms. Dovie when I get inside. I'm pretty sure I saw her run in there earlier."

James had turned to see if he could help Bill and Lou Anne when he was thrown to the ground and surrounded by the black dirt. He tried to yell for Bill, but the grit filled his mouth and choked him. Pulling his handkerchief out of his back pocket, he tied it around his nose and mouth. Unable to keep his eyes open, he threw his arms over his head to cover the rest of his face. His mind raced, should he go toward Elmer or Bill and Lou Anne? Elmer was so close to the door, surely he'd be okay. James tried to remember which way he had fallen so he could find Bill and Lou Anne, and then the house, but the noise made it hard to concentrate. He had to be close to the corral.

Reaching up, he felt for the wood fence and grazed it, leaving splinters in his fingertips. He turned slowly to the right and began to crawl along the corral, feeling for the fence posts. When he reached the barn, he turned again to his right and felt for the stock tank. Bill and Lou Anne had been just on the other side of the stock tank the last time James saw them. He prayed they hadn't crawled in the wrong direction.

The stock tank buzzed with electricity, shocking James constantly, but he had to stay close if he wanted to find them and get them all out of there. He found an arm and could tell it was Lou Anne. She grabbed his arm and pulled herself closer. Through the grit he could see she was alone and terrified. He continued to belly crawl toward the spot he last saw Bill. Lou Anne's grip tightened on his arm, begging him to not leave her. He pulled gently and prayed she'd realize he wanted her to come along. She did.

Finally, he felt Bill's hand. He squinted though his eyelashes and crawled closer to Bill while keeping one foot touching the stock tank. James pulled on Bill's arm trying to get him to follow him to the barn, but Bill didn't move.

Elmer was on the second step of the stoop when the duster smashed into him, knocking off the stairs. His left arm cracked as he landed, and he cried out in pain as the storm surrounded him in the black dust. Quickly, he clamped his mouth shut, swallowing his scream. He knew the stairs were close, but he couldn't see anything. It had gone from afternoon to night in an instant. The musty smell of top soil filled his nose. He got to his knees only to be knocked down again.

Reaching out he felt for the stairs, but instead of air he felt the warm flesh of a hand grip his fingers. He scooted on his butt toward the hand and latched onto it. He felt someone pull. Soon he was face to face with Dovie, a towel over her mouth and nose. She was lying on her belly with her feet still in the kitchen doorway being held tightly by Evalyn.

Grabbing his waist, she said something, but all he could hear was muffled sounds. She motioned for him to climb over her and reached down to give him a boost. Using his good hand, he grabbed the doorway and pulled himself inside the safety of the house.

Dovie was right behind him, kicking the big kitchen door shut. "Are you okay? Where's is everyone? Are they close?"

"I hurt my arm, but I'm sure it's fine." He rubbed his arm. "Bill and Lou Anne were still by the windmill, and Mr. James was near the barn." Elmer explained before going into a coughing fit.

"Oh, dear Jesus," Dovie gasped, handing Elmer a wet towel for his mouth and nose. "Put this on."

"We have to go get them." Evalyn motioned to the door. "We can make a rope with the sheets."

"Nonsense, child. I doubt we could walk against that wind, and even if we could, we'd only end up getting lost ourselves." Dovie said as she grabbed a fresh towel and started making a sling for Elmer's arm. "Evalyn, start puttin' some towels over the windows, or we'll all suffocate in here. Dad and Bill will make sure Lou Anne gets to the barn. Once they get in the barn, they can look after Alice. I'm sure she had enough sense to come out of the loft. They'll be fine." She looked at Elmer. "Now let me tend to that arm."

"Alice isn't in the barn! I thought she was in here with you!" Elmer ran to the window, ignoring Dovie's attempts to care for his arm. "I was in the barn cleanin' the stables. She never came in, or I would've seen her."

"You mean she's out there?" The color drained from Evalyn's face. "We have to go find her!" She ran to the door.

"Make a wish, Mr. Norman." Alice picked a dandelion and blew at the seeds. "I wish Evie would like it here. She takes the fun out of everythin'. It's like she's got a bee in her bonnet all the time. Never has nothin' nice to say 'bout anythin', especially Quail Crossings."

She threw the stem on the ground. "I don't know why I worry 'bout her. She's nothin' but a big meanie. You know she said she'd share her fingernail polish, and she ain't painted my nails one time." Picking up another dandelion, she blew again.

"Sometimes I wish I could fly like a dandelion seed, just float on the air. Then I could see both Mama Dovie and Evie, no matter where we lived. You could fly with me, Mr. Norman. I wouldn't want to leave you behind."

She lay down on her side. "It don't make no sense to leave here. Bill's buildin' that big ol' house so we can all live together. He don't want us to go nowhere. Besides I'd have to leave school, and I like Mrs. Spaulding and Joan.

She's my best friend." She patted Mr. Norman's side. "Except for you, Mr. Norman. You're my bestest friend ever, and I don't want to leave you."

She sat up again and crossed her legs Indian style. "I bet if Ma and Pa saw the house, they'd want to live here too." A smile caressed her face, causing her dimple to go deep. "I know, I'll ask Bill to write them a letter, explainin' the house to them. Once they read it, they'll want to come here, and we can all live together as one big ol' family." She slapped her knee and giggled. "Yep, that's what's gonna happen. I can feel it. Then everybody will be happy, including Evie. I just love a good happily ever after, don't you Mr. Norman?"

Norman honked at the sky, causing Alice to look up. "That sure is a lot of birds, Mr. Norman. I wonder where they're all goin'. Bet it ain't California, maybe Old Mexico. I heard once that all birds fly south for the winter. Guess not all birds, since you stayed here with the chickens, but that's your job." Alice tilted her head. "Well, that don't make sense, winter's over."

Norman honked again and flapped his wings wildly. Alice looked over her shoulder. A wall of black was barreling towards them. She glanced toward the house and then back at the duster. Her bottom lip began to quiver. "I don't think we can make it home, Mr. Norman." She scanned the horizon looking for shelter, and her eyes fell on Bill's house.

She hopped up and ran toward the house with Norman flapping on her heels. "Hurry, Mr. Norman! Fly if you can, we gotta get someplace safe."

She looked at the dirt clouds again and tripped, falling hard on the cracked ground. Norman honked wildly as he waddled beside her. She pushed herself up and continued running, trying to ignore the burning of her scraped knee. Tears raced down her face as the monster duster swallowed the fields.

Finally reaching the house, she looked for a place to hide from the storm. Every room seemed to have an open window pane. She spotted the small closet where Bill kept his tools and supplies, the only room without a window. She opened the door and shoved the tools to one side. Mr. Norman waddled into the small space. Closing the door behind her, Alice sat in the corner by her friend.

Looking around the dark closet, she patted Norman on the head. "We'll just wait here till the storm is over." She shivered. "Don't be scared, Mr. Norman. We'll be safe in here. Bill made this house strong. Remember I helped."

The house creaked in protest as it was hit by the wind. Alice screamed as the house was swallowed in dust.

Chapter Thirty-five

James pulled harder on Bill's arm. His wrist ached in protest, but he was able to move Bill's body closer. "Lord, give me strength," he silently prayed.

Tugging harder he felt resistance. He patted Bill's hand, and then placed Lou Anne's hand on Bill's arm, trying to tell him she was okay and to follow him. It seemed to work as Bill rolled over and belly crawled closer to James and Lou Anne. Together, the three followed the stock tank back to the corral fence and into the barn doors.

James put Bill's hand on the south door of the barn and together they pulled. The door flew open, colliding with James's shoulder, before slamming into the side of the barn. James grabbed his shoulder as pain bolted down his back. He could no longer feel Bill and Lou Anne's hands. He wondered where they had gone. Had they lost him in the duster? He tried to belly crawl forward, but with only one arm he was making little progress. He coughed hard, feeling dirty mucus cling to his throat and mouth. Suddenly, hands grabbed his good arm and pulled him forward into the barn. Bill helped James to a hay bale. Lou Anne leaned in front of James, trying to keep his focus. Before James knew what was happening, Bill snapped his shoulder back into place. James thought he was going to black out from pain but held

Lou Anne's gaze. As soon as he was steady, Lou Anne built a sling out of a feed sack and tied James's bad arm. James squinted through the haze. Lou Anne shook as she gingerly fingered Bill's head, a small trickle of muddy blood flowing from his temple.

"Are you okay?" James yelled. He grabbed a rag off the gate, dumped it in the drink bucket, and handed it to Lou Anne, who placed it gently on Bill's forehead.

Bill nodded and pointed to the south barn door. "We've gotta get that closed."

James grabbed a rope off the stall. "Attach this to my waist, and I'll make my way to the handle. Once I grab it, I'll give you two hard tugs. Then y'all pull me in, and I'll bring the door with me."

"I'll do it," Bill reached out for the rope.

"Are you sure, Bill?" James ran his good hand through his hair. "You was out cold earlier."

"I'm sure. No offense, James, but we can't afford to have you lose the door due to your hurt shoulder." Bill grabbed the rope.

Lou Anne grabbed the rope from Bill. "And we can't have you blackin' out and losin' the door either." She began to tie the rope around her waist. "I'll do it."

"No, Lou Anne, if anythin' should happen to you..." Bill couldn't finish his sentence.

"I'll be fine. You boys just don't let go." She wet a bandana in the bucket and tied it around her nose and mouth.

James looped the end of the rope to a stall and pulled his leather gloves out of his pocket. "We ain't losin' her, son," he said to Bill.

Bill looked at James, eyes begging for a different answer. Finding none he embraced Lou Anne. "I love you," he said before kissing her gently on the lips.

"Just hold onto me, Bill," Lou Anne pleaded. "Whatever happens don't let me go."

Bill nodded at James and grabbed the rope.

Lou Anne stepped back into the storm.

Dovie grabbed Evalyn's arm for a second time. "Are you crazy, girl? You can't go out there. Did you see the effort it took just to get Elmer in from the stoop?" Dovie shook her head. "I want Alice in this house as much as you do, but we don't even know where she is. It's suicide to go out there lookin'."

Evalyn yanked her arm from Dovie's grip. "This is all your fault!"

"My fault?" Dovie gasped. "You're the one who forced her to choose between us."

"You did what?" Elmer yelled. When Evalyn didn't speak, Elmer looked at Dovie. "Tell me."

"If you don't tell him what you did, I will," Dovie said to Evalyn.

Evalyn sighed. "I told her Ma and Pa bought a house in California and wanted the two of us to join them. I showed her a letter sayin' they missed us and wanted us back. I told Alice that Ma would hate her for callin' Mrs. Grant, 'Mama Dovie'. She came in all upset and told Mrs. Grant everythin'. We got into a fight over it, and Alice came in durin' the middle of it." Evalyn looked down. "I made her choose, me or Mrs. Grant, and Alice ran off."

Elmer blinked and tears streaked his dirty face. "How could you? You know as well as I do, they don't want us. Bill knows it too, though he won't say it 'cause he don't want us to hate them. Alice is the only one who don't know better. She's too little to understand!" Elmer sat at the table and laid his head on his arms.

"I know. I'm so sorry, Elm." Evalyn tried to rub his back.

"Get off me! If she dies, it's on you. I'll never forgive you and neither will Bill. I was only out there for a minute, and it was like a bad nightmare, except I wasn't dreamin'. I was livin' it. Do you have any idea what she's goin' through right now? That dirt felt like gettin' stung by a thousand bees all at once. We don't know if she can breathe or if she's bein' buried alive under all the dirt, and we can't do nothin' about it!" He banged his hand on the table and let out a yelp. Dovie hurried over and began to tie the splint.

"All right, that's enough," Dovie said. "We've got to get towels over the windows and sheets over the door, or we'll all be down with the brown plague. Lord knows the others are sure to get it bein' in the drafty old barn. Helen had the dust pneumonia once. Thought she was never gonna stop coughin' up dirt."

She looked at Elmer, "Do you think you can handle wetting some towels, while Evalyn and I nail them up?"

Elmer nodded.

"Okay, then," she patted Evalyn on the back, "let's get busy."

The wind pinned Lou Anne to the barn door, but she managed to stay on her feet. Carefully, she slid along the big wood door feeling for the handle. Splitters dug into her back and shoulders, ripping her shirt, but she fought the urge to jerk away. She felt as though she'd walked for miles when her hand finally brushed over the old iron handle. She grabbed it with her left and gave two hard tugs with her right, before clutching it around the handle as well.

She felt the men pull, as the wind pulled her the opposite direction, trying to yank the door from her delicate fingers. She tightened her grip on the handle and tried to walk backwards, pulling the door shut. The dirt pelted her body like BB's. She could feel the door sliding from her hands and fought to keep her grip. She would not let them down. Without the door shut, they would all suffocate. The barn door was slipping as something wet and slippery slid down her fingers. She must've cut her hand on the old brass handle. The stinging in her hand confirmed her suspicion. The pain grew as she felt the rope go slack. Where was Bill? She couldn't do it. He had let her go and the pain was too much. Her fingers slipped. She struggled to keep hold. Finally, Bill grabbed her around the waist and with one last hard tug, Lou Anne fell in the barn, the door closing behind her.

James quickly tied the two doors together, keeping the south one from blowing open again.

"Are you okay?" asked Bill, scanning Lou Anne's torn shirt and bloody hand.

"Just a cut and a few splinters," she said, dipping her rag into the water and retying it around her face. "What happened? The rope went slack, and I thought I was gonna lose the door."

"The rope broke," said James. "We tied the remainin' rope to Bill. He got to you just in time it seems."

"How's your head?" Lou Anne asked Bill.

"It hurts. All I remember is reachin' for the pipe wrench and then James pullin' on my hand." Bill hugged Lou Anne. "I was so scared we'd lose you when the rope broke."

Lou Anne collapsed into his hug. "Haven't you figured out yet that'll you'll never lose me?"

Bill kissed Lou Anne again, before turning to James. "Did the kids get inside?"

"Elm was on the stoop the last I saw of him, and he said Alice was inside." James rubbed his neck.

"Good. Guess we're stuck here till it ends," said Bill.

James nodded, took off his handkerchief, rinsed it in the water bucket, and tied it back on. Bill sat on a stack of hay, and Lou Anne curled up next to him. Bill put his head in his hands.

"You have to stay awake, love," Lou Anne said gently lifting his head. "I know it's hard, but don't give in to the black."

Alice stuck her face in Mr. Norman's soft feathers. "It's gettin' hard to breathe in here."

Her voice was less than a whisper. The fine grit hung in the closet, causing her throat to feel raw. She fought back tears.

"Maybe I should go to California and be with Ma and Pa. Then I wouldn't have to worry 'bout no dust storms. I hate dusters, always makin' me miss school and have to clean house and do all the laundry and dishes."

Norman laid his head gently on her back.

"I think we need to find somethin' to block that crack. That's what we do at the house." She pointed under the door and looked around the closet. "But I don't see nothin' to use."

Norman let out a low honk as Alice coughed. She

slowly unbuttoned the front of her dress. Pulling her arms through the sleeves, she slid it down to her feet, leaving only her tiny slip to protect her from the cold. Carefully, she rolled the dress and leaned forward, placing it at the door seam.

"There, that ought to do it." She slid back into the corner by Norman. "I wish I had some water. I'm so thirsty, I'd drink that nasty ol' milkweed milk we used to get with Ma and Pa. All our cows had to eat was milkweed, so their milk started tastin' all funny. It was yucky, but Ma made us drink it anyway."

She coughed hard and laid her head on Norman's back. "I'm gettin' sleepy, Mr. Norman, but I'm afraid if I go to sleep I'll never wake up. I just don't know if I can fight it."

Chapter Thirty-six

"I think it's settlin' down." James took off his handkerchief.

Bill got up and walked to the door. "I believe you're right. Here, hold onto my belt. Let's try the door."

"Be careful, Bill." Lou Anne grabbed his arm.

"I'll be all right."

James grabbed Bill's belt and held tightly as Lou Anne untied the doors. Bill nudged the door open a crack before being met with a drift.

"It's stuck," he said. "You can let go, James. I'm not going anywhere. None of us are, unless I can get this door open."

He slammed his shoulder into the door again and again, trying to bulldoze it past the mound of dirt. Conceding the door wasn't going to move, he peered through the crack, trying to make sense of the dirt covered scenery.

"I can see the moon. Lou Anne, I can see the moon!" Bill laughed, swung Lou Anne around and took another shove at the door. "I can't believe it ain't daybreak. It felt like we was in there for a coon's age."

"Take it easy, Bill," said James. "You don't want to black out again. Here let us help."

James and Lou Anne leaned against the door with Bill. The top part of the door bent forward, but the bottom stayed put.

Bill stepped back. "It's no use. We'll have to wait for Dovie and Elmer."

"Maybe not," said Lou Anne. "I'll just go up to the loft and jump down. If the drift is as big as I think it is, then it shouldn't be too far down. I've jumped out of many an apple tree with a far harder landin' than a mound of dirt."

Bill and James stared at Lou Anne, so she continued. "For all we know, Dovie and Elmer are trapped in the house. I could dig them out, and then the three of us can work on this big door."

"I tell you, I'm marryin' the biggest tomboy in Knollwood," Bill said with a smile. "But I'll not let you have all the fun. Lou Anne's right. If that dune's high enough, then all three of us can get out of here. Come on, James, let's give it a shot."

James nodded and the three climbed the ladder to the loft. Small mounds of dirt had made their way through the cracks, making a miniature desert. Bill slid the loft window open and gasped. Everything was covered in thick black dirt. James whistled behind him. "Looks like we've got quite a clean-up job on our hands."

Bill looked down. "Well, here goes nothin'."

Taking a deep breath, he leaped out of the loft and into the soft dirt, rolling with gravity at the end. "It's a little farther than it looks," he yelled up. "Just roll at the end the way I did, and you should be okay."

"I haven't been this nimble since I was a little boy, Lord help me," James yelled down before jumping. He landed with a thud and rolled as Bill instructed. Standing up, he brushed himself off. "Looks like I've still got some spring in my step after all."

Lou Anne peeked over the edge.

"It's okay, sweetie, you can do it," Bill encouraged. "But, if you don't want to, we'll dig you out down here."

She shook her head. "No, I'm fine. I can do it. Just seems a lot further down than all those apple trees."

Bill watched her tiptoe to the edge. Right before her plunge, she hesitated causing her to fall out of control. She let out a harsh scream as she hit the dirt on her side.

Bill rushed to her. "Are you okay?"

"I think I just knocked the wind out of me." Lou Anne tried to get up, only to let out another loud yelp as she grabbed her ribs.

"Lie still," said James. "You might have broken a rib. Let's get the house opened up, so we can get her inside and have Dovie take a look. Hopefully it's just a crack. I doubt the doc can make it here tonight."

The two men hurried to the house where they could see Dovie trying to push the screen door open, a drift blocking her progress. Bill and James scooped with their hands until the door gave way.

"Is Alice with you?" Dovie asked, hurrying down what was left of the steps and hugging her dad. Elmer and Evalyn stood on the stoop, each with a lantern.

"We thought she was in here." James said as he took the lantern from Elmer. "What happened to your arm, son?"

Elmer shook his head. "It's nothin'. We need to find Alice. She ran off right before the duster."

Bill's world began to spin, and he grabbed his head. "You mean she was out in the storm?"

"Oh, Bill, your head!" Evalyn rushed down the steps and tenderly touched the cut on her brother's forehead. He waved her off.

"I'm fine. Oh, God, I can't believe she was out here." He cupped his hands over his mouth and yelled, "Alice! Alice!"

James put his hand on Bill's shoulder. "Don't panic! She's a smart kid. I'm sure she found shelter. First we need to get Lou Anne in the house. She might have some broken ribs."

Bill nodded and ran to Lou Anne. Gently lifting her in his arms, he high-stepped through the dunes to get her into the house. Setting her on the sofa, he stepped back so Dovie could take a look. Watching, he held his breath every time Lou Anne winced.

"Thank the Lord, I think they're just cracked," said Dovie. She looked at James. "We need to go find Alice. Lou Anne will be okay."

"All right," said James, "we stay in pairs. Bill, you and Elm, go southwest. Dovie and I'll go northwest. I doubt she went east, but we'll check that way next."

He looked at Elmer. "Go get our guns, son, and fire three times if you find her. We'll do the same. Evalyn, you stay here and ring the dinner bell if she comes back."

"But I want to help," protested Evalyn.

"You've done enough," snapped Elmer. "For once just do as you're told."

Evalyn opened her mouth to speak, then closed it, looked at the ground and muttered a small, "Okay."

"You can help, Evalyn," said Dovie. "Lou Anne needs her ribs wrapped. You'll find some wraps in the hall closet. Get them as tight as you can, while still allowin' her to breathe. It's very important that they're tight. Can you do that?"

Evalyn nodded her head yes, as Bill hurried past her to fetch the guns.

"Shouldn't we get the dogs?" asked Elmer.

James shook his head. "They won't be able to pick up a scent with all this dirt."

Bill returned with the guns and handed one to James. "Let's go."

Dovie and James headed toward the orchard, calling Alice's name.

"I've got to be honest with you, Dad. I hope we don't find her over here. There's no place for her to hide from the storm."

"But there's nothin' but wheat fields and pasture in the other direction. At least here she could've made some kind of shelter from the trees."

Dovie choked back a cry. "How could she breathe out here? It was hard enough in the house. She's so little."

"Keep it together, Dovie. I need you to keep a sharp eye," James snapped.

"It's my fault she's out here," Dovie shouted.

James stopped and looked at her daughter. "What do you mean? Nobody knew that duster was comin'. Whatever you sent her out to do, you couldn't have known. It's not your fault."

"She wasn't doin' a chore. Evalyn and I were fightin'. I shouldn't have let her get to me like she did, but she told Alice their parents want them back. It was the straw that broke the camel's back, and I let Evalyn have it. Alice heard us fightin' and wanted us to stop. Evalyn told her she had to choose between us - and I let her. I wanted Alice to pick me. When Alice ran out the door, Evalyn wanted to go after her, and I stopped her. If I wouldn't have stopped Evalyn, then at least Alice wouldn't be alone. Evalyn would've kept her safe."

James hugged his daughter, and her tears broke free.

"It'll be okay. We'll find her and work this whole mess out."

"What did you mean when you told Evie she had done enough?" Bill rubbed his temple as they slogged through the dust. His headache was getting worse.

"She told Alice that Ma and Pa wanted them to move to California. That upset Alice, and I guess she talked to Dovie about it. When Evie came in the house, Dovie let her have it for lyin'. Alice came downstairs durin' their argument and wanted them to stop fightin'. Then Evie made her choose between her and Dovie, which caused Alice to run off."

Bill lowered his head. "I don't know what to say."

"You don't have to say anythin', Bill. We just have to find her, and she has to be safe. There ain't no other option. Anythin' else might just tear our family apart."

Evalyn hugged her knees as she sat on the stoop and shivered. It was a cold night for April, but that wasn't why she shivered. She hadn't stopped crying since the others left to search for Alice. Lou Anne had tried to console her while she was wrapping her ribs, but it was no use. Evalyn needed to be alone, so she went outside, leaving Lou Anne to rest on the sofa.

She let out another loud sob as she thought of little Alice climbing out of the haystack. She looked to the sky and stared at the stars.

"Dear Lord, it's me, Evalyn Brewer. I know I don't talk to you as often as I should, but I need you now more than I've ever needed anythin' in my entire life. My little sister, Alice, is out there, and I'm prayin' to you to bring her home safe. She is such a sweet little girl, and I was a monster to her. Please let her be okay, and I'll stop all this talk 'bout goin' to California. I'll tell Alice I made it all up – that I lied."

Evalyn hung her head and swallowed another tearful gasp. "In fact, I'll tell the truth from now on, pray every day, and stop all this nonsense. I won't cause any trouble for Bill anymore, or for Mr. Murphy and Mrs. Grant. I've been so wrong, so very wrong, not to appreciate these kind people and my family. Please, dear Lord, just let her be safe. Just let her come home. Things will be different I swear."

Evalyn buried her head in hands, rocking back and forth, and still swearing to God that things would be different, when she fell asleep.

Bill and Elmer continued to walk as they called out Alice's name.

"Look, Bill, I bet she's in there." Elmer started running toward the unfinished house, holding onto his hurt arm and picking his knees up high, so he wouldn't stumble in the loose dirt. Bill was right on his heels.

He flew up the steps and went from room to room on the ground floor, screaming Alice's name. Bill ran upstairs to the second floor, doing the same. The boys met each other back at the door.

"She's not here," said Bill. He walked to the door and scanned the horizon. Everything was covered in mounds of black dirt. "How will we ever find her?" He sat on the front step. "I've let her down," Bill cried. "I've let all y'all down."

Chapter Thirty-seven

Elmer laid his hand on Bill's shoulder, not knowing what to say.

Bill rubbed his eyes and cleared his throat. "Let's keep lookin'. Maybe James and Dovie are havin' some luck. We'll make our way over to the east side."

Elmer turned to close the front door and something caught his eye. Stopping at the supply closet, he pointed at the pink flowered fabric peeking through the crack of the door.

"Look, Bill, it's Alice's dress!"

Bill rushed past his brother and flung the door open. "Alice, honey, are you in here?" Dust hung in the stale air, and he squinted to see in the dark. "Bring the light, I can't see nothin'."

Elmer held the lantern over his brother's shoulder. As Bill's eyes adjusted, all he could see was a pile of dirty white rags in the corner, but no Alice.

"Norman?" He said weakly, hoping the large pile of laundry would turn into the big bird. Nothing moved and Bill picked up the dress.

"Where else could she be?" he yelled as he threw the little dress at the stack of dirty cloths.

The goose slowly lifted his head and let out a weak

honk.

"Elm, it is Norman! Alice can't be far!"

Norman turned and raised his broad wing to reveal the little girl in her dusty white slip. Alice coughed and blinked as the light reached her face. Raising her hand to shield her eyes from the lantern, Elmer saw her mouth move, but heard nothing.

"It's okay, sweetheart, don't talk." Tears streamed down Bill's cheeks. "I'm so glad we found you. You were so smart to come in here. Don't move. I need to let the others know to stop lookin'. I'll be right back."

Elmer watched his brother run outside but still flinched as the three shots were fired in the air. Bill hustled past Elmer and back to his sister.

Reaching in, Bill picked up Alice. "We'll get you and Norman to the house. You'll be right as rain in no time."

"I'm so glad you're okay." Elmer pulled on his sister's braid. "When we get home, I'm gonna make you a whole parade of wooden critters. Would you like that?" Alice nodded her head and then laid it on Bill's shoulder.

"We need to get her to the house." Bill tried to sound calm, but his voice betrayed him with a crack.

Norman let out another weak honk, and Alice looked at him and then at Elmer.

"It's the least I can do for a hero." He put the lantern out, set it down, and he swept the exhausted goose up with one arm.

James looked in the direction the shots had come from. "Well, I'll be."

"What is it, Dad?" asked Dovie. "Doesn't that mean

they found her?"

James let out a loud laugh and twirled Dovie in a circle. "It does indeed. I bet she was in Bill's house. Alice is as smart as a fox, I tell you. Praise Jesus!"

Dovie pushed her father away and hung her head. "We don't know she's okay, only that they've found her."

"We've got to have faith, Dovie. Let's go," said James, grabbing Dovie's hand. She pulled it away.

"What's wrong, sweetheart?" asked James.

"I can't do it." Dovie bowed her head.

"Do what?" James ran his hands through his hair.

"I can't lose another child. I was barely makin' it without Helen when the Brewer's came along. I let myself become attached. I knew it was a mistake. The whole time I was tendin' to Elmer, I was fightin' the urge to run away. I can't face death again. I can't do it, Dad!"

"We don't know she's hurt…" started James.

"We don't know that she isn't!" Dovie's shoulders slumped, before a loud sob filled the air.

James grabbed his daughter's shoulders. "You keep it together. Now the good Lord has seen it fit for us to find Alice when it looked impossible. Don't let go of your faith now."

"How can you keep talkin' 'bout faith when He keeps takin' the ones we love away? He keeps takin' and takin' while we're just supposed to sit here and have faith. Well, I can't do it anymore, Dad. I can't blindly follow someone who does nothing but cause pain."

James stared sadly at his daughter, searching for the right words. He knew her heart still ached for her mother, daughter, and husband. His did as well. He just refused to believe God had done all this to spite them and that Alice was hurt in any way. She just had to be okay.

"Dovie, I understand your anger. Losin' so many loved ones in such a short amount of time would challenge anyone's faith in God. But I believe that having faith in Christ means I will get to see them all again. Not only see them again, but spend eternity surrounded by nothin' but love, their love and the love of God.

"I know it's hard right now, but we have to go and see about Alice. If she is hurt, then you're the best person to help her. I not only have faith God will see us through and that He has protected Alice, I have faith that if she is hurt, God has given you the knowledge and strength to make her better."

A weak smile crossed Dovie's face. "You always know what to say, Dad."

She wiped her eyes and headed toward the house. James watched her walk away before looking at the sky. "Please let me be right this time, God."

Three loud bangs woke Evalyn and she stood. Rubbing the grit out of her eyes, she tried to remember which direction the shots had come from. Stepping off the stoop, she paced. Just because they found Alice, didn't mean she was okay.

"Did I hear shots?" asked Lou Anne from the doorway.

Evalyn nodded her head yes as she bit her nails and looked from the northeast to southeast. Finally, she saw a light bobbing towards her from the direction of the orchard. She ran to Dovie and James. "Did you find her?"

Dovie nodded her head. "It was Bill and Elmer. Aren't they back yet?"

Evalyn shook her head no.

Dovie turned to Lou Anne. "You should be lyin' down."

"There will be plenty of time for rest after Alice is safe," said Lou Anne as James helped her down the steps.

Evalyn hurried to the south side of the barn to watch the pasture. Dovie, James, and Lou Anne followed. Soon all were pacing, except Lou Anne who leaned against the barn.

"What's takin' them so long?" asked Evalyn, feeling the tears returning.

Dovie put her hand on Evalyn's arm. "She's gonna be okay. I'm sure Bill's carryin' her over all the loose dirt. They have to be careful."

"Shouldn't we at least see the lantern? Something's wrong, I just know it." Evalyn buried her head in Dovie's shoulder and began to sob heavily again. Dovie closed her arms around the young girl.

"I think I see somethin'," said Lou Anne.

Evalyn looked up. As James held up his lantern, she could barely make out the shape of two people walking towards the barn, both carrying large objects.

"Alice!" she screamed and ran to her sister.

Hugging her brother and sister both, she said, "I'm so sorry, Alice. I shouldn't have done that. You don't have to choose. You can have us both. And I shouldn't have lied. Ma and Pa never wrote us. I was so wrong. I'm so sorry."

Dovie hurried over. "Let's get her in the house. I'm sure she needs some water."

James took Norman, and Elmer shook out his good arm. "Norman needs some lookin' after too. He protected Alice from the storm."

"All right," said Dovie, "bring Norman in the house too."

Bill laid Alice on the sofa, and Dovie gave him a glass

of water. "See if you can get her to sip. Her throat's probably pretty raw. I'll see if I can't get a bath prepared. She'll feel better once all the grit's off her, but it may be a bit before that well comes up with clean water. Lou Anne, why don't you go lie down on my bed for a spell. You're lookin' mighty pale."

Lou Anne gave Alice a little peck on the forehead before retreating to Dovie's room.

Evalyn kneeled by her sister's feet. "I don't know how you can ever forgive me, Alice. I'm so sorry. I could never forgive myself if somethin' happened to you. I'm just so sorry I ever lied to you."

Elmer put his hand on Evalyn's back. "Evie, it's all right. Alice is okay, and I'm sure she accepts your apology." He looked at Alice who nodded her head yes and smiled weakly.

"But how can you?" Evalyn asked Alice. "I was so mean and hurtful. I'm sorry I was like that to you."

Bill looked at her. "We can forgive because we are family, and that's what family does."

"I couldn't have said it better myself," said Dovie. "The water is nearly clear. We'll just need to heat some up. Evalyn you want to help me?"

"Yes, I do, and please call me Evie."

Chapter Thirty-eight

Alice set her book on the coffee table and leaned against the blue arm of the sofa. It had been a week since Black Sunday, and she still tasted the grit as it burned her throat and chest. Not a day went by that she didn't soil a hanky by coughing up dirt. Dovie said it was good for her to cough the gunk out of her lungs, but Alice longed for the day it didn't hurt to breathe. She had missed the whole week of school. But Dovie helped her keep up with her studies at home, which included reading Peter Pan together.

Today Alice was surrounded by her brothers and sister. They were having a family meeting, so her book would have to wait. She looked at Bill, sitting in Dovie's sewing chair. He looked worried and that worried her.

Elmer was the last to take a seat. "Sorry, Mr. Norman didn't want to take his medicine."

"Well, I don't blame him," said Alice, her voice raspy. "It's icky."

"Good, now that everyone's here, we can get started," said Bill, leaning forward and placing his elbows on his knees. "I've called this family together because I haven't been fair to y'all."

His siblings looked at him in confusion.

"What do you mean?" asked Evalyn, sitting in the

corner in James's rocker.

"Well..." Bill ran his hands through his hair, stood, and began pacing. "Since Ma and Pa left I've been makin' the decisions without askin' y'all what you want to do. I thought it was up to me, as the oldest, to make those decisions. Now, I see it's up to us as a family to decide things. I've always tried to do right by y'all, but I never once entertained the notion of goin' to California. I've talked to Lou Anne, and she's gonna go with us whatever we decide, so that's not an issue."

"The way I see it, we have two choices: stay here or go to California and search for Ma and Pa. We all need to be in agreement. I'm not splittin' up this family."

"There's nothin' to discuss. We're stayin' here." Evalyn folded her hands in her lap as her siblings stared at her opened mouthed. "Y'all better shut your traps before you start collectin' flies. You heard me right. There's no reason to go halfway across the country to look for parents who want nothin' to do with us. We're better off with these fine folks here at Quail Crossings. We have a house and land, which is a lot more than most hard-workin' folks can brag about nowadays. We are truly blessed, and I for one intend to stay that way. I vote we stay here."

Alice couldn't hide her grin as Evalyn looked at her. "What's your vote, Alice?"

"To stay here." Alice giggled, coughed and then looked at her brother. "And you, Elm?"

"Stay, of course. What about you, Bill? I don't reckon you want to leave with your weddin' coming up."

"It seems we are in agreement." Bill laughed and motioned for Evalyn and Elmer to join him in a group hug with Alice on the couch.

Alice snuggled into the family hug, fighting back her

happy tears. She knew crying even happy tears, would send her into a coughing fit.

Dovie walked in wringing a dish towel, James standing behind her. "Is the meetin' over?"

"Guys, I can't breathe under here," Alice cried. "I need some air."

Evalyn rose from the hug and wiped her eyes. "Yeah, and I couldn't be happier."

James walked past Dovie. "Now listen, y'all are makin' a mistake. California is a big state, and there's no guarantee you'll find your parents. Y'all don't even know where to start lookin'. Y'all need to think about this."

"There's nothin' to think about. We voted and everyone agrees." Evalyn danced to James and kissed him on the cheek. "We're stayin' put, and there ain't nothin' you can do about it. You're stuck with us."

James slapped his knee and then swung Evalyn around. "You mean it? Y'all are staying?"

"Yes, sir," said Bill, standing up.

James crossed the room and grabbed Bill's hand. "Enough of that 'sir' stuff. I want you to be my partner, fifty-fifty."

Bill stood, mouth gaped. "James, I don't know what to say. You've already given us too much."

"He says, yes," said Elmer from the couch, smiling. "He ain't as stupid as he looks, just slow sometimes."

Bill ruffled Elmer's hair. "Of course it's a deal."

Alice skipped down the stairs in her favorite pink church dress as she twirled a new white rope decorated with blue bows.

"You look lovely, Alice," said Dovie, straightening her own dress of sky blue and yellow. "Is that for Mr. Norman?"

"Yep." Alice held up the rope. "You don't think it's too girly, do you?"

"He'll be the best lookin' goose there."

Alice cocked her head. "Won't he be the only goose there?"

Dovie nodded and laughed. "Let's go get him and try it on, shall we?"

Grabbing Alice's hand, the two went outside. There sat Mr. Norman, picking at his newly washed feathers.

"He didn't really feel a bath was necessary," said Elmer, drenched from head to toe. "But he's clean now, and I've got to hustle or we'll be late."

Elmer ran up the stairs to the back door almost knocking Evalyn over.

"Wow," said Elmer, "you sure look pretty, Evie."

Evalyn blushed and smoothed the wrinkles out of her emerald green dress. "Oh, hush and go get ready. Bill will be mad if we're late."

"You do look lovely," said Dovie as she tied the decorated leash around Norman's neck. "You've got quite the skill with a needle. Most women would kill to be able to sew dresses so glamorous."

"Really?" She spun around. "Thank you, I do feel lovely. I'm still a bit surprised Lou Anne asked me to be her maid of honor. I was sure she'd ask one of the girls from her class or at least her little sister. But I'm glad she asked me."

Elmer hopped out the door in a new starched white shirt and black slacks. "One good thing 'bout washin' Norman was I got my bath in too."

Dovie wrinkled her nose. "Elmer Brewer, are you

tellin' me you took a bath with that bird?"

Elmer laughed and then winked. "Gotcha!"

A vision of Elmer washing his armpit while Norman swam around him in the pond, popped into Dovie's mind, and she began to giggle. The giggle grew into a fit of laughter that didn't stop until her sides hurt. Wiping the tears from her eyes, she looked at the three children who stared at her as if she'd gone mad. She looked up at the sky and said a silent thank you.

"Come on. Let's go."

The church was decorated with a variety of spring flowers, and the scent of lilac and honeysuckle filled the air as Mrs. Spaulding started playing the organ. Bill stood at the front by Pastor Spaulding, James and Elmer beaming by his side.

The sanctuary filled with adoring "ahs" as Alice walked down the aisle carrying a little white basket filled with flower petals with Norman by her side.

Norman strutted down the aisle with a shallow basket filled with more petals attached to his back. As he waddled, the petals fell to the ground. He and Alice stopped and stood in their places at the front of the church.

Next came Evalyn, carrying a small bouquet of purple lilacs. The crowd stood as Lou Anne and her father approached the doorway, and Mrs. Spaulding boldly played the "Wedding March".

Lou Anne's ivory dress flowed over her small frame as she slowly walked down the aisle. A lace blusher lay delicately over her soft face as her eyes locked with Bill's. He shifted his feet, holding back the urge to run down the aisle and swoop the woman of his dreams into his arms.

Finally, she stepped to the front of the church where her father placed her hand in Bill's and sat by his wife in the first pew. Bill could tell through the blusher that Lou Anne was smiling with tears of joy wetting her hazel eyes. Taking a deep breath, he listened to Pastor Spaulding ask him the most important question of his life.

Reciting their vows, Bill then placed his grandmother's ring on her left finger, and all that was left were those five little words. "You may kiss the bride."

Bill lifted the blusher and dipped Lou Anne into a long passionate kiss as the congregation clapped and cheered.

"It is my pleasure to introduce Mr. and Mrs. Bill Brewer."

The crowd erupted again in cheers as Bill and Lou Anne hurried down the aisle and outside where a lovely outdoor reception waited. Hannah Garber's breath-taking three layer wedding cake was surrounded by cookies and pies the town ladies had brought, all laid out on the church's picnic tables. A small basket sat at the end for donations to the happy couple.

Bill and Lou Anne stood by the basket and were congratulated by the townspeople.

"I can't believe she came," Bill whispered into Lou Anne's ear.

Lou Anne looked down at the end of the reception line, and there stood Charlotte.

"This should be interestin'," she whispered back to Bill.

Charlotte approached and embraced Lou Anne in a huge hug, then Bill. She looked from side to side to see if anyone was listening, but all were busy eating fantastic goodies from the buffet.

"You better keep him warm at night, Lou Anne. If you don't, he knows where to go," said Charlotte, resting her hand on Bill's chest. "My door is always open."

Bill grabbed for Charlotte's hand when she let out a loud scream. Everyone turned in time to see Norman latched onto Charlotte's rear.

"Get this bird off me!" she screamed, knocking Norman off and running. Norman followed with loud honks as he chased her around the church.

"Somebody help me," she screamed again. "Bill, do somethin'!"

Bill turned to Lou Anne. "Would you like some cake, Mrs. Brewer?"

"I would love some, Mr. Brewer."

Chapter Thirty-nine

May 1935

Dovie let the wind blow her hair from her face as she sat once again in the cemetery. No need for a blanket today, she thought, as she pulled weeds from her family's graves.

Wiping the sweat from her brow, she looked over her shoulder at Alice and her new puppy, Nana, playing around the big cedar trees surrounding the small cemetery.

"Watch for snakes, Alice," she hollered, and the little girl nodded.

"Remember I used to tell you that all the time, Helen?" She pulled another weed from around the stone marker. "I always worried about you, but now I don't have to anymore. No harm can come to you in the arms of the Lord."

She moved over to Simon's stone and began pulling at a milkweed. "Besides you're there to watch over her too, honey, aren't you?" She sat back. "My heart still aches at not being able to hold y'all in my arms. But it's gettin' better. I don't know if it'll ever go away, but the good Lord is bringin' me more peace every day. It doesn't hurt that we've been so busy with the weddin' and finishin' up Bill's house. You should see it. It's so lovely, a great home for a great family."

"Dad hasn't stopped singin' the Lord's praise since the Brewers agreed to stay. And Norman, well Norman is his ornery ol' self, but I don't suppose we'd have him any other way."

"Alice is readin' at a third grade level. I think she got bored when she was stuck at home after the dust storm and just took up readin'. Her favorite is Peter Pan. Even named her pup after the one in the book. She's a doll."

"Elmer's becomin' a wonderful young man, takin' up more responsibilities since Bill's been workin' on their house. Trained another litter of pups and wants to start his own breedin' business. He's so good with those dogs. And what a chatterbox, can't hardly get a word in nowadays. Sounds a lot like Tiny, if you ask me."

"Evalyn has surrounded herself with everythin' Hollywood. Says she's gonna be a world famous actress. She and Alice do plays for us all the time, and she's very talented. I can see her bein' in the picture shows one day. Though I've only seen one, I can see the appeal. Her ornery ways seem to be a thing of the past. Lou Anne is lucky to have such a good helper in the kitchen."

"Bill and Lou Anne are so happy, like a couple of love birds, always gigglin' and stealin' kisses when they think no one is watchin'." Dovie smoothed her dress. "Reminds me of us when we was young. But I'm thankful, Simon, oh so thankful that I have once again found love at Quail Crossings."

Acknowledgments

I've come to the impossible task of thanking everyone who helped make Quail Crossings what it is today. To thank everyone who had a hand in it, would be writing another book just of thank yous. So to everyone who read even a paragraph of the first drafts (and basically I shoved it in front of anyone who would read it), thank you for your patience, time, and honesty.

A special thank you to Linda Boulanger for believing in me and holding my hand through this crazy publishing world. To Diana Purser, you are the Grammar Diva and I love you for it. I can't imagine the mess this manuscript would be without your help. It would be a huge mistake to leave out the WordWeavers; Denise Jarmola, Heather Davis, Rita Durrett, Marilyn Boone, Diana Purser, Barbara Shoff, and Tawnya York. I couldn't have done it without your support, encouragement, and most of all your brutally honest critiques. An author is only as good as her critique group, and you ladies rock.

To Ester Miller, Fay Schoenhals, and Margie Cook, thank you for taking me on a journey down your memory lane. The best part of my research was talking with the three of you lovely ladies. Speaking of lovely ladies, Claressa Carter and Rubina Ahmed, a girl is nothing without her besties. Thank you for all your support and love.

And now for my family. I am truly blessed to have such a kind, caring, supportive, and helpful bunch on my side. To my numerous aunts, uncles, cousins and in-laws, thank you for being yourselves, although sometimes quirky, and feeding my imagination with your awesome stories and personalities. To my grandparents, to whom the book is dedicated, as I said before, thank you for sharing your stories. I hope Quail Crossings does your experiences justice.

Thanks to my dad, Randy Collar, who taught me to not just do, but to think about what you're doing. A priceless lesson I hope I'm able to pass on. To my mom, Cathy Collar, for giving my imagination an appetite that can never be filled and for helping me see the story in everything. To my sister, Brandy Walker, thanks for all your love and support but most importantly for making me look glamorous in my wonderful headshots. You are an artist in every sense of the word. I would be remiss not to thank my dearly departed sister, Anna. Even though I can't see you, I know you stand with me always, and I miss you every day.

To my dear sweet daughter, Annaley, thank you for being the best kind of motivation. You are the sweetest little punkin, and I appreciate you sleeping through the night, so Mommy can get some work done and not feel like a zombie the next day.

Finally, to my husband, Mike, to say I am blessed to have you in my life is an extreme understatement. Thank you for your countless edits, support, love, and understanding that dreams don't always start with a paycheck. I love you.

If you enjoyed Quail Crossings
watch for Winter Song
coming in 2013

Also by
Jennifer McMurrain

Winter Song

Enjoy an Excerpt from
Winter Song

Sage McKennan stared into the fire place and shivered. Cooper knew the one-bedroom house he shared with her was warm enough. It was an internal chill that raced through her body. It happened every time they fought and tonight was no exception.

"Come sit by me," said Cooper, patting the couch cushion beside him. Sage didn't move.

Cooper sighed and bit his lower lip. "Okay, you were right. I shouldn't have gone. I just thought I could earn us some money for the bed and breakfast. I don't want you to have to work graveyard at the hotel for the rest of your life. You deserve better."

Sage moved from the fire to the window. The snow was coming down harder now. The lights blinked and Sage gave a worried glance at the lamp. Cooper walked up behind her.

"Don't worry, baby, this storm will blow over soon enough," he whispered gently. "Just another Wyoming winter. Nothing to worry about."

Sage turned away and rushed to the china cabinet, gathering candles from a top drawer.

Cooper chuckled. "I know. I know. If you light all the candles now the lights won't go out. If you wait and don't light them, the lights will go off and you'll be scrambling around in the dark." He smirked. "Of course, you know how I like to scramble in the dark."

Sage set the candles around the small den and began

lighting them.

"Come on, Sage!" Cooper groaned. "How long are you going to keep giving me the silent treatment? I've been through hell. I don't even know if anyone else made it off the boat. The only thing I could think about was getting to you. Speak to me! Tell me you love me! Let me hold you, damn it."

Sage looked up as headlights fell through the window.

"Who in the world is that?" asked Cooper.

Sage hurried to the back door, opening it in time to let the Deputy in out of the snow. He stomped his boots off before stepping out of the mud room.

"Deputy Park," said Cooper. "I bet you're here to ask me about the accident. Sage, get the man some coffee."

"Please sit down, Richard," said Sage gesturing to the small kitchen table. She hurried to get the coffee pot that sat warming on the stove. "I'm sure you're chilled to the bone. I hate nights like this."

Richard sat, holding his hat in his hands.

Cooper leaned on the door frame. "I really don't remember much. You should've called. I would've saved you the trip. All I know is the alarm went off and I grabbed my survival suit. This kid by the name of Gavin Hart was my bunk mate, couldn't have been more than eighteen. He did the same. Then he started freaking out 'cause his suit had a hole in the foot. So I traded with him. Next thing I know, we're both swimming in the Bering Sea."

Sage handed Richard a large cup of steaming coffee. "Well?" she asked.

Richard placed his untouched coffee on the table, grabbed Sage's hand and shook his head. "It's not good, Sage. You better sit down."

Sage sank to a chair.

Richard rubbed his thumb over the back of Sage's hand

and cleared his throat. "They found one life boat. Captain Mullis and some kid named Gavin Hart were the only ones in there."

"Oh good!" Cooper gave a sigh of relief. "Glad the kid made it out."

Sage took in a deep breath. "What about…?" A loud sob finished her sentence as Richard shook his head slowly.

"You mean he's dead?" Sage gasped. "Cooper's dead?"

"What are you talking about? Sage, I'm right here." Cooper closed the distance between him and Sage. He reached out to hug her but caught nothing but air as his hands passed through her body. "What the…"

Sage shivered.

"Do you have someone I can call?" asked Richard.

"She doesn't need to call anyone. I'm right here!" Cooper yelled. "I don't know what kind of shit you two are trying to pull, but it's not funny."

Cooper reached for Sage's hand and again it passed right through. He stared at his hands.

Sage shook her head as Cooper walked to the window, trying to wrap his brain around the news. "I'm dead," he repeated. "How can I be dead?"

"I don't know if this is going to make you feel any better," said Richard. "But that Hart kid is alive, thanks to Cooper. I guess he had a hole in the foot of his survival suit, and Cooper switched with him at the last minute. Cooper's a hero."

Sage managed a small smile. "He was always my hero."

The electricity blinked a couple of times before calling it quits. Candlelight filled the room.

Richard meet her gaze. "You don't have to be alone tonight," he said, placing a hand on her arm.

Sage shook her head again, and patted Richard's hand. "I'm not alright, Richard, but I'll be okay. Thanks for driving out here and telling me. I know you're a busy man."

"I don't feel right leaving you here alone," protested Richard. "Really, I think I should stay."

"I want to be alone!" blurted Sage. Taking a deep breath she looked at the deputy. "Please Richard. I need to digest this in my own way."

"I understand," he said, putting his hat back on. "I'll be back in the morning to check on you. No arguments. Call me if you need anything, and I mean anything. It's really no trouble."

Sage thanked Richard before firmly shutting the door. Cooper watched Sage pick up Richard's coffee cup, dump it into the sink, and wash it. The candles flickered around her, giving her blonde highlights an amber glow. Setting the cup in the drainer, she made her way to the den, and started picking up the scrapbooking material that covered the coffee table. She'd been working on the albums when Cooper came home.

Gathering up the pictures, she came across one of Cooper sitting in a meadow. Wild flowers bloomed all around him as he smiled at her, hiding behind the camera. Dropping the pictures, she fell to the floor.

"Why?" she cried. "Why'd you have to leave me?"

Sage pulled herself onto the couch and curled in a ball. "I told you not to go. I told you it was too dangerous. Why didn't you listen? Why'd you leave me?"

Cooper sprang to the couch, anxious to touch his love again. "I'm right here, baby. I would never leave you."

He looked around, trying to find a way to show her that he was there. Spotting the candle nearest her, he bent down and concentrated as he blew. The fire went out.

Sage stared at the candle through wet eyes. None of the others had even flickered. Picking up the candle, she examined the wick. It was fine.

Cooper leaned in close, aching to hold her. "I will never leave you again."

About the Author

Having a great deal of wanderlust, Author Jennifer McMurrain traveled the countryside working odd jobs before giving into her muse and becoming a full time writer. She's been everything from a "Potty Princess" in the wilds of Yellowstone National Park to a Bear Researcher in the mountains of New Mexico. After finally settling down, she received a Bachelor's degree in Applied Arts and Science from Midwestern State University in Wichita Falls, TX. She has won numerous awards for her short stories and novels. She lives in Bartlesville, Oklahoma with her husband, daughter, two spoiled cats, and two goofy dogs. Quail Crossings is her first novel.

Author photograph by Brandy Walker Photography

Friend Author Jennifer McMurrain on Facebook:
https://www.facebook.com/pages/Author-Jennifer-McMurrain

Follow Jennifer's tweets -
https://twitter.com/Deepbluejc

Visit her on her website:
http://www.jennifermcmurrain.com